# Out of Time

*A Novel*

*by*

# Bernice Erehart

# Out of Time

Published by Bernice Erehart

Front cover photo by © Geraldas G. Fotolia.com

This book has been fictionalized and all persons appearing in this work are fictitious. Any resemblance to real people, living or dead, is entirely coincidental.

ISBN-13: 978-1500809188

Second Edition

## DEDICATION:

I would like to dedicate this, my first complete novel, to my mother. Who, before her death, listened to everything I wrote with pure love and knew that one day I would have a book published. I love you, Mom, and I miss you so much.

# Contents

# Out of Time

"Everyone is a genius. But if you judge a fish by its ability to climb a tree, it will live its whole life believing that it is stupid."

–Albert Einstein

# PROLOGUE
## Friday, August 4th, 2201. 9:30 PM
## THE CURE

Miranda Jordan, better known as MJ, was ranked the ninth smartest person on the planet. She felt the rankings were stupid and bordering on the barbaric, but that was the current government.

She paced the observation deck of the planetarium with gloom in her heart. MJ was so distracted by the ominous feeling in the pit of her stomach that she was hardly aware of the other scientists and guests milling about the deck. She had the sick feeling that what they were about to do was not a cure, but a disease.

Fourteen months of study; cheek swabs and genetic screenings in ninety percent of Earth's female population seemed a very short span of time, considering what they were looking for. But they had found what they were looking for – that one DNA marker.

Then, eight months of round the clock work to create the vaccine that would target that special marker and rid the world of the so called 'surplus' in the world. It was a top secret assignment; if word got out about what was really going on in the labs at Albany, there would be a mass panic. Much like the great panic of 2183. Worse yet, they were six months ahead of schedule and that couldn't be good.

But they said it was the humane thing to do. MJ wondered what possessed her to take part in this. She was chosen to be part of the team because she was a chemist.

She knew about chemicals and formulas, and this formula was not right on so many levels.

Alan Barker, ranked the second smartest person in the world, was an arrogant jackass, and the most stubborn person MJ had ever met. He had made it a contest and insisted that the cure was ready, and nothing anyone could say would change his mind. MJ wondered what made his opinion so distinct than say hers – her IQ was only seven points less than his.

Alan had convinced the governments of all nine regions that 'the cure' was ready and no matter what objections had been voiced by at least half of the team, the 'powers that be' were unduly consumed with its purpose to question Alan's assurance of its completion. They were all too ready to agree and give the orders for the launch.

It had been proposed that the vaccine would be disbursed into the night air, whatever the weather; it really didn't matter as the weather could be controlled. A natural jet stream was needed to carry the vaccine around the world, but a manmade stream would also do the trick.

No one would be hurt, as it was colorless and odorless. It would inoculate anonymously and no one would even know. Sure, it would take at least a year before the effects would be known, but the government was confident that if Alan said it was ready, then it was ready. He was, after all, the second smartest person on the planet – and MJ agreed he was number two.

This evening the weather grid had to be activated because the laws of nature were not cooperating. MJ wondered, as she watched a colony of bats fly by if that could be a sign of bad things to come.

The exquisite stemware, crafted especially for the occasion, were being filled with the champagne that had been chilling in the ice buckets lining the observation deck of the new planetarium in Albany, New York, awaiting the launch. The hors d'oeuvres were set on a buffet table nearby, being consumed by the anxious crowd.

MJ's boyfriend, Ryan Carter, who was ranked the twenty-fifth smartest person on the planet, took two glasses and handed one to her. Ryan had only become part of the team because Alan's wife Amelia, who was ranked the smartest person on the planet, refused the project; citing moral issues.

Now twenty-four of the planet's top scientists – including MJ, Ryan, and Alan – had gathered, along with many others from the science community, to observe the secret disbursement. The top twenty-four were fifteen men and nine women. The team had been commissioned by the collective governments to secretly design a cure for the condition the planet was in.

Sixty billion people, give or take a few hundred million, was the condition the world was in and not enough resources to care for them. And tonight that condition would be treated. It would take years for results to be known, but that was okay. They had all the time in the world.

The rest of the team were inside the planetarium and watched as the capsule containing the cure slowly moved along the conveyor belt. Its destination was the newly constructed syringe; a giant replica of the smaller model designed especially for this project.

Alan beamed with pride; although a bit lonely, his wife and son were back home in Toronto, where four year old Arthur was being tucked into bed. Amelia's refusal to join in the celebration had been the breaking point for Alan and he decided this was it – the marriage was over.

Alan loved his son, and now that Arthur was showing tendencies toward being a genius and not some dumb as a stump athlete or momma's boy psychic, Alan was determined more than ever that Arthur would grow up with him and be just like him.

Forty-four eyes beheld the marvel of the capsule being sucked into the vacuum where it traveled two stories up. They ran up the stairs out to the deck where MJ and Ryan waited. As it made its final boost, MJ wondered if she should try and stop the launch, but she kept quiet.

"Don't worry, it won't do anything, it's not ready. You know as well as I do that this celebration is premature," Ryan said. "There's a timetable to these things and a protocol to follow."

He could see his words fell empty on her ears, so he put his champagne on the rail and took her in his arms, kissed her neck, and softly said, "Nothing is going to happen. Let's just enjoy the beautiful night and free champagne."

Together, they watched with bated breath as the capsule was guided to the pointy nubs that punctured the capsule and released the vaccine as a fine mist. One, two, three, ten times until all of the formula had all been disbursed. They watched as the mist integrated into the air and became one with the breeze.

The people applauded. They hugged and kissed each other. The man standing next to MJ, his name was John and was ranked the twelfth smartest person on the planet, clinked his glass with Ryan's and together they drank.

The colony of bats was coming around again, and as they flew over the crowd, one fell out of formation and hit Ryan's glass; causing it to fall to the deck, shattering.

MJ's glass never reached her lips. Her knees had buckled, forcing her lifeless body forward. Both Ryan and John heard the snap when her nose broke as her face hit the deck, just a few inches from the dead bat and the broken glass.

The first casualties of 'the virus'.

# CHAPTER ONE
## CURSED IN ATLANTIC CITY

My name is Emily Leigh Ann Gibbons and on the thirtieth day of October in the year 2010, I turned fifty years old. I am short for my age, a mere five foot three. At the moment, I have short, wavy blonde hair. My normal color is light brown with grey patches, but I colored it last night just for this day of days.

It was a day like any other day. Like any other day at the end of October. Like any other day at the end of October when you are turning a half century.

You never really think you'll ever be fifty when you're seventeen, not even when you're twenty-five. But if you're lucky, it happens. Because what's the alternative? Death. But nobody really wants that.

So, here it is, the day of my birth, only fifty years later.

Yes, fifty years later and I'm a bit more than pleasingly plump, single, never been married, tired of that second job called 'looking for love in all the wrong places', and my sisters are grandmothers and I'm not. Still working, because God knows I'll never be able to retire. How can I? It's ten years into the twenty-first century and the economy is custom made for living on two and a half retirement funds – I barely have *one* going. Thank you, President Bush.

When I woke up that day, the day I turned fifty, I looked out the window to a very beautiful fall day. The leaves were all just the right shades of red, orange, and gold. The squirrels were running around, gathering food for the winter and doing the mating dance for the long, cold winter ahead.

My cat, Bandit, was stretching out on the bed and greeted me with his squeak of a meow – he didn't have a normal meow. He lost that sometime before the day I found him at my front door that winter day, cold and hungry, wet and near death. Even though his fur had been matted to his body, I could tell he was beautiful; all beige with an orange highlight and calico colors around his eyes, making him appear to be wearing a mask.

I took him to the animal hospital in Tinton Falls where they nursed him back to health. His biggest problems were malnutrition and dehydration. So, with a little food in his belly and fluids, he was ready to come home with me after just two days and become my sidekick.

He loved me. He loved only me. He wouldn't even give my sisters a chance, hissing at them and showing his claws. Jill would get a sniff and a tail in her face as he walked away from her.

I was his and his alone, and he was mine. From the first night at home with me, he had slept on the bed with me. Our five years together have been wonderful.

The year Bandit and I became a family, I turned forty-five and I started giving myself special gifts for my birthday. That year, I went to Atlantic City for the night. I saw Keith Urban in concert and went to a psychic for a reading. At which time, I was told that I would finally meet love that year. Yeah! It's not like I really believe in those readings or psychics – it's just for entertainment purposes, right? I didn't meet the love of my life that year, but I was entertained.

By the way, Keith was much better than the psychic reading.

At forty-six, I went to Atlantic City and saw Cher in her farewell concert (little did I know it would only be her first) and got a psychic reading, where I was told that I would meet the love of my life – and I would be his world. Wrong again!

Cher was great!

At forty-seven, I went to Atlantic City to gamble and get a psychic reading, at which time I was told I would meet the man of my dreams and yadda, yadda, yadda. And, well, you know what happened there.

At forty-eight, I went to Atlantic City to walk the boardwalk and get a psychic reading (you would think by now I would have learned something about psychics), and maybe a little gambling. That birthday trip to Atlantic City would prove to be the time I would promise myself *no more psychics*.

I had decided to do the psychic thing first and get the "you're going to meet the man of your dreams very soon" out of the way first. So, I went out to the boardwalk and began my search for a new and improved psychic. Whatever made me think that anyone with real psychic abilities (if there was such a thing) would be working the AC boardwalk surely had to be the product of a brain disorder. Anyway, I hadn't gone very far when I saw a young woman sitting outside her shop, looking like she could be the 'real thing'.

I was sure I had never seen her there before, because on her head was a gold chained headband with hanging rhinestones with long, dangling hoop earrings that I had to assume were heavy as they pulled her earlobes down. She was wearing a white bra fringed in sequins with a matching sequined belt. She was also sporting a full turquoise chiffon layered maxi skirt. She was dripping in multi colored scarves and she was barefoot. I could only assume she was wearing genuine Gypsy garb or it was her Halloween costume. Either way, none of my prior readers had been wearing anything so dramatic.

I went in to find that her clothes weren't the only difference in my choice of psychics. After I paid, she asked me to think of a question that I wanted her to answer. My question was, *would I win money this time around in the casino?* She began to get her reading out of me – I told her it was my birthday and I was single and never had children. (These seem to be important aspects of a person's life in order to get a true reading.) She began to flip the cards and I could see concern growing on her face. I almost laughed.

"What is it?" I asked.

"The cards!" she squeaked. "I never, never see. Oh, oh, I was only told dis could be. I never thought it could really be true, that dis curse could be *for real*." She really put the emphasis on the last two words.

"What?" I asked again, stifling a laugh.

"The cards, they no lie."

I opened my eyes wide in mock anticipation, which, of course, she was totally oblivious to. I looked down at the cards to see if I could see what she saw. What I saw were very used and worn cards, bent edges and tiny tears. She was gripping the deck tightly in her left hand, the six cards she had on the table were laid out in a three on top two underneath and one under them pattern.

The one on the bottom showed a court jester type character in colorful clothes, which she explained was the fool card; of the two above the fool, the card on the left showed the magician who steals the fool's possessions; the fool continues his journey and encounters the empress card, where he stops and shares his story with her.

She points to the three cards above the two and starts with the one in the middle, stating it's the emperor card and it's a warning that something unwelcomed has happened. She then points to the card to the right and says it is called the hierophant card and basically it says to give up. The card on the left, she says, is the lover's card, but because it is on the left and not the right of the emperor card, it means that I should give up on love.

"Why is that?" I asked.

"It is all right here, in da cards." And this is when the over acting and the what I assume was a gypsy accent began. Pointing down at the cards, she said, "It is all in da cards. Yes, da reason you will never find love."

Okay, that wasn't my question, but I was curious now.

"Why will I never find love?" I asked in an innocent voice.

And this is when the wailing began and the accent got really thick, "Oh, oh," and her head swung back and forth in an arc that I wouldn't have thought possible. "You have been in da presence of a very powerful witch, no?" she cried.

"NO!"

"Yes, you played her the fool, as the magician you tried to steal her lover," she clutched at her chest and real tears, big and fat, rolled down her cheeks.

"I did?" I tried to match her despair. I really could not remember a time when I would try to take anyone's lover away. You just didn't try things you already knew would never happen. It's just not who I am.

"A curse!" She went on. "A curse she put on you, a very horrible ting, only a very powerful witch could have cast dis curse on you." I'm sure she said 'ting' and 'dis'.

"What kind of curse?" I continued with the game.

"I can no say da name," her face was glistening now. "I can no say it." She put her hands up to her face and began to weep.

Only she didn't really weep. She looked at me through her fingers and I could see there were no tears on her face. When she didn't get the reaction she wanted, she actually got up to let me know the reading was over, but abruptly sat back down. "But I can tell you how you got it. And I can tell you how to overcome dis, dis horrible ting." And she spat.

I was riveted now – she was good. She wasn't psychic, but she was the best over actor I ever saw.

I sat back down. She went through the pretense of drying her face and I could see her trying to compose herself. After a few minutes, she looked me straight in the eyes, looked over my right shoulder (to somewhere outside her shop, I have to assume), then back into my eyes, and in a slight whisper, said, "Dis is a curse, which is against our laws to cast."

"Whose law?"

She shushed me and went on, "Only the most powerful of our kind would even have da power and da influence over da elements to cast it," she paused to see my reaction.

This got me thinking. I had a curse put on me that the actual elements were involved in. Ah, I must be special.

When she didn't get the reaction she wanted again, she sat straight back in her chair and said in a very matter of fact voice, forgoing the accent, "This curse is stuck in your vagina," and blew air out of her mouth and fell back in her chair again.

I was shocked! Every year, when I went for my annual physical, I just always assumed Dr. Clarke was looking, so if it was in there, he never saw it or took it out. Or, at least, he never said.

"You must have really pissed her off to get dis horrible ting done to you."

She was back to the gypsy language.

The thought that I was really getting my monies worth this time popped into my head. She said 'pissed'.

"The curse is cast upon an article of clothing, a hair scrunchy, a pin – or in your case – a pair of panties. So, when you put them on, the curse became lodged in your vagina, which guaranteed that you would never find love." She paused again for affect.

I wondered what the correlation was between love and my sweet spot.

I wondered how and where someone could have gotten a hold of my underwear. And which pair was it? Did the curse leave my panties when I washed them? Or do I keep reinforcing the curse by continually putting that pair on. Food for thought.

For a second, I actually thought about throwing all my panties out (cutting them up first, of course, so no other unsuspecting girl could get dis horrible ting stuck in her whoha) and buying all new ones when I got home.

When there was no reaction, she went onto say, "I can remove this curse from your vagina."

Okay, now she had said 'your vagina' one too many times and I was starting to feel a little uncomfortable.

"Okay," I said. "How do you do this?" I figured she would dance around me, singing words in a language I couldn't understand; maybe even burn some incense and throw holy water on me. A part of me was also afraid she was going to lay me down spread eagle and try to gouge it out with her fingers.

She got up and turned her back to me, making sure I could see exactly what she was doing. First, she took a salmon colored pillar candle (probably bought at the dollar store) out of a cabinet above her. She then opened a drawer and took out a handful of what appeared to be small stones that she carefully picked and chose special ones from. When she brought nine or ten of them to the table, they turned out to be colored glass; rounded and smoothed by the ocean – probably picked up on the beach right outside her shop. "I have the necessary tools," she said. "Brought from the old country."

Then, in that same slight whisper, she said, "Take these stones and place them around the candle in a circle; then, and only then, light the candle with a small wooden match." Then, her voice rose an octave, "Follow my instructions just as I have given them to you."

She looked at me again for affect. She was very detail oriented.

"Okay." It was getting harder and harder not to laugh in this girl's face. Really? A small wooden match? As opposed to what? A long fireplace match?

"When the candle has been burning for no less than five minutes, say these words." She took a piece of scrap paper from the left cup of her bra and handed it to me. It had three words written in capital letters on it – "CURSE BE GONE."

*Strange magic words.* Not even, "CURSE LEAVE MY VAGINA." But who am I to judge?

I had to wonder how many people came to her with a curse stuck somewhere in or on their body.

She put the candle, the ten pieces of glass, and the 'boob' note in a small brown bag, and gave it to me with a smile, saying, "That will be nine tousand dollars. I take credit cards."

"Excuse me!?"

"The money is a donation to my church," she said.

I was almost sure she was lying. But when it came to church, you couldn't be too sure if extortionists actually went to church. I handed the bag back to her.

"What?" she asked. "God told me you could afford to pa—uh, make the donation. If you don't have it with you right now, my cousin, Marco, can come to your home and pick it up."

"First of all, God would not tell you something that wasn't true," I said to her, "And second of all, nobody named Marco is coming to my home."

There was a quizzical look on her face as I forced the bag back into her hands.

"My question was not about love. Honestly, what makes you people think that just because a woman is single she can't be happy?"

That day, I won thirty-five hundred dollars at Bally's – you think she would have seen that one coming.

# CHAPTER TWO
# FIFTY YEARS LATER

At forty-nine, I passed on the boardwalk the nice room, the concert, the gambling, and – most definitely – the psychic reading; and treated myself to a full body massage, facial, and manicure. I never got a pedicure because the second toe on my right foot, my ugly toe, kept me out of the pedicure chair and in shoes that always covered my toes.

Not going to Atlantic City was cheaper. I didn't have to drive very far and the girls were Vietnamese, and so didn't speak very much English, let alone tell me I would find love anytime soon or that I had a horrible 'ting' stuck in my wazoo. And I didn't have to leave food and water out for Bandit. That made him happy.

No more psychics for me. I don't believe in them – anyone who thinks he or she is a psychic is a criminal and should be locked away where no one can hear them make promises they can't keep.

So, on the morning of my fiftieth birthday, I did what I always did. I got on the scale to see if yesterday's meatloaf put me over two hundred and fifty pounds – nope, still the same. I looked down at Bandit, who seemed to be as happy about that as I was.

Then, a nice cup of tea with the new pumpkin spice Coffee-Mate out on the balcony to enjoy a perfect fall morning. I liked the new flavor – it tasted good and went down smooth, and quickly became my favorite flavor.

It was then that I talked to God – I was grateful for all I had and, as always, I was very quick to tell Him. But I also wanted Him to know about the things that I wanted. I told Him I felt I needed something different in my life, telling Him that things had gotten a little stale, a little too mundane. I needed a real change in my life. No, maybe not love (considering I still had a curse stuck you-know-where). Maybe I could win the lottery or finally write that book that had been writing itself in my head for years.

I had once thought about writing a book about teenage vampires in love – but I did not like vampires, didn't really know a whole lot about vampires, and wasn't sure I wanted to do the research. And anyway, how long could that craze last? What did I know?

I just wanted something different, maybe even a little freaky, "You choose," I said out loud. "I trust you to do what's best."

Next stop – breakfast at IHOP for their new pumpkin pancakes. Everybody knows that no one makes pancakes quite like IHOP, so the new pumpkin pancakes had to be wonderful. And I was just the girl to find out.

I was right! The pancakes were great. I knew I would be visiting IHOP again real soon. Then, I was off to the nail salon for my manicure. I did not get pumpkins painted on my nails. Pumpkins do not belong on your nails.

After that, I was off to the spa for my full body massage and facial – I so love being pampered. So, around two in the afternoon, I got to go home and rest until dinner at the food court in the mall with my sisters. Why the food court? Well, this year my birthday fell on a Saturday, so I was being taken to see *Hereafter* with Matt Damon. I was totally in love with Matt Damon – that would change in 2012 when I would see *We Bought a Zoo*. Don't ask, the book was so much better.

Every year I wasn't in Atlantic City, I spent my birthday, or some part, with my older sisters, Charlotte and Lucy – just them, my nieces and nephews had better things to do. Their husbands, Bob and Kris, also always found better things to do on my birthday. How could anyone have better things to do than share Aunt Emily's fiftieth birthday at the movies? I mean, how often am I gonna turn fifty? Yes, that was sarcasm.

Honestly, I was very happy that Lucy's husband, Kris, wasn't coming – he and I are not the best of friends. Actually, Kris is an ass; he's so full of himself, he can't see anyone else. And he's worse when he's drinking.

I wanted to go to Buffalo Wild Wings, but I wasn't paying, so it wasn't my choice. It's just my birthday, my fiftieth birthday, but not my choice. They got big parties, thrown for them by their husbands for their birthdays, but I didn't have a husband, so I got the food court and a movie… lucky me.

Yes, more sarcasm.

Here is where I would like to say that I believe everything happens for a reason. You see, God already knows what's going to happen, what is supposed to happen. He just makes sure one way or the other that you are right where you're supposed to be when that something has to happen. So, we were going to have dinner at the food court. That is exactly what I was supposed to be doing that night. So, we were at the food court.

I knew that's what we were doing, I knew there wasn't going to be a big surprise party that year because there was no *"why don't we have cake at the house this year*" or "*let's go to the community center*" or some other ploy to get me to an outside venue with caterers and real gifts. It never happened before and I assure you it hasn't happened since.

I wonder sometimes if I had given them a list of my friends' names and addresses, if they would have considered a party for me. But that's neither here nor there now. Because if they had given me a big party, I wouldn't have been at the mall and I needed to be at the mall. Because things happen the way they are supposed to happen when they are supposed to happen. Right? I know it's a little confusing, but it's true.

I wanted something different to happen and something really different, really freaky did happen. That was the day I had been waiting for my whole life, because that was the day I met… *Sam.*

My life didn't really start until the day I turned fifty years old. Sometimes it just works out that way.

The story I'm about to tell you is true. I know it will be hard to believe. It's still hard for me to believe. I never expected anything like this to happen to me – who does? So, sit back and relax because you are about to be blown away.

# CHAPTER THREE
# FALLING APART

To get the full and true picture about my story, let me give you some background information on the main character – me. It won't take long, I'm only fifty.

I was born Emily Leigh Ann Gibbons, on the thirtieth day of October in the year of our Lord, one thousand nine hundred and sixty. I was also not born to win any beauty contests and the proof is in the six pictures taken of me from birth to five years old. Then, after that, there were only school pictures and the family holiday pictures and oh, yeah, that one birthday picture of me and the cake that my mother took of me when I turned sixteen. But they aren't really important.

I guess I began to lean toward being chunky when I started school – five years old and my mom had to make my clothes because I was of the "husky" variety, hence only the school pictures. How lucky was I that my mom was a seamstress. Yup, that's right, more sarcasm.

What's new is that between the hot flashes and the night sweats that qualify me for a good hosing down by the local fire department, I don't sleep well – I'm up every two hours going potty. I can't remember the last time I slept through the night. Oh, yeah, that was August nineteen eighty-nine. I'm just saying.

And hardly anything I put in my stomach agrees with me. When I'm not constipated, it's the total opposite. I still eat whatever I want – well, mostly whatever I want, knowing full well that there may be consequences.

And my 20/20 vision said 'good bye' when I was forty and bifocals said 'hello' when I was forty-five. The dark circles under my eyes are a direct result of not sleeping well.

My hearing is going, too. The only thing not dying down is my sex drive. This, in truth, is the only part of me I'm not using. My gynecologist, Dr. Austin Clarke, promised me when I had my hysterectomy that my desire for sex would decrease. What does he know? He's a man!

I'm falling apart, nothing works any more, and sometimes I'd have a senior moment and not even remember what I was talking about. I guess that's why they call it a senior moment.

My blood pressure is out of control. Oh, not so bad that I live in Heart Attack City or the Village of Stroke, but bad enough that I have to take medication for it. The dosage of my thyroid medication has been changed four times this year and I mostly feel awful. I love my life!

My legs are the legs of a, well, of a fifty year old. I have arthritis in both my knees and it's killing me. Living in a second floor apartment isn't helping either. I guess I'll have to give it up some time before my legs give out all together.

My face is starting to succumb to gravity and I now have more than one chin, and the dark spots and patches, which began to show up four years ago, are slowly coming together. I'm hoping by the year twenty twelve all the dark patches will be completely together and I'll look like I have a tan. Yup, sarcasm.

And there are the various other little 'tings' that happen as you grow older. My hair was thinning and getting grey, my nails were always chipping and breaking, and my skin feels like it's about six layers too thin. And don't even get me started on how I'm farting like my grandmother.

According to my sisters, Charlotte and Lucy, they also lean towards the heavy side, but the five or six pounds they always fuss about confuse the crap out of me. I have never been less than twenty-five pounds overweight, probably not even on the day I was born. And my weight doesn't even bother me any more. Well, okay, not too much.

Charlotte and Lucy have both been married for what seems like forever and they seem happy, so I guess chubby doesn't bother their husbands.

I have three nieces and two nephews. I love them so much sometimes it hurts. I know they love me, they just have their own lives now. They are starting to have their own kids now and their own set of problems, so Aunt Emily is just not a priority any more. Well, I never was, but I'm still their aunt – and that's something.

# CHAPTER FOUR
## HAPPY BIRTHDAY

So, now that I'm fifty, the big five oh, and my only wish is for something different to happen. I didn't know what, but remember I did ask God this morning if this couldn't be the day that something really freaky happened to me. His choice.

Well, this was the one time I'm convinced He was listening. Because something did happen. I didn't know just how freaky it was at the time, but believe me, it was freaky.

I was at the counter of the Street Corner kiosk at the mall by the food court, getting ready to buy my mega millions lottery tickets – because *it could happen.* So, I was just standing in line, minding my own business, and that's when the freaky thing happened.

First, I heard what sounded like the rushing of air going through a tube behind me and then, I felt a hand on my back, *his* hand, flat on my back. It was the first time I had been touched by another person and actually felt something pass between us.

I would like to tell you it was heat coming from his body, but that's not the way it was – it was just the opposite. It felt like something left my body, which caused me to become dizzy and I began to sway – and as I was falling, in what seemed like slow motion, I turned my head to look at the person who touched me.

My first thought was *I know this guy,* but I couldn't place him – then, everything went dark.

When I opened my eyes, the first thing I saw were his eyes. They were big and blue, and they were looking right into my eyes. Apparently, I had passed out in his arms and we were both on the floor. Well, he was kneeling on the floor, and my upper body was in his arms and my legs were stretched out in front of me. He was smiling and talking. I couldn't hear him, but I knew he was talking because I could see his lips moving. It was like my ears needed to pop.

And when they did finally pop, I was suddenly aware that there was a crowd of people around us, murmuring and speaking in low voices. I didn't see my mother or father, so I knew I wasn't dead and boy was I glad because this guy was really cute. And it had been quite a while since I had been held like this by a cute guy. Okay, so, it was never. I was never held like this by a cute guy, but I liked it.

"Are you ready to get up?" he was saying.

"Are you all right?" I asked him, then laughed. "I mean, am I all right? Not are you all right – you didn't pass out. I passed out. You are just fine," I babbled. "You are all right, aren't you?"

"Yes," he said, continuing to smile as he lifted me up.

I realized he was having no trouble getting me up off the floor. He didn't look abnormally strong – in fact, a man his size probably shouldn't have been able to lift me up all by himself so easily. But I was on my own two feet in record time.

The thought came to me that I didn't have my purse, "Where's my purse? I have to buy my lottery tickets."

Someone handed me my purse and I saw it was Lucy, white faced and visibly shaken. "I saw you go down and I didn't know what to do. I screamed for Charlotte, but I

23

didn't know where she was. Oh, I think I might have a heart attack," she said, fanning herself and grabbing her chest.

Well, what do you know? She made it about her.

I told her I was okay and turned to tell her that this magnificent man caught me and his hand was on my back again. And this time, I can truthfully tell you I did feel something coming from his hand into my body. But I didn't jerk away like you would think. It was pleasant, the only other word to describe the feeling his hand gave me is maybe "orgasmic." I do know that when he finally took his hand away, I wanted a nap and maybe a drag on a cigarette. And somewhere deep down I knew this man would be important to me.

"I'm Sam. Sam Malone." I heard him say and I remember thinking, *like the bartender on Cheers?* But the fact is, he looked like a Sam. "Are you feeling better?"

God, he was cute. I noticed his skin was smooth and unblemished, except for the small, red boomerang shaped scar on his right temple. His eyes were huge and the brightest blue I'd ever seen. They looked like they could look right into my soul.

And his hair was thick and full, sandy blond waves that framed his flawless face. Long, but not too long, styled nicely around his neck – hair you just want to run your fingers through.

His lips were full and kissable. His nose, well, all I can say is it was perfect. His voice was the voice I dreamed of listening to in the dark, saying the last words I would hear every day and saying the first words I would hear every morning.

"Yes, I'm okay," I said sheepishly. "I'm just getting old. You know I turned fifty today." I chuckled, not knowing why I told him that.

"It's your birthday? Well, happy birthday," he said and he put an arm over my shoulder and placed his other hand on my chin, and turned my face slightly away from him, so he could plant a light kiss on my cheek. If I had been ready for it, I would have turned my head and let him kiss me full on my lips. My mama didn't raise no fool!

It turned out to be the best birthday I ever had, even if it did happen at the mall.

By the time I got home, I was exhausted, from which I had to assume was from my little tumble into Sam's arms. My head hit the pillow and I fell fast asleep.

That night, I dreamt Sam was standing over me as I slept, watching as my chest rose and fell in an even motion. He crouched down and I heard him whisper as he placed his hand on my belly, "You're doing fine – vision, blood pressure, oh, a urinary tract infection, facial dark spots, corns… the ugly toe – all right on schedule."

When I awoke the next day, I realized that I had gotten up only twice to go to the bathroom and no night sweats – an amazing feat for me. I got on the scale to see if yesterday's birthday dinner put me over two hundred and fifty pounds, for surely it had to – Lucy brought cupcakes. So, we ate cake.

I looked down at the scale and did a double take. Thinking I wasn't seeing the number properly, I put my glasses on and got back on the scale. I had to squint, but yeah – two hundred and forty-seven. Damn! I had to go buy a new scale and a new pair of glasses – happy birthday!

There was something else I noticed as I was looking down at the scale. The second toe on my right foot – the one I called the ugly toe, the one I never wore sandals because of, or got pedicures because of, deformed from birth – was no longer deformed. I chalked it up to being fifty years old. I just knew that when I looked at it again it would surely be ugly. It always was, it always will be.

# CHAPTER FIVE
## THE NEXT TWO WEEKS

As I drove to Bed Bath & Beyond to buy the new scale, I realized that I couldn't see the road very well, so I pulled over and took my glasses off. I cleaned them with my shirt and put them back on – still couldn't see. So, I took my seatbelt off and looked into the rear view mirror to see if there was something in my eyes.

I didn't see anything in either of my eyes, but that's when I first noticed that there was something missing on my face. I looked and looked for them, but I couldn't even remember where they had been. The dark spots were gone and so were the patches. Just freckles – my freckles. My fifty year old acne was gone, too – with no scars. And I had one perfect chin.

I remembered my dream and shook my head – can't be, he'd have to be some kind of miracle worker. And in my bedroom? *Please.*

And just to prove the dream was just a dream and Sam was gone and never coming back, I drove the rest of the way to Bed Bath & Beyond with my glasses on. But because it was just so uncomfortable, when I pulled into the parking lot, I yanked my glasses off. I was getting a headache.

I found the scales and made my purchase. When I got home, I took my clothes off and stepped on the scale – two hundred and forty-five. I jumped off. How could that be? The scale was new and I couldn't possibly have lost two pounds walking through Bed Bath & Beyond. If that could happen, every woman in America would be walking through Bed Bath & Beyond – every day.

I considered taking the scale back, but it was the same day, so I kept it – for one more weigh in.

It wasn't that I didn't want to lose weight. I had lost weight before, many times as a matter of fact. I'd take it off, put it back on, then take it off again. I got tired of that, so I decided to stay where my body was comfortable. Two hundred and fifty pounds seemed like a good round number on the scale, I could still enjoy the foods I liked and I didn't have to buy new clothes or run to the gym on a regular basis. Or run anywhere, for that matter.

Losing weight isn't just about physical changes, it's about the emotional changes you go through, too. Oh, sure, I always looked better and I felt better after I'd lost a lot of weight so, *of course*, I must need a man now, right? No, NO! I did the online dating thing… two years of it. Constantly thinking about it – nonstop!

I did the personal ads, too. Most guys would love me on the phone and then, when they got a look at me, it was over before it started. I did not want to go through that again.

I mean, really, if it is ever going to happen, some guy is going to come up to me and say, "I love you. Let's get married and have a baby – let's save the world together." If it's real love and it's meant to be, it should happen that way. And no long courtships – I don't believe in them. There's time for dating after a very short engagement and the babies will come when they are ready. Well, at least, that's how I, an outsider of all this love crap, saw it.

No, losing weight and dating for me is like kicking a dead horse.

Besides, there's a curse stuck in my doodah!

I was pacing around my room in the nude when I noticed my underwear drawer was open about halfway. I know that an open drawer is not really all that strange, but ever since the day I caught Bandit climbing into one of my open drawers, I've been afraid I would shut him in one and suffocate him. And I would just hate that. He's just a little guy – he's my little guy and I love him.

So, not only was it strange that I would leave the drawer only half way closed, but there was a pair of panties thrown carelessly on my bed.

There was no explanation for it, except to blame it on old age, so I went over to Charlotte's house to see her daughter Jill (a delightful accident), who was still a teenager and loves Halloween as much as I do. She always put together the best costumes, and as always, I wanted to see it this year. By the time I was in Charlotte's living room, Jill had already been to a few houses and showed me her stash.

She was dressed in black thigh high boots, red leggings, with pink shorts – a pair of pink jeans she had cut the legs off of – and a form fitting blue top that showed a lot of cleavage. She may have only been fifteen, but when it came to breasts, she took after her favorite aunt. The outfit was topped off with a headband that had three black stars with silver glitter on them. It made her blonde hair look enchanting. She had what appeared to be a red cape falling down her back.

She looked fabulous. She was a very pretty girl and a genuinely nice person, and the only person in the world who made me wish that I had a child.

I'll admit, I had to ask her what she was, "So? What are you this year?"

She put her hands on her hips, looked into the distance, and said, "I'm a time traveling superhero." She smiled that smile I loved so much. "Saving the world one century at a time."

Interesting! I wondered if there really were time travelers, if they could be half as beautiful as she is.

When she was a little girl, I would go and get her and take her to McDonald's or Burger King, where we would buy a kid's cheeseburger meal and a medium soda. We'd take it all to our table with ten packets of ketchup. I would eat the cheeseburger and drink the extra soda, and we'd sit for about an hour and I would listen to Jill talk about herself and watch her suck the ketchup off the fries. I love kids, and I love my nieces and nephews with a passion, but my passion for Jill was different. I couldn't love her more if she had come out of me head first.

It's not that I don't love my other nieces, Lynn and Annie, and my nephews, Eli and Brian. It's just that when they were little kids, I was doing the dating thing, trying my damnedest to find the man I would save the world with. Jill came along when Brian, the next youngest, was fourteen. By that time, I had almost given up completely on finding the love of my life.

Spending time with Jill made my heart ache, because she was calling me Aunt Emily and not Mommy. Now fifteen years old, I still loved spending time with her, but like most girls of her age, beauty, and personality, she had her own friends. Hanging out with old Aunt Emily was almost a thing of the past.

Whenever I saw her, I would always think that if I had a daughter, I would want her to be just like Jill.

Jill had only a few fun sized candy bars and offered them to me. I took them, tore the wrappers off like a champ, and ate them greedily. Charlotte looked at me, puzzled.

"Starving, haven't eaten anything all day," I said with my mouth full.

I realized I hadn't eaten anything all day, so I took myself out to dinner for a very fattening meal – I had to get back to my favorite weight.

So, my choices were McDonald's, Burger King, Wendy's, or Taco Bell. I chose Wendy's. I ordered a Bacon Cheeseburger, Biggie Fries, and a huge Frosty. It took me quite a while to eat it, but I finally got it down – and just for good measure, stopped and got ice cream on the way home. I was sick, but I was determined to keep it down. I had to get back up to my weight. Yeah, I know – never thought you'd hear a woman say that.

Yes, I did weigh two hundred and fifty pounds, but I didn't eat like a horse. It was just my metabolism, my makeup, my gender, and my heritage. That's my story and I'm sticking to it.

The next few pages are excerpts from my journal.

_Monday, November 1st, 2009_ – Welcome to a new month. I woke up, went potty, and got on the scale – 240. I hate this scale. This is the worst scale I have ever had. I'm throwing it in the garbage.

Bandit looked surprised that I was stomping around the apartment naked. (Author's note – I always weighed myself naked, but that would end starting tomorrow.)

On my way to work, I stopped to buy a bagel with butter and a carton of 2% chocolate milk. For lunch, I had a cheesesteak sandwich with peppers, onions, and mayonnaise with a large order of fries and a bottle of diet wild cherry Pepsi I bought at the cafe. It took me my whole lunch hour to eat it all. The girls I worked with had a good laugh watching me eat all that.

After work, I stopped to get a pizza for dinner and actually thought about eating the whole thing, but thought better of it when I realized I would probably just throw it up. So, I stopped and got a half gallon of mint chocolate chip ice cream and a bottle of diet wild cherry Pepsi and proceeded to have that when I got home.

I'm sure I'll be back up to 250 in the morning.

Thought about Sam today. I still think I know him from somewhere.

<u>Tuesday, November 2nd</u> – got up at 6:10 am, went to the bathroom, then got on the scale – 236. My mouth fell to the floor. I refused to believe that I lost 14 pounds in 3 days. It was the scale – it had to be the scale. And that's exactly what I told Bandit.

As I got off the scale, I heard a racket in the kitchen. Bandit heard it too as he looked toward the bedroom door and hissed. It sounded like all my dishes and glasses and all the cans and bottles in my pantry fell to the floor in a flourish of noise. I ran in there to find everything the way I left it, except for a lone spoon in the middle of the floor. Weird!

Stopped to get a bagel with butter and cream cheese and a carton of whole milk chocolate milk for breakfast. Lunch consisted of a whole order of chicken fingers (6 pieces) and a large order of fries. Again, a lot of food, but I am determined to keep it down. For dinner, I had some of the left over pizza and a half gallon of Tin Roof Sundae ice cream and a bottle of diet wild cherry Pepsi. I'm sure I will be back up to 250 in no time.

Where is Sam?

Wednesday, November 3rd — got up at 6:08 am, went potty, and jumped on the scale — 233. OMG! Why is this happening to me? Bandit had no answers.

Breakfast — hard roll with butter and a carton of chocolate milk with an orange juice chaser.

Lunch — grilled cheese sandwich with bacon and an order of fries and a bottle of wild cherry Pepsi.

Dinner — got a pepperoni and cheese sub with mayo and a bottle of Pepsi at Wawa.

I noticed my clothes are beginning to get loose on me — damn! I'll have to buy some new clothes — and where will I find money for that, since I've been buying so much food???

Sam... Where do I know you from?

Thursday, November 4th — up at 6:02 am.

Potty.

Weight — 228.

Bandit and I just looked at each other.

Breakfast — scrambled eggs and cheese wrap with mayo and a carton of chocolate milk and a small bottle of orange juice. The sugar will bring me back up to my real weight. I just know it.

Lunch — pepperoni and cheese sub with mayo from the cafe (Wawa is better) and a bottle of wild cherry Pepsi.

Dinner — chicken with cashews with an egg roll. I can't believe I ate the whole thing. Ugh!

How come with all the Pepsi I'm drinking, I don't have gas any more?

I noticed today that stairs no longer bother my knees — did Sam do this to me? God, I miss him!

I also noticed that Bandit is no longer sleeping on the bed with me. What's that all about?

Friday, November 5th — up at 6:00 am.

Weight — 250.

Slept all night, feel refreshed, feel like I could run 10 miles — what is happening to me? Bandit did not give me an answer.

When I was brushing my teeth this morning, I heard that same ensemble of dishes, cans, and bottles crashing to the floor in my kitchen. But when I went to investigate, everything was still just as I left it.

I'm not doing any kind of exercising, but I seem to be toning up — well, as toned as you can be at 225 pounds.

This is freaky... Even my calves seem to be slimming down... I want Sam.

Saturday, November 6th — out of bed at 5:58 am.

Why so early? It's Saturday.

Tried to sleep late, but had too much energy. Decided not to get on the scale — went to IHOP for pumpkin pancakes instead.

For lunch, I went to Lucy's and had a sandwich with them. Lucy noticed I lost some weight. When she asked me how much, I lied and said, "Only about 5 pounds." Well, I didn't want her to worry. And by the way, she bought it.

Dinner — had dinner at the food court in the mall — a hot dog with cheese fries and a Pepsi.

Was hoping to see Sam again, but I didn't. It's only been a week since my birthday and I miss him and I still have that nagging feeling that I know him.

I noticed I haven't had a hot flash in days. Bandit is still not sleeping on the bed with me.

Sunday, November 7th — up at 5:50 am.

Slept all night again.

Pretended I didn't see the scale, but it seemed to be calling my name, and Bandit was sitting next to it like he wanted me to step on it. But I got dressed and went out for breakfast instead. That's right, pumpkin pancakes.

For lunch, I searched through my pantry looking for something fun to eat. (Like I haven't been eating fun things since the first) Found one of those Mac 'N Cheese cups and made that. It was good. I haven't had one of those in a while.

For dinner, I went to Charlotte's — Lucy was there, too. Jill cut her hair, still looks perfect. Charlotte served spaghetti and meatballs with salad and garlic bread. I had 2 helpings of spaghetti and garlic bread. Tried to pass on the salad, but both Charlotte and Lucy looked at me like I had 2 heads, so I took a little salad and poured a boatload of dressing on it and topped it with a ton of croutons.

On the way home, I stopped at Scoops and got a small cone with vanilla ice cream topped with chocolate sprinkles.

Really want to see Sam — I want Sam in so many ways — how can I want someone so bad when I don't even know him? Or do I? I asked Bandit what he thought, but the question embarrassed him and he covered his face with both paws.

<u>Monday, November 8th</u> — up at 5:50 am.

Weight — 215.

I dreamt about Sam again last night. He was standing over me as I slept again, looking down at me — I wanted to tell him that I missed him and went to the mall hoping to see him, but the words wouldn't come. He put his hand on my belly again and whispered, "Right on schedule." What could that mean? I can't be dying, I feel so much better — in just a week.

Before the dream ended, Sam looked right at my face and said, "You will." What did that mean? I'm dying? Can he read my mind? Yeah, right! He'd have to be psychic or something and I'm not having any of that. Bandit was on the bed getting frisky with Sam?!? What was that about?

Sam looked great! <u>I WANT HIM!</u>

When he wasn't playing with Bandit, he was looking around my room like he smelled something funny. <u>My room does not smell!</u>

Breakfast — I wasn't hungry, so I just had an instant breakfast.

Lunch - still wasn't hungry — bought a small bag of chips at the cafe.

Dinner — wandered over to the mall and had a salad.

Thought about having my way with Sam in the back seat of my car. Where are these thoughts coming from? I don't even know him. And besides, I've never been in the back seat of my car.

<u>Tuesday, November 9th</u> - 5:50 am.

Weight — 208.

If I didn't feel so good, I would swear I was going through chemotherapy. Nothing against chemo patients, but why is this happening? Bandit still doesn't have answers for me.

For breakfast, I ordered scrambled eggs with cheese and wondered where I was going to get some money to do the shopping with.

For lunch, I broke down and got a salad off the salad bar and put lots of croutons and blue cheese dressing on it. I have to put the weight back on or I am going to need new clothes <u>real</u> soon.

For dinner, I searched the pantry again, hoping to find another Mac 'N Cheese cup, but no luck. I did find a pouch of mashed potatoes — so, mashed potatoes it was.

I hope I dream about Sam tonight...

<u>Wednesday, November 10th</u> - 5:50 am, already up and showered. I never shower in the morning. I'm sick, I have to be sick.

Weight — 205.

It is 1 day short of 2 1/2 weeks and I have lost 41 lbs. I think I'll call the doctor and get some blood work done. Bandit doesn't think that's a good idea. But come on, really, it's not normal to lose so much weight in this short amount of time.

I noticed my 'ugly' toe is never ugly when I look at it now — I think I may need a pedicure. There's no way Sam did that. Or did he?

I stopped and got French toast and bacon (crispy) from IHOP for breakfast and ate it at my desk. I noticed

I'm not falling asleep in front of my monitor any more. I miss my mid morning naps and my mid afternoon naps.

For lunch, I went to Wawa and got a bagel with cream cheese.

For dinner, I had left over mashed potatoes. How come I have leftover mashed potatoes? Am I not trying to put the weight back on?!

I have an appointment to see the doctor tomorrow at 3:00. I'll have to leave work early – yay! It'll be like a mini vacation.

When I came home tonight, I found a fork on the kitchen floor. Spooky! I'm almost sure I didn't leave one on the floor this morning. Why would I?

I hope I dream about Sam tonight – if I wish it hard enough <u>it could happen!</u>

<u>Thursday, November 11th</u> – 5:45 am.

Weight – 202.

I feel so good I have to wonder why I need to see the doctor. Why should I have to remind myself that I've lost almost 50 lbs in less than 2 weeks? What is my problem? Bandit doesn't know either.

Breakfast – scrambled eggs, bacon, and cheese on a wrap with extra mayo for good measure.

Lunch – chicken cheesesteak on a nice fluffy roll with extra mayo. Seemed like a lot of mayo, but who am I to judge – and, of course, a bottle of wild cherry Pepsi.

Dinner — went to Taco Bell and got a couple of soft tacos and a wild cherry Pepsi.

When I was at the doctor's, I told Dr. Berger how much weight I've lost and he gave me a look like I was crazy — like I had always been this weight. Doesn't he ever look at me? No one else does, why should he? He took blood and I made him weigh me, so the next time I come in there will be something to compare.

I want Sam so bad, I had to take a cold shower — which is really not like me at all. And it didn't help.

<u>Friday, November 12th</u> — 5:40 am.

It's payday — thank God — I have become very poor in the last 2 weeks.

Just couldn't face the scale today, couldn't stomach any food, and could only do a half a day at work.

I am having Sam cravings and going through Jill withdrawals — since I have no idea how to get in touch with Sam, I called Jill and invited her to dinner. She already had a date planned, of course — she's 15, isn't that too young to date?

The doctor called to tell me my blood was fine and normal and told me to stop worrying <u>because nothing has changed.</u> Well, maybe not yet, but I'll be changing doctors tomorrow.

I headed over to the mall at around 5:00 to grab a salad at Salad Works and realized that if I was going to see Sam at the mall, I would have to hang out awhile. I tried to remember what time it was when I found myself in his arms. I seemed to be lost in my memories because it took a little girl's giggles to bring me back to reality.

I miss Sam!

Bandit is still not sleeping on the bed.

<u>Saturday, November 13th</u> – 5:30 am.

Okay, this is ridiculous. I like to sleep – all this energy is killing me.

Weight – 200.

And I don't think anyone really notices – how could they not notice? My clothes are huge on me. What is wrong with these people? What is wrong with me? Okay, Bandit noticed and I think he's okay with it.

I really have to buy new clothes – the few articles of 'small clothes' I had in the back of my drawers and closet are running out. Sure, I can wash them – but I need more. I'll go to Wal-Mart tomorrow

Breakfast – back to IHOP for pumpkin pancakes.

Lunch – Mickey Dee's for a quarter pounder with cheese meal – super sized. Really, how do people drink this much soda? Should have gotten a shake. That I can finish – it's only ice cream.

Dinner – I found 2 cups of Mac 'N Cheese in the pantry. Weird... they weren't there the other day. And there was a 2 liter bottle of wild cherry Pepsi in the fridge – when did I buy that?

All day I thought about the Go-Go's and their song, 'Vacation' — "<u>Two weeks without you and I still haven't gotten over you yet.</u>"

If I don't see Sam Malone soon, I am going to explode.

# CHAPTER SIX
## PLAY IT AGAIN, SAM

By the time Sunday the fourteenth rolled around and I got on the scale to find out that I had now lost a total of fifty five pounds in two weeks, I decided that I really did need to go to the store – I just couldn't put it off any longer. There was no denying it. Not only was I losing weight, I was looking better and feeling better. But my heart was sick. I didn't really understand it, but I wanted Sam. I looked up Sam Malone on the internet and there were just too many to figure out which one is the Sam my heart (not to mention my body) was aching for. Because truthfully, I really needed Sam.

I had been shopping at the Wal-Mart in Neptune for just a little while, thinking about Sam, wondering what it would be like to run my tongue over his… And that's where I was in thought, when I heard a rush of wind going through a tube behind me and I heard his voice – the voice I wanted to hear in the dark, saying all kinds of sweet and dirty things. Okay, I know that's a bit nauseating, but I really do like his voice. And I had been aching to hear it.

"Well, look who's here, the birthday girl. How are you feeling?"

I turned to face him. He looked good – *good enough to eat*, I thought. He was wearing a green polo shirt with blue jeans and slip on navy sneakers. His eyes were bright and shiny, and almost looked like they were dancing. His lips were full and kissable, and his skin was flawless (except for that boomerang shaped scar, but I decided that it worked), with just a hint of a five o'clock shadow. Man, he *was* good enough to eat.

"I feel good." I felt great, now that I was looking at him in the flesh again.

"You look good," he said and I really wanted it to be true, but how could it be? My clothes weren't fitting properly.

"What are you doing here?"

Embarrassed, I said, "I lost some weight, so I have to buy some new clothes."

"Ooh, new clothes are fun to buy." He sounded very excited, like we were buying him a new wardrobe.

When I only shrugged, he said, "Is something wrong?"

"I'm losing weight, but I'm not dieting."

"Well, as long as you're not dieting, how about you let me take you to lunch?" He smiled.

I must have given him a blank look because he said, "Did I say something wrong?"

"I don't usually get asked out by men in the Wal-Mart," I chuckled. "Oh, who am I kidding? I haven't been asked out by a man anywhere in a very long time." I laughed a very nervous laugh.

"I can't believe that, but if it is true, I am honored to be the first." He stretched his arms out to the side and gave me a mock bow.

"Okay." I suddenly thought that there might be something wrong with this guy. I started to look at shirts again.

"Just a slice of pizza?" he asked, sounding hopeful.

What the heck. I was hungry and I didn't have to see him again, if afterwards I still thought that there was something wrong with him. But it was Sam and I had been missing him – and wanting him.

Lunch was at my favorite little Italian place on West Park in Ocean Township. I had a salad, two slices of pepperoni, and a garlic knot with a cherry coke. Sam had two slices of sausage and peppers, one slice of pepperoni, and three garlic knots with a cherry coke.

"Mmmmmmmmmmmmm," he kept saying, drawing the Ms out like a lover. He made it sound like eating was a very intimate affair.

"The food not this good where you come from?" I asked with a giggle.

"Not at all," was all he said and I could see he meant it.

"So, what do you do?" I asked.

"I'm a doctor, a baby doctor," he said.

*Really?* I thought, *what doctor describes himself as a baby doctor?*

"A baby doctor?" I asked suspiciously. "You're a pediatrician?"

"No, I just deliver babies," he said between bites. "It just makes me happy to help deliver babies."

"You help deliver babies?"

"Yeah, I just help." He continued to eat. "I don't have my own practice, so I'm just on call when my partner, Austin Clarke, is delivering a baby."

"Dr. Clarke is your partner. He's my doctor."

"Really?" he asked, but it sounded like he already knew that.

He talked me into ice cream after lunch (after all, I hadn't bought any new clothes, so I really had to put fifty five pounds back on), so I met him at the Carvel in West Long Branch where I had a brown bonnet over vanilla soft serve and he had a large chocolate sundae with nuts, strawberries, hot fudge, peanut butter sauce, and two cherries. He ate it like he'd never had ice cream before.

"Mmmmmm," he said, licking his lips. "That was good," he sighed. "The only thing better would be getting your number, so we can do this again sometime."

I was caught between a rock and a hard place. Here was this guy who I had wanted to see for weeks. He made me feel like I mattered and made me want him more than anyone else, and at the same time was weirder than anyone else I knew – and I knew some pretty weird people. On the other hand, who was I to judge? And after all, I had asked for something freaky to happen, and damn it, if he wasn't freaky, no one was. So, I was going to see this thing through.

We exchanged numbers. Sam had one and he got all mine – I'm old fashioned, so I still have a land line. And as we were walking to our cars, I realized I still had to buy clothes. And I heard him say, "If you'd like, I'll go shopping with you. I don't mind."

I thought I might really like that. But then, I started thinking again about how much weight I had lost in so little time.

My heart started to race. I must be sick. I must have cancer – a very fast moving cancer. I was going to dwindle away to nothing. I would have kept thinking that way, but my cell phone rang and brought me back to the present.

It was Sam. *He must be calling me from his car*, I thought.

"So, when did you want to go shopping? We could go back to Wal-Mart right now. I'm not doing anything."

I really had to shop, they were really getting upset about my clothes at work. Just the other day, my boss had taken me into a conference room and said, "Emily, this is ridiculous. You look sloppy – what is happening to you?"

So different than the time he took me in the conference room to tell me my clothes were too tight. Damned if I do, damned if I don't. I just couldn't win with this guy.

He didn't even ask me if I felt all right or even if I was sick. He didn't even suggest that maybe I should go to see a doctor. I liked him, but come on, I had worked for him for ten years and you'd think he'd have at least a little real concern for my health.

"What are you doing? Going to the big girl shop for your clothes now?" He was in my face.

*Well, yeah, where else would I shop?*

"Don't you realize how the way you look reflects on me?" he said, exasperated.

And just like that, he made it about him.

Sam met me at my apartment, so we could go back to Wal-Mart together to help me get a few new outfits for work.

I got into his car and the first thing I saw was what appeared to be a TV screen where the radio/CD player should be. But it was double the size of your average radio/CD player and looked just like a flat screen, only smaller.

In fact, nothing was right on the dash board – the ignition was missing and there was no gear shift. There appeared to be no air and no heat. There was what I thought was a clock only because it had the numbers 2010 on it and I thought it must be military time. But I didn't know military time, and I really didn't want to ask and appear to be stupid.

I leaned back to get the belt, but Sam stopped me and pushed one of only two buttons on the dash in front of me, and the belt came out of nowhere and I was belted in.

"What just happened?"

"Oh, don't give it another thought. There are very few cars like this in the world right now," He said waving his hand like he was waving it all away. "It's a new model, probably not going to turn into much for quite a while."

"What kind of a car is it?" I asked.

"It's a Honda, it's one of only two makes left."

"What?"

"Uh, it's the only make I'll own."

Ok, fine, I had a 2000 Honda Civic myself and I understood where he was coming from. But even if my car was ten years old, I was pretty sure the new Hondas didn't look like this.

"What year is this car?"

What came out of his mouth was muffled, and I think he wanted it to, but I was sure he said, "Twenty-two fifty-seven."

"Huh?"

"Oh, um… it's, um… a twenty thirteen model," he stammered.

"Twenty thirteen? Sweetie, it's only two thousand and ten."

"Oh, I know, but all the car makers test cars that will be future models."

I wasn't sure if that was true, but I wasn't sure it wasn't true, so I had no choice but to accept it.

He was smiling at me.

"What?"

"You called me sweetie."

He placed his hand over the circle near the flat screen and the car started up.

"What was that?" I asked.

"Oh, they're testing out new ways of preventing cars from being stolen. There's a finger print recognition program built in," he said. "Eventually, no car will ever be hijacked again."

Hijacked? A car? Didn't he mean carjacked?

"That seems like a step in the right direction," I said. "I hope they pull that off."

"They do. I mean, will – they will," Sam said. At that moment, I heard what sounded like wind chimes and a face all of the sudden filled the blank screen – a black face, sweet, with huge brown, puppy dog eyes and large white teeth.

"Sam?" he said in a sweet voice that matched his eyes. His neatly trimmed goatee was more visible as he moved his head to see me.

"Hi, Kurt, be selective. I'm with Emily."

What the heck did that mean? Well, I guess it could have been worse – he could have said, *spell everything. I'm with Emily.*

Sam looked at me and smiled. "I didn't mean anything by that."

"Dolly is getting a little antsy," Kurt said. "She's really scared."

"Dolly is fine. There's nothing to be scared of," Sam said in a soothing tone. "I've done this hundreds of times before."

"I know, but this is her first time."

"And I promise she is doing great. She's going to be fine," Sam continued with the soothing tone. "The baby is fine, too"

"I'll tell her," Kurt said with a sigh.

"Emily and I are going shopping, then we'll probably have something to eat. After that, I'll stop by if that would help Dolly to feel better."

Kurt smiled and disappeared from the screen with the sound of wind chimes.

I knew a girl named Dolly – worked with her for six years until she got married and mysteriously quit five weeks ago. I wondered if they could possibly be the same person. If that were the case, it really is a small world.

Sam then said, "Wal-Mart in Neptune," and the car started, and Sam placed his hand over that circle again and put the car in gear.

The screen now showed a map of the area with a red line showing the way to Wal-Mart. In the left hand corner was the temperature at fifty-eight degrees and the right hand corner had the date.

"What was that?" I asked calmly.

"Bluetooth and face time," Sam said with a smile.

"Dolly?"

"Yeah, she's one of our patients – she's having a baby." Sam smiled.

I found that very funny as Kurt looked to be at least fifty years old. But maybe he had a lot of money. Or did something special real good.

"And what did you mean when you said, *be selective, I'm with Emily.*"

"Oh, I meant be short, I'm doing something important."

Okay, that made me feel better. I was important. It didn't make any sense, but I felt better.

"What is face time?" I thought I could figure it out myself, but since I had never heard of it before, I wanted to be sure.

"It just means that you can be face to face with the person you're speaking with."

"Oh, cool!" I said.

On the way, I noticed that words appeared and disappeared on the screen with no rhyme or reason. Some of them popped up for just a second and some stayed for longer.

*Sam, want to go hit a bucket of balls?*

"You golf?"

"No."

*Beam me up, Sam.*

*Sammy!* After this word appeared, a man's face came onto view, with the muffled sound of glass falling to the floor and breaking, he seemed to look at me, then at Sam, rolled his eyes, and disappeared. Sam got an odd look on his face.

*Where are you?*

*Good news! My boy is now a vet.* Sam seemed to smile at this.

*So, what about Boo?* Sam got a confused look on his face.

Sam's eyes actually shifted from the road to the screen. Wow, he was good.

We shopped for almost two hours and for once, shopping was really a lot of fun. Sam picked out pants, tops, dresses, and skirts – and I put them on and modeled them for him. I decided on all the things he liked the best.

At the register, I was sure I used my credit card to pay for my new clothes, but I never got the bill for them.

As we walked out to the car, Sam announced he was hungry.

Shocker!

"I was thinking the Windmill and their world famous cheese fries. Mmmm, mmmm, mmmm," he said, licking his lips.

I watched him lick his lips and thought we barely had ice cream just a few hours before, but the best cheese fries in the world were now calling my name, too. And I had to get the scale back to normal.

"So," he said. "The Windmill?"

I nodded my head to say, yes, and he reached out a finger and touched the screen on the dash board and said, "The Windmill on Ocean Avenue in West End."

He ran his finger over the start circle and the car started up; and what I now figured was the GPS, commenced to give us directions.

The Windmill is on Ocean Avenue in the West End part of Long Branch, next to the Tasti D-Lite, which is across the street from a park that used to be a movie theatre. I have to assume they called their restaurant the Windmill because it looks like a windmill, but I guess they could have decided to call their restaurant the Windmill, and then built it to look like a windmill. But it really does look like a windmill – it's red and has the four blades. The blades don't move, of course, but that's how you know it's a windmill.

I ordered a hot dog, cheese fries, and a Pepsi. Sam ordered a hot dog, a cheeseburger, cheese fries, and a Pepsi. And we sat at the counter that runs half way around the place against the windows. The other half was the cooking area.

I found that eating with Sam was very entertaining. I ate half my hot dog in the bun and half without the bun, and I ate my fries slowly as to savor the taste, because they really are the best cheese fries in the world. In the same time, Sam ate his burger, his fries, commenced to get the attention of the guy behind the counter to order more fries; ate his hot dog, ordered another one when his second fries came, and got a refill on his Pepsi.

We didn't talk much while he ate because he just enjoyed his food so much. It would've been hard to get him talking anyway. I didn't have a problem with that. I enjoyed my food, too, but for as big as I was, I couldn't eat the way he did. I had no idea where he was putting it all. He was a slim guy – a very cute slim guy.

Yeah, sure, there was that old saying about how it was going down his leg or something like that, but I'm sure if that were true, he was filling both his legs. He took a last sip of Pepsi, picked up his napkin to wipe his mouth, and he leaned back a bit and smiled.

"That was a great meal. Want some ice cream now?"

The Tasti D-Lite right next door used to be a Carvel, so we wouldn't have to go very far. "Can we let our food settle first?" I was sure he would at least have to go to the bathroom before we got ice cream. Because I did.

I used the bathroom at the Windmill, then Sam suggested we take a walk on the beach before going over to the Tasti D-Lite. I agreed. Even though it was November and it was a bit chilly, I love this time of year – so, why not take advantage of it? Besides, I had been eating so much lately, it just felt like I should. So, we walked across the street and found a nearby stairs down to the sand. Before we got down there, Sam looked out at the ocean, closed his eyes, and took a long, deep breath through his nose.

We took our shoes off and went down to the water's edge. Sam stopped and looked out over the ocean again.

"It's so beautiful," he said.

I wasn't sure I agreed, but said, "Okay."

We turned and walked toward the beach at Bath Avenue and we chatted. Sam's voice was gentle and soothing, and much better than a stress ball.

"Did you always want to be a doctor?" I asked him.

"No." He smiled, stopping and looking out over the ocean again. "I wanted to be a surfer. But the pay is bad, as my dad told me on a daily basis. And besides, the water's not safe."

"What?" I asked incredulously.

"Well, you know," he said. "There are sharks and guppies in there."

I giggled. I couldn't help myself, putting guppies in the same category with sharks – that's funny. He was just so cute.

"What about you? Are you doing what you always wanted to do?"

"Me? I went to Montclair. I wanted to be a writer, but I just never seemed to get that one great idea for my first book." I shrugged my shoulders. "But it could still happen."

He seemed very interested in what I had to say, which was very unusual, because no one ever cared about what I had to say.

"It will," Sam said, almost without thinking about it.

Twenty minutes later, we were back across the street and walking into the Tasti D-Lite. It being November, they weren't busy, so we were waited on right away. I ordered a small hot fudge sundae with vanilla ice cream, and Sam said, "Make it a large."

"No, I won't be able to eat all that ice cream."

"It won't go to waste," he said, and ordered a large banana split and a chocolate shake. We went to the car to eat our ice cream and we didn't talk, until he tipped my cup over his mouth to let the last of my melted sundae drip into his mouth. He smacked his lips and smiled. I was beginning to hope that someday soon I could make him do that.

"The food is so good here."

"Here? You mean here on planet Earth?"

He laughed, then looked at me tenderly. I was a little uncomfortable because no one had looked at me like that in years.

"What?" I asked.

"I think you are very special."

"Oh, I get it. You're going to kill me?" I asked.

He smiled and asked, "Why would you say that?"

"Because no one talks to me like that."

"That doesn't mean it's not true."

I wasn't sure what to make of that, so I eyed him curiously.

"What do you mean by *your food is good here?*" I had to ask. "Are you from another planet?"

"Do you mean, am I an alien? From another planet? No! Of course not. I'm human," he said.

"Okay, if you're not an alien, where are you from?"

"I was born in a suburb of, um… Philadelphia."

I gave him a questioning stare. "How old are you? If you don't mind me asking."

"I don't mind you asking," he said. "I'm fifty-three.

"Are you an only child?" I thought it was a good time to get to know him better.

He looked at me tenderly. "No," he said, shaking his head. "I had a twin brother."

"Had?"

"Yes, my brother, Seth, died when we were three."

"Oh, Sam, I am so sorry." I wanted to take him in my arms and comfort him, but he didn't look like he needed to be comforted. But I still wanted to take him in my arms. Weirdo or not?

"How did he die?" I asked.

"I'm not ready to talk about that with you yet," he said sincerely. "But we will talk about it. It is important that you know."

"So, tell me now."

"When it's time, I will tell you everything."

I told Sam about my sisters and Bandit, and my nieces and nephews.

# CHAPTER SEVEN
## BANDIT AND THE WATER BOWL

Sam took me home and I found Bandit's water bowl in the middle of the kitchen floor when I went up to my apartment. I was almost sure Bandit couldn't be doing it. So, I asked him, and he looked at the bowl and hissed, and gave it a rude paw gesture.

I put the bowl back on the mat I bought special for Bandit, even had his name put on it, and headed to my room to change. On the way, I heard a clatter of dishes falling to the floor and breaking, along with all the cans and bottles in my pantry; and I ran back to the kitchen only to find Bandit's water bowl in the middle of the floor again. Bandit was hissing at it again.

I know this may seem a little silly to you, but it was this event that made me go back to Wal-Mart and buy a Louisville slugger. Yes, I know that a famous bat would do me no good against Casper the tricky ghost, but it made me and Bandit feel safer.

Two nights later on the sixteenth, Sam called and wanted to have dinner with me. I suggested IHOP.

"You hop?" he asked excitedly.

And I said, "No, silly, let's go to the International House of Pancakes for their new pumpkin pancakes."

His eyes glazed over and he said, "Ooh, pancakes. Can we put syrup on them?"

"Yes."

"And whipped cream?"

"Yes, of course, when you buy them, you can put anything you want on them," I said.

He had treated me to the Windmill's world famous cheese fries and I wanted to introduce him to the best pumpkin pancakes. I would have treated him, but recently I had spent a lot of money on food and clothes, and I still had to pay bills.

Breakfast is my favorite meal of the day, so I ordered two eggs over easy with hash browns and sausage, with my favorite pumpkin pancakes. Any meal is Sam's favorite meal of the day, so he ordered the pumpkin pancakes, the eggnog pancakes, a BLT on rye with mayo, French fries, and hash browns. I smiled – you had to love the way Sam ordered food.

While we waited for our food, I asked Sam what he had been doing the last two days. As soon as the question came out of my mouth, I felt bad for being so nosey.

But Sam didn't care. "Austin and I delivered two babies, a male and a female." I thought that was a very peculiar way of describing human beings, but he wasn't wrong. Not technically, anyway.

I decided to tell Sam about the mysterious goings on in my apartment, but didn't quite know how to start, so I blew air out of my mouth.

"What's wrong?" Sam asked.

"Well," I began. "There are some very weird and strange things going on in my apartment." I deliberately left out the part about how they started the night of my birthday – the first time I saw Sam.

"What kind of weird and strange things?"

"Well, the first thing is I hear bizarre noises coming from another part of the apartment," I told him. "Which is crazy because my apartment is small."

"What kind of noises?" Sam seemed very interested.

"It sounds a lot like what dishes would sound like if they were falling off of shelves and crashing to the floor. Also, it sounds like all the cans and bottles are falling off the shelves in my pantry. Weird, huh?"

"And you've heard this more than once?" he asked.

"Yes, a few times."

"Anything else?"

"Yes, once, when I came home, I found my underwear drawer halfway open," I said.

"Why is that weird or strange?"

"Because I have Bandit and if I left drawers open all the time, he could crawl in one and fall asleep. I might not see him and shut the drawer with him in it, and he might suffocate or something."

"Okay, so, you found the drawer open…"

"Well, that in itself wasn't weird because I may have gone to close the drawer and just not have pushed it all the way in. What was really weird was the pair of underwear I found on my bed."

Sam's eyes widened just a tiny bit. I'm not sure if he knew I noticed.

"Anything else?"

"The other night when you took me home after dinner, I went upstairs and found Bandit's water bowl in the middle of the kitchen floor."

"And you don't think Bandit did it?" he said, shaking his head from side to side.

"Well, he might have, except that I moved the bowl back and went to change for bed – and I heard dishes crashing to the floor and when I got back into the kitchen, Bandit's bowl was back in the middle of the floor." I was talking very fast now. "I was only out of the kitchen for a few seconds… I can't explain it."

Now Sam's eyes got very wide.

"So, I went out and bought a Louisville slugger – not that I think it will do me much good."

"You can buy those?" To this day, I still don't understand the question. Sam seemed very unsettled now. "Is this just since we met?"

"Yeah," I said. "Since that night at the mall – since my birthday."

"Oh, it's probably nothing to worry about," he shrugged. "Probably just a few tricky ghosts." But his breath came out hard and I just felt like he thought there was a problem.

Sam said he would be out of town until Saturday and if we could spend the day together.

I brought Sam down to the beach, so we could walk on the sand and pick up shells. It was my favorite thing to do after a storm and especially after a hurricane – you never knew what would wash up on shore.

At around 11:30, Sam was hungry again, so we went to the mall to eat at the food court. Sam liked to mix it up and try different places. Sam got Chinese, while I got a kid's meal at Burger King. I wanted to see what toy I would get.

As we were leaving the mall, I noticed one of those picture booths and suggested we get in and take some silly pictures. They were silly, but I loved them and couldn't wait to go home and put them on my dresser mirror. Silly, I know, but I had never taken those pictures before.

When we got back to my apartment, I asked Sam if he wanted to come upstairs.

"Sure, I'd love to see your apartment," he said excitedly.

When we got up to my apartment, I went right into the bedroom to put the pictures on my dresser mirror. Sam followed.

"So, what do you think?" I asked.

"I like it. It was fun taking them."

Then, I realized that I had all the pictures and I tried to give half of them to Sam.

"No," he said, putting his hands out in front of himself. "You keep them. I'll visit them." He smiled.

I smiled back at him biting my lower lip, "Would you like to kiss me?" I asked. You can learn so much about a guy from that first kiss.

"Yes," he said, moving closer to me. He was so close I could smell his soap. Man, he was clean.

He put his face right up to mine, but hesitated.

"You have done this before, right?" I asked softly.

"Yes," he said, then put his lips against mine; taking my lower lip gently between his lips and with just the tip of his tongue, he lightly and expertly licked; sending serious sparks of excitement up and down my spine. It had to be the chastest kiss I had ever gotten, but easily the best first kiss I had ever gotten.

Oh, who am I kidding? It was the best kiss in the history of kissing.

When the kiss was over (way too soon for me), Sam pulled my lip with him as our lips parted. He put his forehead against mine and said, "And, no."

I took a deep breath and asked, "What does that mean?"

"I will tell you someday soon," he said as he walked out of the bedroom. I followed. "I promise."

He gave me a hug at the door and I went back into my apartment, feeling on top of the world. That's when I heard the clatter again coming from the bedroom.

I ran in there and found my beautiful black and white pictures ripped into little pieces and on the floor. I looked around the room and only saw Bandit, and I knew he did not do it. I grabbed my phone and ran out of the apartment. I dialed Sam and practically screamed into the phone, "Sam, you gotta come back!"

# CHAPTER EIGHT
## FONZIE AND THE HAPPY DAYS GANG

I don't know where he came from, but Sam pulled into the parking lot in just a few minutes. He was barely out of the car when he saw my tears.

"What's wrong? What happened?"

"You have to come back upstairs."

"I can't make love to you tonight," he said apologetically.

"Do I look like I wanna make love?" I almost screamed.

Sensing my annoyance, he said, "Lead the way."

As we went back upstairs, two things went through my mind. First, I had left Bandit upstairs to fend for himself – what kind of a mother was I? And second, the Louisville slugger is in my room right next to my bed and I didn't even think to pick it up. But what would I have used it on?

"Right after you left, I heard that noise again – you know, the dishes crashing to the floor. And when I went back into the bedroom, I found the pictures on the floor in little pieces," I told him.

Sam stopped on the way into the bedroom and grabbed my arm and turned me toward him, stopping me in my tracks. "Did you see anybody?"

"What?" I sneered. "Did I see anybody? How would I see anybody?" I asked as I walked into the bedroom. "I live alone."

The thing I remember the most before everything went black was somebody saying, "I see you haven't told her the good news yet, Sammy."

When I came to, I was lying on my bed with Sam at my side (ooh, déjà vu), with a cool damp cloth on my forehead.

"Are you okay?" he asked.

"I thought I saw Fonzie and the Happy Days gang in my bedroom."

When Sam and I walked into my bedroom, I saw six or seven guys in a 'V' formation. They were wearing white t-shirts, jeans, black leather jackets, and their hair was cut long in a 1950's style. In the instant before losing all control, I wondered why men, who looked to be in their fifties, were dressing like teenagers.

He gave his head a minimal shake.

"Yeah, well, that's not what we call them," Sam said. "But, yes, they were here. I made them leave."

"But how? And why? And who are they?" And even as the words came out of my mouth, I knew the questions were pointless. Just the fact that they were in my bedroom was impossible.

"Why? Because he doesn't like me – in fact, he hates me."

I couldn't imagine anyone hating Sam. "How did they get in my apartment? I ran out my only door and stood outside waiting for you right there in front of the apartment door. I was outside the whole time. I would have seen them."

"Well," Sam said. "Not exactly."

"What do you mean, *not exactly?*" I asked.

"Well," he started. "They have a different mode of transportation." He paused a moment, then continued, "It's called time travel."

I chortled at this.

"Time travel isn't real, it's science fiction," I said point of fact. But then, meekly asked, "Isn't it?"

Sam screwed up his face and shook his head back and forth. "It's science fiction here in the twenty-first century and made for quite a few real good movies," he began. "But in the twenty-third century, where I'm from – where knucklebrains is from – time travel is a reality."

I was pretty sure he meant knucklehead, but it's Sam, so I let it go.

I knew he was weird and loved him for it, but this was a bit much. "Sweetie, maybe you should lie down and I'll put the cool cloth on *your* forehead."

"I was hoping we'd be a little bit more along in our relationship before this," he started. "But I find it's time to let you in on a very well kept secret."

Yes, because a little more time would make that easier to handle. He took my hand and helped me off the bed. He stood behind me and took my left hand in his. Oh, what fantasies I would have about this – is all I could think about.

Our hands reached up. "Now, which one do we want to peek through?" he asked.

"What are you doing?"

"We are going to open a time rift, so you can see just how real time travel is." I wasn't sure if I believed in time travel, let alone want to open a time rift to make it real.

"Ah!" I heard him say. "Now just let me guide you."

"NO, Sam, I don't want to. I'm scared." Yes, scared about what would happen. What if Sam couldn't open a rift? How would he feel, then? But what if he could open a rift and time travel was real? How would I feel, then?

"It's okay. I know it can be scary, but I'm right here and I'm not going to let anything happen to you. We're not going anywhere. We're just gonna take a little look see." His breath was on my neck and I could smell him – the manly scent of him and at that point, I would have let him do anything he wanted to do.

"So, we're gonna just reach up and gently close our fingers on it," Sam said in a gentle voice.

Sam pressed my fingers together and oh, my God, I actually felt something between them. "Sam," I said. "I feel something."

"Yes, I know. That's the fabric of time."

The fabric of time? *Oh, please.* I snickered, but quickly felt silly and wished I could take it back.

As I thought these things, Sam guided my hand, so we were gently pulling on whatever it was my fingers had a hold of. And, oh, my Lord, there was a soft ripping sound – like tape being pulled off of a flat surface. As we gently pulled our hands away, I saw my bedroom like it was another bedroom and I saw Sam easily lifting me up onto my bed.

The last thing I heard before floating in the blackness again was what sounded like a shade snapping back and rolling up to the top of a window.

When I came to, I was back on my bed and Sam had the damp cloth on my forehead again. Bandit was close by, giving himself a bath; impervious to what was happening.

"I'm dreaming, right? Time travel doesn't exist in real life. You can only do it in the movies."

Sam was looking at me tenderly again.

"What?"

"No, it's real in the twenty-third century – where I'm from," he reminded me.

"You can't be from the twenty-third century. That would mean you had traveled a very long way to get here. And why would you?" I asked.

"Among other reasons, I came here to meet you."

"Why would a guy from the twenty-third century want to meet me?"

"Because you're special."

I wasn't buying it. I had never been 'special' to anyone before. Maybe my parents, my sisters, but not any of the guys I ever dated. So, no, certainly not special enough for anyone to come from that far away to meet me.

"You're gonna have to do better than that," I said.

"Okay, you can do something for me that no one else can."

"Like what?" I was a bit skeptical. With all the women in the twenty-first century – that's assuming he really was from the twenty-third century – only I could do this special thing for him.

Sam actually blushed at the question. He looked around the room, like he was trying to think of the right words. Bandit finished up his bathing and put his front paws on my upper arm, as if to soften whatever it was Sam had to say – because it was going to be hard for me to hear.

"I need you," he finally said. "To have a baby with me."

At first, I didn't think I heard him properly. But then, I burst out laughing.

"Sweetie," I said with a smile. "I can't have a baby with you or anyone else. I had a hysterectomy a few years ago. I'm not even sure I'd want to have a baby if I could."

I got up off the bed and looked at him. "But you got me, that was a good joke. Haha! Time travel and fifty year old women having babies," I snickered. "What a hoot. Maybe you should go."

Sam was very patient with me. He sat down on the bed. "What if Fonzie and the Happy Days gang come back?"

"I don't know how you did it. How did you get those guys in here? Did you drug me? Because, really, time travel isn't real and none of this is… can be real."

"Do you feel drugged?" he asked calmly.

I didn't, so I put my lips together and shook my head.

"Remember the night of your birthday at the mall?" he asked. "Remember I touched you? I put my hand flat on your back?"

I did remember, but I didn't want to. Too many freaky things had happened since that night. But I also had to admit that a lot of nice things happened since that night. Like the kiss, the best kiss I ever had, and how just knowing he was on the planet made me delirious at times. I began to cry.

"Yeah, so?"

"I gave you something that no one else could give you. I gave you a gift," he said.

# CHAPTER NINE
## THE GUY WITH SOMETHING EXTRA

"Oh? And what gift was that? Not a baby I hope?" I asked petulantly.

"I gave you back your health," he said gently.

Wait. What?

"What? What does that mean?" And even as the words were coming out of my mouth, I knew what he meant. Since that night, about three weeks ago, I had lost almost eighty pounds, my skin was clear of all my brown spots and patches, the arthritis in my knees was gone, and my eyesight was perfect.

"Did you make my ugly toe pretty?" I asked shyly.

"Yes, I threw that in for giggles," he said with a smile.

"But how?"

"I am a psychic healer," he said.

*Oh, dear merciful God in Heaven.*

"No, no, no, you're not. Psychics are not real, that I know for sure," I practically shouted at Sam. "And anyone who thinks he is one is a criminal."

Sam's expression changed from illuminating to hurt and I knew I had to stop talking. I didn't want to hurt him and there was no denying the things he had already told me. So, maybe he was a psychic or a psychic healer like he said.

"I'm not just a psychic. I'm a psychic *healer*. Think of me as the guy with something extra."

"Do you see dead people?"

"No, I'm not a medium."

"I've seen on TV where they debunked psychic healers as charlatans and scam artists, pretending to help people just to get their money," I informed him.

"Yes, but I'm the real thing. I'm not doing this for money or fame," Sam said, getting off the bed. He took me by the shoulders and guided me back to the bed, and pretty much forced me to sit down.

"Sam," I asked. "Why do I keep thinking that I know you from somewhere? Have we met before?"

Sam gave a snort. "That was your last thought just before you passed out that night and I wondered what you meant," he said. "But that was before I harvested your eggs."

Wait. What?

"Before you did *what?*"

"Think back to that night you were in Boise Idaho twelve years ago. You were on a business trip for the company you were working for at the time."

It was true, before my current job, I was an administrative assistant at an advertising agency and I occasionally had to travel with my boss, Michael Santini. Michael was the kind of guy who was not a Mike, but absolutely a Michael. Michael was almost six foot tall – weight was not then nor has ever been anything I could guess, so I won't try. But he was fit. He made sure every day that he was.

Michael said his suits were Italian, as were his shoes, and fabricated flying to Italy to pick up his custom 'designed' suits, when in fact they were off the rack in one of the better stores at Monmouth Mall.

Michael was a man who enjoyed being pampered, mostly by women he did not employ, so facials and manicures were a weekly treat for him. He enjoyed having his nails buffed and polished to a shiny gloss. Not my kind of guy, but his wife seemed to be able to tolerate him, at least for the first five years of their marriage. After that, I just couldn't feel sorry for him.

Michael was all about being the best, but sometimes, as in Michael's case, the best means you're an ass.

On this trip, my last trip, I began to feel pain in the lower part of my belly early on the morning of the day of an important meeting – and my boss kept saying, "Nothing can go wrong today." Wow, was he wrong.

The pain became increasingly agonizing. It had started on the right side of my belly, but by the middle of the day, the pain had spread all the way to the left side of my belly. I told Michael I couldn't handle the pain any more and he said, "You're joking, right?" And pretty much told me to suck it up. And if I didn't, I could get myself back to New Jersey and find another job tomorrow.

I tried, I really did, but I just couldn't. And it wasn't long before I was fading in and out of consciousness, and not long after that I rolled out of my chair onto the floor.

I came to on the way to the hospital in the ambulance. The attendants had plugged an IV bag of some clear solution into a vein in the back of my hand and hooked me up to a heart monitor. I had an oxygen mask over my face and the pain was unbelievable. On a scale from one to ten, the pain was well within the fifteen to twenty range.

The female attendant, who introduced herself as Aggie, explained to me that I had passed out and I had been on the floor for an undetermined amount of time when she and her partner, Ken, got to the conference room. Sadly, Michael didn't know anything important about me – too bad, I had only been working for him for fifteen years. So, they needed to ask me a few questions. He couldn't even tell them how long it had been since I passed out. That actually made me happy, because a man who didn't know me would not fiddle with me in my incapacitated state.

At the emergency room, it was determined that my appendix was bursting and I was prepped for surgery. As they were wheeling me into the operating room, we passed a man who seemed to be watching intently as they pushed me passed. As I was caught in between what I like to call, the here and there, feeling kind of like I was drunk, I noticed he was cute with sandy blond hair, big blue eyes, and a very cute smile, so I said, "Hello," in the sexiest voice I could muster.

Oh, my God! I had flirted with a guy I didn't even know while being wheeled into surgery. "That was you? But how? You haven't changed a bit."

"For you, that was twelve years ago. For me, it's been just a few weeks," he smiled confidently.

"So, why were you there?" I still was not exactly sure if any of this could really be true.

"I was the assistant surgeon for your surgery. I harvested seventeen of your eggs at the time."

"And the surgeon didn't realize you were doing it?" I asked, getting riled up.

"He didn't know."

"How could he not know? You were right there with him! Did he leave the room to go to the bathroom?" My voice had risen a couple of octaves, as it always did when I had trouble understanding something.

"Well, no, but he wasn't aware of what I was doing because he, like you, lives and moves in real time.

Whereas I, not only live and move in real time, I can also live and move in what I like to call travel time," Sam explained.

"What does that mean?"

"It means that I can slow time down or speed it up – depending on what the situation calls for," Sam said. "So, right after Dr. Parker made the laparoscopic incisions, I went into travel time, meaning I slowed time down, so I could harvest the eggs while he was none the wiser," he finished proudly.

"Who said you could do that, anyway? What if I had needed them?" My voice was still up there.

"I'm sorry to say that Ariel had looked into your future and knew you wouldn't need them." He looked very concerned.

"Ariel?" I asked sarcastically. "The little mermaid?"

He grimaced. "Ariel is my wife—" He stopped almost as soon as he said it.

Wait. What?

*"YOUR WIFE?!"*

*Oh, my God! This just gets better and better.*

I had let this man kiss me. I had many dreams about him standing over me in my bed and watching me sleep, not to mention the naughty daydreams I had been having for weeks now at my desk to make up for the loss of my mid-morning and mid-afternoon naps.

*Oh, dear Lord, I'm going to Hell in a hand basket.*

His face took on a contorted look. "Yes, I know," he said out loud. "I know what you're thinking and I knew this part would hurt you. That's why I wanted to wait until we knew each other a little longer."

"A little longer?" I asked. "Because a little more time was going to make *finding out that you're married* better for me?!"

"Please let me explain."

"Sure, why not? Go right ahead. It's not like everything you've already said was a piece of cake," I said.

"You have cake?"

# CHAPTER TEN
## THE VIRUS

"Sam," I said. "You've already come this far, please, please enlighten me.

"How many people would you say are on the planet right now?" he asked. I had no idea what this had to do with harvesting my eggs and his wife.

"I don't know. A few billion. Why are you asking that?" I asked, stunned at the question.

"Because in the year two thousand two hundred and fifty-four, the year I come from, there's less than five hundred thousand people left on the planet," he said humbly. "The youngest male on the planet is thirty-seven and the youngest female is forty-three."

I was confused. "Why are there no children? Don't you people have sex?" I almost screamed it. After all, he wouldn't have sex with me. But then, why would he? He had a wife.

"Yes," he smiled. "But the women in the twenty-third century are barren."

Where had I ever heard that word before?

"At the risk of sounding stupid, what does that mean?" I asked.

"It means they're infertile. They can't have children. They can't conceive."

Not having any children of my own, I could understand that these women probably felt like failures. That is, of course, if this was all true.

"Why not?" I asked.

"On the night before mine and Seth's third birthday, the government released a virus into the night air…" he began.

"What?" I sat myself upright. "That's quite an accusation. I know the government is capable of many things, but a virus? For what purpose?"

"In the year two thousand two hundred and one, there was close to sixty billion people on the planet." I was amazed. Not really surprised – he was talking about almost two hundred years in the future. It could happen.

"We don't really have an exact number as a great number of the planet's citizenship didn't live within the city walls. So, records weren't kept," he continued.

"Where did they live?" I heard myself ask.

"As you can imagine, there wasn't enough resources left to maintain any kind of a normal life for all of us. By the year two thousand one hundred and seventy-one, most jobs or occupations had become automated. Progress, you know. They figured out a way to keep things running without human help." He stopped for a moment to catch his breath. "Are you okay?" he asked.

"Yes. Where did these people live?" I asked again slowly.

"They lived on the outskirts of the cities, in the foothills and in caves." He grimaced again. "In tents on blankets at the beach."

"Why?" It was just too unbelievable and I wanted to catch him in this mockery of my feelings for him.

"There was nowhere for them to live. They couldn't afford their lifestyles any more, so we just have to assume that they were forced out of the cities to live off the land. There was still a lot of what you might call natural foods." He really didn't look well. At the time, I was sure he had the countenance of a man deluded.

"Like?" I asked.

He blew air out of his mouth. "Like bugs and roots." He really looked like he was going to throw up. "Flowers, bugs, did I mention bugs?" His voice cracked. "Bunnies, deer, raccoons, and rats – anything they could find."

I just looked at him, not knowing what to think or feel.

"And then, what?" I asked.

"They actually began to thrive, but when the natural resources began to falter, they would come into town and break into stores and houses to take what was left of our commercial food. At first, they only came into town in the night when everyone was asleep in their beds, but they got bolder. They started to come in the daytime, not caring who saw them. They got violent and brought weapons. Murder had to have been on their minds." He took a breath here.

"Wow!" I said. "That's a great story – you should write a book," I said, getting off the bed and walking away from him.

"I don't have to," I heard him say. "You're going to write the book."

Okay, now he had my attention. I took a bottle of Pepsi out of the fridge and started back for the bedroom. He was now in my living room, sitting comfortably on my loveseat. Bandit was right next to him.

"Traitor," I said, sticking my tongue out at him. I sat down on Bandit's other side and he laid his head on my thigh. "I'm going to write the book?"

"Yes," he said. "I've read it. Several times and I've seen the movie several times."

At this statement, I practically lost my soda, but choked instead.

"There's a movie?" I asked incredulously. "Who plays you?"

"It would be easy to get ahead of ourselves," Sam responded. "First things first, let's talk about the virus."

"Okay, so they live out of town, eating off the land. Tell me, why would the government do that? I mean, besides the fact that there's a gazillion people in the world and there isn't enough food for them." Did I just answer my own question?

"Yes, precisely, because there were just too many people in the world. And no way to keep them alive and healthy." He had listened to my thoughts, but I was okay with that. "Now, I am not saying what they did was right. I'm not saying it was wrong, I'm just saying."

"So, there are too many people in the world, let's kill them off," I said. "Is that what the government said?"

"The official papers say that the virus was created to prevent conception in certain women." Sam looked at me and I could see pain in his eyes.

"Certain women?" I asked. "Are you kidding me? You're telling me that in two hundred years people still haven't gotten over their petty prejudices? That people still can't get along with each other?"

I wanted to vomit.

"Well, yes," Sam answered weakly. "I'm sorry to say that it's true."

"Why are you sorry? You were only three years old," I comforted.

"Well, to be honest, it started long before Seth and I were even born, before our parents got married," Sam continued. "Women from all walks of life, all around the world were called into what they were calling command centers for all kinds of screenings and blood tests. People thought they were going to start up the cloning process again."

I will not go into the cloning process here. When Sam explained it to me, I did not like it and I don't think you will either. Unless you've always wanted a twin. Even then, you still shouldn't want to know.

"What they were looking for was a certain DNA marker. DNA markers are a specific gene that produces a recognizable genetic trait and they use to test for it to find people who would develop certain cancers and late in this century, developmental disorders like autism, retardation and Down syndrome. Which, by the way, they will find a cure for by the year two thousand and twenty-six," Sam explained. "Robin Cook wrote a great book about DNA markers. You should read it."

I did not know any of this and was quite mesmerized listening to Sam explain it. How could anyone think he wasn't a genius? Or at least intelligent?

"So, they found the marker they were looking for?"

"Yes, by end of the twenty-second century they found their marker and began to develop the virus that would attack only the reproductive system of females with this marker. They didn't want to kill anybody. They just wanted to prevent offspring of what the official papers call 'undesirables'." Sam actually winced. It hurt him to tell me this and I loved him more for it.

"They think that at least one of the scientists on the team jumped the gun, and tried to speed up the process by using inferior components. Maybe incorrect measurements or maybe it just wasn't ready," Sam took a sip of his soda. "Whatever happened, what we know is that it all went terribly wrong." He raked his fingers through his hair. "Originally, they had scheduled the release of the virus six months after the actual disbursement."

Wow! That was a lot to take in at one time. I really didn't think I could listen to any more at the moment.

"I need a break," I said. "You should go." At this, Bandit got up, and stretched and yawned big.

"Can I continue tomorrow?" he asked.

"You tell me – you read the book," I said, walking into my bedroom. "Please lock the door behind you."

# CHAPTER ELEVEN
## FOR YOUR ENTERTAINMENT

I could not get to sleep. I kept tossing and turning. I flipped the pillow a couple of times, but it didn't help. I kicked the covers off and stared up at the ceiling, and didn't remember hearing the rush of wind through a tube.

I got up and went back into the living room – I honestly could not believe what I saw. Bandit had been sleeping on the back of the love seat, but was now awake and yawning. Sam was stretched out on the love seat, his head up on the arm.

"Sam?"

Sam stirred, but didn't wake.

"*Sam?*" I said a little bit louder.

Nothing. The man sleeps like a log.

"SAM!" I shouted.

Slowly, his eyes opened and as he focused on me, he smiled. But the smile soon disappeared and with a rush of wind through a tube, Sam was gone.

*How did he do that? I didn't even see him reach up for a time rift.*

"Not funny, I already saw you." I said to no one. I waited. He had to come back. I wanted to talk about this.

"Sam?" I said out loud. "Sam, I want you to come back right now."

Nothing.

"Sam, come back right now or never come back again." And with a rush of air through a tube, Sam was back.

We looked at each other for a few minutes. He sighed, and I, with my hands on my hips, continued to stare at him.

"Well?" I finally broke the silence.

"Well, what?"

"You want to explain why you're sleeping on my couch?"

"Not really." He smiled, but he went on, "I had been staying with Austin before we met, but after that day at the mall I've been staying here."

"Why? Don't you have an apartment?"

"It never seemed prudent to have one, since I move around so much."

"Do you not have an apartment because you don't have the money?" I asked. "I mean, it's not like you have a regular job."

"Oh, no, I have lots of money – that's not the problem. I'm just not in one place for very long," he explained.

"Why didn't you tell me?" I asked. "I don't think I would have been upset about it. But as long as you're already in the apartment, shouldn't you just sleep in the bed with me?"

"I can't, not until we get married."

"But still, I don't think I would have been upset." I looked down on my love seat and saw the sheets. "Do you make the couch up every night?"

He smiled and nodded his head. "Yeah, I do. I like sheets."

"And you're the reason why Bandit doesn't sleep in bed with me any more." I looked at Bandit. He had his paws in front of his eyes.

"Bandit and I have been catching up," Sam said.

Wait. What?

"How could you have lots of money?" And as soon as the words were out of my mouth, I regretted them. "I'm so sorry, that was a really personal question. But how could you have lots of money?"

"I have an unlimited supply of gold, silver, diamonds, platinum, pewter, and pearls." ·

I didn't understand. "And that means what, exactly?"

"In the twenty-third century, gold, silver, diamonds, platinum, pewter, certain coins, and pearls have no value," Sam started.

"Yeah," I said. "I'm not sure pewter and pearls have that much value here. But go ahead, sorry I interrupted you. Gold and silver have no value? Diamonds have no value? They're worth a lot here."

"Exactly," Sam said. "And I have an unlimited supply. Here in the twenty-first century and the late twentieth century, there are all these convenient little stores that will buy it from me, and Boo and the other guys."

*Boo and the other guys?*

It took me a few minutes as I have never had anything to sell. I never really gave those stores a thought. I never even thought they were legitimate.

"Yeah, they're legit," Sam chuckled at this. "We needed a legal way of getting money from whatever time period we were in. Not just me, the other guys, too."

"Isn't that changing history? Wouldn't that create a paradox or something?" I asked.

"This isn't a movie. It's not science fiction. Just because somebody thinks it might happen, doesn't mean it will," he explained gently. "We did some testing before we sold the first pieces of gold and silver, and it really didn't make that much of a difference. We just had to be sure we didn't sell anything from this time period. You know, make sure it doesn't belong to anyone who is, say, still alive."

"So, it's okay to do something as long as it doesn't make a difference?" I chuffed. "When did it happen that gold and silver had no value at all?

"It was about the middle of the twenty-second century. I couldn't tell you the exact year. I'm not an historian. There just wasn't a need for it any more. And by that time, all the natural resources were hoarded either through legal means or pilfering, anyway." By this time, Sam must have been dry. So, he got up and went to the fridge and got himself a wild cherry Pepsi. "Haven't you even noticed that your fridge is always full?" he said, when he came back. "Your pantry is always full?"

My fridge was always full and so was my pantry – trips to Foodtown were becoming less frequent for me. "You're buying me food?" I asked weakly.

"Well, I do seem to eat a lot of it now," he chuckled.

"Now?" I asked.

"Yeah, since we met I have discovered all kinds of different foods," he said excitedly. "We should get Chinese food. I have never had Chinese food. Have you?"

"Yeah, once or twice," I sighed.

"Okay, so, you have all the money you will ever need, a virus killed a few billion people in the twenty-third century, and I write a book about it," I recapped. "Tell me about the entertainment center."

"The entertainment center is a very busy place – every book ever written, every song ever recorded, and every movie ever made; and games, every game ever created. It's all there – well, every one that survived is in that building. They are open every day but Sundays. That's our day of worship." He was still smiling and I wanted to punch him.

"Yeah."

"Well, Ariel had been begging me for months to participate and I kept saying no, because I didn't think I could love anyone else."

"So, what changed your mind?" I asked.

"For four months, I had been traveling through time and meeting a lot of women. And they were good women – sweet, smart, fun women, willing to help repopulate the world, and we didn't have to offer anything in return but love and health. And I thought, well, we could at least have the genealogy done to see who could be found." He paused.

"Genealogy?"

"Yes, all the women have to be in our wives' direct lines. The world leadership really wanted to make it a family affair."

"Okay, keep going." I admit, I'm a very inquisitive person and I needed to know more.

"So, on Sunday, June eighth, I told Ariel that I would participate in the program and meet somebody." He was nodding his head like I finally got it. I had not.

"You need to spell this out for me."

He got a curious look on his face and said, "Which part did you need me to spell out? The month?"

"Sam," I said. "I still don't get it. What is so special about June eighth and ninth?"

"On the day I finally told Ariel I would take a more active part in the project, so we could be a family, the entertainment center was closed. It was a Sunday, the eighth day of June. The very next day, a patron – who just happens to be a friend and colleague of Ariel's – found the book, checked it out, and read it. She loved it and thought she recognized me and some of the other characters – and suggested Ariel take it out and read it." He paused, for effect, I think.

"After Ariel read the book, she admitted to doing the genealogy and announced she had found the perfect person. That was you. This, by the way, genealogy is a job for a psychic profiler, like my mom. They have to find the right person, but I have to admit, Ariel did a pretty good job." He was still smiling.

*A pretty good job?*

"So, what you're saying is that there was no book until you said yes to meet me. So, you changed the past – isn't that like against the laws of nature?" I wondered.

"Tiny changes are fine, they are actually expected. It's catastrophic changes that are against the laws of nature. Like, I wouldn't be able to go back in time and stop the planes from flying into the World Trade Center towers. While I am sympathetic to the families of those lost that day, putting those people back into the time line could possibly change things dramatically. Does any of this make sense to you yet?" he asked.

In a strange way, it did.

"So, tell me about the movie? Who plays you?" I asked with a glint in my eye.

He smiled at me and said, "Who do you think?"

"What you do mean?" I asked.

"Well, you know me, you're attracted to me – who do you think would play me well?"

I was getting tired, but I was also feeling a little playful and still wanted to catch him in a lie, so I said, "Denzel Washington?"

"Ah, great actor, but too tall," he said with a chuckle.

Denzel is truly a great actor.

"Um, Ron Howard?"

"I think he stopped acting a long time ago. Besides, he doesn't have enough hair to be me and it's red."

True.

"Dennis Quaid?" I asked. The man was one of my favorites, so it would only stand to reason that if I wrote the book they were going to make a movie out of, I might have something to say about who played the leading man.

"Too sexy," Sam said.

Even though Sam is a very sexy man and very cute, he falls short of that movie star look, so I had to agree.

"Simon Baker?"

"Not old enough."

True, but very cute.

This was kind of fun and for the time being, I forgot Sam had a wife and he was from the twenty-third century, and there was a virus that had wiped out billions of people, blah, blah, blah.

"Blair Underwood?"

"Way too sexy."

Also true.

George Clooney?"

"Not Sam."

I wondered what that meant.

"Hugh Jackman?"

Sam just smiled and shook his head from side to side.

"Ryan Gosling."

Another favorite.

"Too young, try again."

"Robert Downey, Jr.?"

I was trying to think of movie stars from some of my favorite movies.

"NO!"

"Johnny Depp?"

"Too dark."

"Brad Pitt?"

Sam's head bobbed up and down, and he was grinning from ear to ear.

Well, Brad Pitt's eyes are blue and he does have sandy blond hair – and, like Sam, could look younger beyond his years. Of course, when it's the movies, I found in Hollywood they could do just about anything they wanted.

Well, I guessed he could pull it off. But the Brad, Angie, and Jennifer triangle drifted through my mind and I almost had to laugh.

"Did I change the names to protect the innocent?" I asked.

"Yes."

"Then, how do you know the book is about us or that I even wrote it?" I asked in that same mocking voice.

"We have a huge entertainment center. You call it a library. It's where all of our entertainment is stored. Books, music, movies, and video games. You name it, it's there. It's for the whole community, so that no one person or couple or family have more than anyone else." He was nodding his head slightly.

"Again, I have to ask how do you know it's about us and written by me?"

"The author's last name is my last name, and no one read it until it was discovered on the shelf on June ninth of this year," he said with a smile.

I still didn't understand. "And why is that date so important?"

"Because for months, ever since the project began, Ariel had been asking me, begging me to participate in a more, shall we say, hands on capacity. She wanted me to be more than just the traveling healer, she wanted me to meet someone and have a baby, so we could be a real family." He was still smiling. "So, we could have a part in saving the world, too."

"I know," I said, "that I'm just a woman from the twenty-first century, but I'm still not getting it."

"The book didn't exist until I said yes."

# CHAPTER TWELVE
## THE ART OF TIME TRAVEL

"How does time travel work? Can anyone do it? Can I?" I asked, still not sure I believed him. How could I? Time travel is science fiction.

Sam and I had been sort of dating on and off for about a week and a half, and I wasn't sure if he had actually ever lied to me. He said things to me that no one had ever said to me before.

"Did Ariel invent it?" I asked, taunting him.

"No, Ariel invented the artificial environment," he continued. "The government." *Oh, no,* I thought, *not the government again.* "Yes, the government", he said again.

"Those rat bastards," I giggled, trying to ease the tension.

"The government started to discuss the possibility of time travel in the year two thousand one hundred and seventy-five. Before the virus, they gathered all the information they could, the written word, all that was stored in the data banks – what you call "the world wide web" right now. About twenty of the top scientists of the time got together and they actually figured it out by the year two thousand one hundred and eighty-six. It took almost eleven years to figure it out. In that time, they built the time machine and developed the chip – the time chip. I know," he continued. "Not a very inventive name, but in eleven years, that's what they accomplished."

"So, I have to assume then that the time machine still exists?" I asked. I couldn't help myself, it really was a very interesting story. I had to admit, he was very creative. "Because here you are."

"Yes, it does," he laughed. "Are you familiar with Mount St. Helens in Washington?"

"Yes, I am. I have cousins up in that area," I said.

"Well, on September twenty-fourth, two thousand one hundred and fifty-four, Mount St. Helens erupted for the fifty-seventh and last time. It spewed up a compound that they later decided to call Helenspew. Because whatever it was, when it mixed with the lava and ash it became a non-destructible material. And there was a lot of it."

"What happened to the people who lived nearby?" I was just full of questions. I really wanted to hear the whole story.

"I'm sorry to say that anyone in a fifty mile radius, perished. And that includes all the animals, insects, and plant life."

This upset me, but it was in no way Sam's fault.

"So, they built the time machine with this non-destructible material and the time machine still exists," I summarized. "And in between, time travel was invented and you came here to meet me." I was still having a little trouble believing everything he was saying, but there was a small voice in my heart telling me it was all true.

"By the time Marty was discovered," Sam continued. "In two thousand two hundred and fifty-three, the government was already trying to figure out how to save the human race. If we hadn't figured out time travel and invented the artificial environment, the time machine would still be there long after the handful of us who are left passed away. But we figured it out and we found we could make it work."

"So, you don't think you're messing with God's work?"

"What do you mean?"

"Well, maybe it's God's will for the world to end this way, maybe the human race is supposed to die out." And even as I said the words, my heart broke thinking about Sam dying in the future.

"Who do you think gave us this knowledge? And because He did give us this knowledge, don't you think we should use it?" Sam asked.

He had me there. I totally believed that if God gave you a gift, talent, knowledge, etc. you were obligated to use it.

"Okay," I said. "So, now you have this still existing time machine, which apparently functions as a time machine, because, well, you're here from the future. And you must have a time chip." I smiled at him. "How does all this make time travel possible?"

"The time machine – which I like to call Marty, because I love the *Back to the Future* movies – don't you?" I nodded my head. "So, Marty relies on the sun or solar power and we've got plenty of that. If you were to stand in the middle of Marty, you could see all the rifts and you could fold space."

"Say what?" I asked.

"Personally, I think it's the Helenspew that makes it possible," Sam said, nodding his head. "It has to be what makes it possible to see the ripples in time and space. There are a lot of them and they are all around us all the time. If you could see one, you could reach up and grab it between your fingers and pull it open and travel through. Once on the other side, you would need another time machine to get back. But since there is only one, you need the time chip to interface with Marty."

I was gripped by this story and couldn't wait to write it – oh, yeah, if he said I was gonna write it, I was most certainly going to write it. I would thank him in the forward.

"Don't you want to know how we figured all this out?" he asked with amusement on his face.

"Sure," I said, because now I really did want to know. Sam sat down on my sofa and patted the seat next to him so I would sit down. I sat down.

"Okay, remember the scientists back in two thousand one hundred and eighty-six, they had built the time machine and developed the one time chip?"

How could I forget?

"Well, they realized that the chip had to be sort of a middle man or go between, so a man or a woman could interface with the machine. So, in order for it to work properly, it had to be connected to the person; be a part of the person. They decided that the chip would work best if placed in the right side of the brain."

"Why is that? Why the right side and not the left side?" I heard myself ask.

"The right part of your brain is called the cerebrum, it's what causes the body to move. And since time travel is about moving your body, they decided on the right side of the brain. If they were wrong, they decided they would develop another chip and place it in the left side of another scientist's brain."

Sam was very excited at this part of the story and quickly went on.

"But they were brilliant scientists and it turns out the right side of the brain is the best side for time traveling.

Of course, all of the scientists wanted to be the first traveler, so they had to draw straws. I'm not really sure if it was straws – we'll just say straws," Sam said with a grin.

Sam's story continued and I will take over from here to explain further.

A man named King, Stephen King – is he related? I don't know. But he won the draw. So, they surgically placed the chip in his brain. No pain, no muss, or fuss. A few days later, he began to see the ripples in space even when he wasn't near Marty. So, he started to grab them to see what would happen. The scientists were mesmerized. They followed him around and watched as he opened up time rift after time rift. Well, after a few days of this, he decided he was going to pick one and walk through it.

The question on everyone's mind was how he was going to get back, but he assured them that because the chip was in his head and he was interfacing with the time machine, it would act as a beacon – he could surely return.

So, he did just that. He opened a rift and stepped through it. To those left behind, it seemed a very short time that he returned. Seven minutes, they said, but he was sporting a full beard and much longer hair than it had been when he left. He claimed to have been gone for nine months. He also said they had to hide the time machine, so that it would not fall into the wrong hands. Because of what he learned, he was certain the world was not ready for this kind of technology. But he told them further in the future, which is where he went, they would be ready and they would need it desperately.

"The time rift Stephen had decided to go through brought him to the year two thousand two hundred and fifty-three. Just thirteen short months before I became a time traveler," Sam said with a smile. "Yes, Emily, Dr. King taught us about time travel first hand. He stayed with our scientists for nine months before he realized that the time machine could be put to better use by us, so he had to go back and make sure the machine was hidden and would stay that way until he came to visit us. Remember how Dr. Brown hid the time machine in the third *Back to the Future* movie in a cave, so Marty could find it in the nineteen fifties? Well, Dr. King and his colleagues did that very same thing."

I felt like my head would explode. At this point, it would have been okay with me if Sam had put a gun to my head and pulled the trigger.

"Okay, I'm confused. You're saying he and the other scientists hid the time machine in their time. But didn't you already have the time machine when he arrived through the time hole, uh, portal whatever?" I forgot what we were calling it. "How else could he teach you about time travel?"

"Yes, we had it, about a year before the doctor arrived. Some friends were back packing up the Atlantic coast on their way up to Niagara Falls where the center is or was."

"The center?"

"Yes, the center for detecting special abilities, where I went when I was twelve – where I met Ariel." He stopped, knowing full well that Ariel was still new information and it still stung.

"So, the six of them were on their way up to Canada and stopped by the Ellis Island Park to have lunch or maybe just to rest, I'm not sure. And Lucas, one of the guys, had never been to the Lady before and decided to walk out there and check the statue out." Sam stopped to take a breath.

When I realized he was talking about the Statue of Liberty, I was confused.

"Uh, sweetie, I don't think you can just walk out to the Statue of Liberty." Remembering the one time I went on a school field trip, I was pretty sure we took a boat out there.

"Well, since the wind machines, or blades, or mills, whichever you prefer to call them, were put up, they had to have a way to get out to each one in case there was a problem, so they built what I think you would call a pier, out to the Lady," he explained. "Although, I don't remembering ever hearing or reading about any problems."

"So, it's really not a tourist attraction any more?"

"Oh, not for at least a hundred years, since the harbor is now mainly in use as an energy source and there is really no one to visit any more, anyway. If you had seen it once, you pretty much saw it and didn't need to see it again, unless you were bored or back packing." Sam shrugged his shoulders. "It's still a national park, I suppose, but not really a point of interest or concern because the windmills are pretty much self sufficient."

Sam nodded his head. "So, no jobs there. So then, Lucas walks out there and goes inside, you know, the base or the bottom and comes running out about ten minutes later, yelling and screaming that there's a 'thing' in there and he saw 'things' in the air. It was Marty."

*No kidding!*

"And the things he saw were the time rifts."

*Really? I hadn't figured that out.*

"So, they all went in, and they all saw it and the time rifts."

"Did they pull on them?" I was almost scared to ask.

"Yes, and what they saw scared them." Sam was really running with the story now and so was I. "So, they called the world leadership office and—"

"They called? They could make phone calls?

"Oh, yeah," Sam said. "Our phones are two hundred years smarter than they are now. In fact, we don't even have to dial any more. Everything is either voice activated or fingerprint activated. No one or very few people left in the twenty-third century can duplicate either."

*Genius,* I thought.

"Okay, so they call the world leadership office and what do they say?"

"Well, I can only guess that they described what they found and all the things they could see. Needless to say, Canada had to wait. They could have went on their way, but they were curious to know what it was. I would have been, too. So, anyway," Sam continued. "The world leadership sent a crew to transport Marty to the center at the Falls."

"Did they even have a clue what it was?"

"No, not at first, but they had several clerks from the WLO searching all the data banks to see if there was anything written about it. It took a while, but they finally found a journal, a hand written journal – guess where and whose it was? It was at the entertainment center under glass to preserve it and it was Dr. King's journal." Sam was practically giddy with excitement.

"How did they know to look for it there?" I was practically giddy myself.

"One of the officials there remembered reading something about it some years back, so they got it and they read it," Sam said with a lot of enthusiasm. "And they waited."

"Waited?"

"Yes, the journal told when he would arrive. So, that's when we realized we had the means to actually save the human race and the plan making became more serious."

"So, in the nine months Dr. King was with us, he discovered our technology was only slightly more advanced than his. Since the human race was practically extinct, there was no one to further the technology. He and my good friend, Doug, developed many more chips as we were now contemplating many, many travelers." Sam took a deep breath.

"We found out earlier that the artificial environment that Ariel created would not mature in our women. In fact, before we stopped the process in the twenty-third century, we lost two of our precious girls. Ariel was heart sick. I was secretly happy we hadn't tried it on her first, like she wanted. But that is another part of our story."

Sam continued, "We are talking about time travel – and you must understand, it wasn't as simple as walking through a rift as Dr. King did for all of us. I don't know why, maybe because he was so brilliant it worked differently. I can't say. I just know it took me almost five weeks to make a successful round trip. And just as an FYI, I didn't want to be part of the group scattering around time to make babies. My interest in the project was purely to protect the health of our men and the babies – and the special ladies. There were so few of us."

"And you could protect their health because you're a…" I just couldn't bring myself to say it.

"Yes, I could, because I'm a psychic healer," he said in that same matter of fact tone.

"No! No, you're not. There is no such thing as psychics. And anyone who thinks he or she is—"

"—Is a criminal. Yes, I know how you feel about psychics. We've been through that." He looked at me with that same calm expression on his face and continued.

"The psychics of your time – most of them, anyway – are con artists who learn to read people, facial expressions, body temps, body movements, or language, all for your entertainment and for your money," he said in a very reassuring tone. "There are a few real ones in your area. I've had to be very careful and stay under their radar."

He continued, "My job was to keep everybody healthy and to prepare the bodies of the women who were selected for the project – to create the artificial environment. They had to be women whose lives would be disrupted in insignificant ways. Like it couldn't be a woman who had a husband – in fact, it was decided that it would be women who had never been married and never had children."

"Why is that?"

"Honestly? Because they would be more likely to want the experience of having someone to love them and have a child."

"But why would you think someone my age would want to raise a child? And wouldn't people want to know how someone who had had a hysterectomy was having a baby?"

"Although the child will be the natural child of the woman who gives birth, it will also belong to the traveler and his wife at home. The wife at home has her DNA inseminated right into the eggs, giving the child two moms and a dad. The child would be taken to the mom in the twenty-third century, so she too can have the experience of being a mom. The child also has time travel built into his or her DNA – no chip will be needed."

My head was reeling – he had really thought this through.

"I didn't see any of the time rifts until the chip was inserted into my brain. For whatever reason, surgery was out of the question – time was of the essence. They took a syringe with a very long needle and inserted the chip through my temple." He pointed to the boomerang scar on his head.

"Did it hurt?"

"To quote the people of the twenty-first century, like a son of a bitch. Hey, I'm nobody, just a psychic healer, but it took another psychic healer to calm the pain. Let's just say if they thought they would have to insert another one into me, they were out of luck. Once was more than enough for me," he said, shaking his head.

"Like I said, as soon as the pain died down, I could see the rifts, they were everywhere and there were a lot of them. We were told not to tug too hard, so as not to tear a hole in space or time. And they wanted us to open rifts that would take us forward or backward just a few minutes to start. A week, a whole week, it took me to get the hang of it, but I was determined – the health of our last few remaining men was important."

"What changed your mind about having a baby of your own?"

"At first, I didn't want to be a part of the program more than restoring health and creating the artificial environment package, because the men really had to care. I've been in love with Ariel since we met – I was twelve and she was thirteen. We met at the center for detecting abilities and I love Ariel so much, I couldn't even imagine that I could care enough about another person and want to have a baby with her," Sam said."

"Ariel did the family history behind my back, behind everyone's back. We have genealogists or psychic profilers for the purpose of finding these women. She found you and wanted to share parenthood with you – she pestered me so bad that, in the end, she beat me down and I promised to meet you. She got permission for me to restore you back to health, even if I didn't want to have a relationship with you, vice versa – unusual, because it could have changed the time line – but the minute I touched you I knew, you were so much like Ariel, I knew I would fall in love with you."

"Why me? What does family history have to do with this?" I was on the verge of tears.

"It was always important to make this a family thing, that all the women in the past – well, my past – are related to the women of my time. Ariel is the many generation granddaughter of your niece Jill."

My heart skipped a beat. This was just too much. He was mocking me and he was using my love for Jill to hurt me.

He looked into my eyes and took my hand, and in that instant, I just knew it was all true.

# CHAPTER THIRTEEN
## GHOSTS OF THANKSGIVINGS PAST

On November twenty-fourth, the day before Thanksgiving, I went over to Lucy's house to let my sisters know that I was bringing Sam over to Thanksgiving dinner as Sam suggested. It was only right that I let them know I was bringing a guest, and to possibly break the news that I was going to marry him and have his baby. I was sure that would go over well, just like a lead balloon.

After all, how could they not have noticed how healthy I was compared to the day we met Sam. I was seventy-five pounds heavier, had horrible vision, stiff legs, and age spots, and even had some grey in my hair. All of that was gone, thanks to Sam. They would have no trouble believing that I, fifty year old Emily Gibbons, was going to finally be married and have a child. *How could they not believe it?*

Okay, sure, it might be hard at first, but after some time, after they realized how healthy I was, it would be easier.

I stepped up to Lucy's door and was ready to knock when I heard Sam's voice in my head saying, *'You can't tell them.'*

*'Can't tell them what?'* I thought to him. After everything that had happened over the last couple of days, this was actually fun, but wouldn't last. I wasn't any good at it.

*'You can't tell them I'm from the twenty-third century and we're going to have a baby.'*

I was blown away. *'They're my sisters, my family.'* I felt my heart breaking. This was something I had wanted to tell them most of my life. *'They'll be happy for me. For us.'*

*'Yes, I'm sure they would be,'* I heard him say. *'But they can't know. The fact that I've come from the future to get your help in repopulating the planet is information that is limited only to those involved.'*

"But that's not fair," I actually said out loud. I knew he could hear me. He was still connected and I was going to have to do something about that.

*'I know,'* he said. *'And I am very sorry about that. But the truth is they won't believe you anyway.'*

He was probably right.

"You don't even know them," I shouted out loud. "They are my sisters and I am going to tell them."

It was then that Lucy's front door opened and Lucy looked out at me like she was expecting someone else to be at her front door shouting at whatever.

"Emily?" she asked. "Who are you yelling at?"

"Nobody," I said to her. But to Sam, I said, *'Get out of my head.'*

I went into Lucy's house to find Charlotte and Jill in the kitchen. Charlotte was chopping carrots and onions for the stuffing. Jill was watching as she always did.

Charlotte looked up and asked who was doing all the shouting outside.

"Oh," I said. "I was just thinking about a conversation I had with my boss yesterday. And I guess it came out."

Jill came over to give me a hug and I squeezed her tight – I really needed some Jill time.

"How are you, Auntie Em?" she asked.

I hated it when she called me that. It made me think of the Wizard of Oz and I hate that movie. So, I stuck my tongue out at her and she giggled.

"What are you doing here?" Charlotte asked. "Did you come to help?"

I never helped. I also never hung out and just watched Charlotte and Lucy get dinner ready. "Oh, God, no," I said. "I just wanted to let you know that I am bringing a guest tomorrow."

Charlotte stopped chopping in mid chop – guess I shocked her. It had been a while since I made this kind of announcement.

"Really?" Lucy asked. "What's her name? Do we know her?"

"Why would you assume I'm bringing a woman?"

"Oh, I don't know. Maybe because the last time you brought a guy to Thanksgiving dinner, it didn't really turn out very well."

"Yeah," I said. "But I have brought women before. And thanks for reminding me."

Charlotte and Lucy had always invited their boyfriends over for dinner, sometimes just their guy friends. I thought that it made them feel normal because everyone would continue to think them normal because they were dating or even just knew guys. So, every year, every holiday, they had a guest and I didn't. I wanted to feel normal and I wanted people to think I was normal and dating (it would be a few years before I got over this feeling), so I decided I would invite someone over for dinner at my house. As my guest.

In 1978, the year I graduated from high school, I decided to take a year off before going to Montclair State College and work at Toys "R" Us in Eatontown. I had been working there three months prior to graduating and I liked it. And I liked the people I worked with, so I wasn't ready to leave and live in a dorm room.

While there, I met a nice girl named Ella. She was very pretty with her dark eyes and long blonde hair. She worked part time while attending Monmouth College in West Long Branch. In the few months we worked together, we got to know each other pretty well, so I invited her home to Thanksgiving dinner.

Everything was going well until we got up after dinner and Lucy told me that all through dinner she had to keep removing Ella's hand from her knee.

And then, after dinner, while we were cleaning up, Ella asked Lucy if she wanted to know what the term 'girl on girl' meant first hand.

Not for nothing, but Ella was my friend.

Three years later, during my third year at school, my roommate Liza invited herself to dinner and I really couldn't say no. There was really no reason to say no. She was from Pennsylvania and wasn't going home for Thanksgiving and I really didn't want her to spend the day by herself.

Liza's major was criminal law and mine was English literature, so I really didn't see a problem. And with all the heterosexual dates she'd been on since moving in with me, I knew she wasn't going to come onto Lucy. Since Charlotte had gotten married that year, she might come onto Bob, but I did talk to her about that on the way home.

My mother said dinner would be at three thirty sharp and I should come early to help set the table. And as I never help we arrived at three twenty-five, just in time to sit down and say grace. The look on my mother's face was the same one I got every holiday, so I wasn't that concerned at the time.

The police arrived ten minutes into dinner and I knew I was wrong about Liza. It seemed Liza was only taking criminal law classes, so she could learn how to get around the law.

Apparently, the classes didn't help. She and her latest lover had robbed a jewelry store in a nearby town using the information she had gotten in class on how not to get caught, but he *had* been caught and she came home with me thinking the authorities wouldn't find her. They had followed us all the way down the parkway and gave us a few minutes to settle in before, smashing the battering ram against the front door. Which I thought was a little much on their part.

Needless to say, we were detained in our own house for five hours as they searched each and every room for the stolen goods. You can imagine the looks of disappointment, disgust, and loathing I got. I wished I could stand in the corner like I did when I was a child and being disciplined, just so I wouldn't have to see their faces.

Now, *really*, this could hardly be my fault.

In 1982, I thought I would try again to bring a friend, a *normal* friend, home for Thanksgiving.

His name was Andrew, not Andy, *Andrew* – a very nice, respectable name. He wore suits bought modestly priced from Sears and JC Penny's, and penny loafers. He didn't smoke or drink and the worst swear word I ever heard come out of his mouth was 'hell' – "Hell if I know." – "What the hell." You get the gist. And he was a Yankee fan like my dad and Bob. So, how much more 'non weird' could you get?

I had been out to dinner and a movie with him a few times and he seemed very likable, and normal. I had no reason to think he would do anything remotely like my last guests.

In fact, I even asked him on one of our dates how he felt about men as sexual partners. The look on his face gave none of his feelings away. It was all in his voice.

"Firstly," he said with disgust. "Men should only be the sexual partners of women, preferably one at a time."

Okay, I wasn't so sure about the 'only' part – people should be able to love whoever they wanted to love as long as they didn't hurt anybody. However, I do draw the line at horses and dogs. But one at a time was probably a good idea.

But I also knew he would not be making inappropriate advances to my father or Bob or Lucy's new husband, Kris.

Andrew worked in another part of the company I started to work for after college. He was not an executive, but he was management. A lot of the girls I worked with had wanted to date him, but surprisingly he had asked me out. I, being no dummy, said yes the first time he suggested lunch outside the office.

Lunch was great. We went to a local sub shop that Andrew frequented. They knew him by name and he ordered by saying, "I'll have my usual."

I ordered ham and cheese on rye with mustard. We got a bag of chips that we split and the conversation was easy. It was shop talk, something we both knew something about, so it kept our interest.

Our next few dates found us holding hands and making out in his car, so it just seemed right that we eventually spent the night together. It wasn't great, which I chalked up to my inexperience. But after that, I almost had to invite him to Thanksgiving dinner. He was the closest thing to a boyfriend I had ever had. And he had nowhere else to go or, at least, he said he had nowhere else to go.

He arrived at our house a half hour before we had planned to sit down to dinner and he immediately sat down in the living room with my dad, and Bob, and Kris to watch the game. I went into the kitchen to see where my baby nephew, Eli, was. He was just three months old and small enough to still fit in my arms, and still young enough to try and nurse. I was an aunt for the first time and I loved him, so I didn't care. I was there early for Eli, not to help.

Lucy, who was pregnant with Lynn, took a peak into the living room to see Andrew, followed by my mother and Charlotte. I picked Eli up out of his carrier and gave him a big wet kiss.

My mother looked at me and wrinkled her nose at me, "Are you sure you're dating him?" she asked.

"You work with him?" Charlotte asked."

"Is he normal?" Lucy asked.

"Yes, yes, and yes."

Charlotte handed me the forks and I wrinkled my nose at her.

"What?"

"I never help."

"Well, there's a first time for everything," she said with a grin.

"How old is he?" my mother asked. My father was eleven years older than she was, so I really didn't understand the question.

"I don't know,' I said honestly. Because I really didn't. I just assumed he was my age.

At that moment, I heard Andrew say out loud, "No, it's true – he's a Jew hater." And after a short pause, he went onto say, "And he doesn't like blacks either. But who does?" Only he didn't say 'blacks'; he then let out a wholehearted laugh.

My mother and my sisters looked at me quizzically and I shrugged my shoulders. I had never heard Andrew say anything remotely like that before and in all fairness, we didn't know what they were talking about. I mean, they could have been talking about Adolph Hitler and Andrew just thought he was telling them something new. At least, that's what I was praying for.

We sat down to dinner at three o'clock sharp. My mother liked to have dinner on time and she was notorious for being sharp. My parents were at each end of the table. Andrew and I were on one side with Kris, who faced Lucy and Charlotte and Bob on the other side. My dad said grace. We bowed our heads and closed our eyes.

"Dear Lord," my dad began. I thought I heard a snigger from Andrew and opened one eye to look at him. He had a big grin on his face. "We thank thee for this food," my dad continued.

Andrew saw me looking at him with an inquiring look on my face and immediately bowed his head. Whether or not he closed his eyes, I couldn't say.

"We thank thee for the hands that prepared it and for Emily's, too."

Wow! My dad had mentioned me in his prayer. I probably would have been excited, but it was at that moment that Andrew erupted into laughter. We all lifted our heads and looked at him.

"Would you like to tell me why you are laughing so hard during a prayer, son?" my dad asked him.

"It's – just – that – you – thanked – a – God – who – isn't – there for hands – that didn't – even help," he said in between cackles. "You do know that 'God'—" His fingers went up in air quotes. "—was invented by religion so dumb schleps would go and give money, so the priest or clergy could drive big fancy Cadillacs." He continued to laugh like a hyena until my dad and Bob physically lifted him out of his chair and showed him the door.

We were all silent for a few moments, then I said, "I put the forks out."

In 1984, when I was twenty-four, I announced to my parents that I was bringing yet another guy home for Thanksgiving dinner. "A boyfriend?" my mother had asked with much excitement in her voice.

*Sure. Why not?* I saw no reason to take away any excitement she felt over something I did. God knows that didn't happen a lot.

The truth is, he was not my boyfriend. He was a guy I knew from high school. Dean Winchester. You know Dean Winchester – everybody knows a Dean Winchester. He's the guy you think is the cutest guy ever and you wish just once that he would know you were alive. But he never even saw you in high school and he would never have even seen you at the mall, except that you got clumsy and you happened to trip over him in front of JC Penny's.

Okay, so you didn't just get clumsy. You actually saw him and he still looked good, and you still just wanted him to know you were alive. So, you fell in front of him. Yeah, okay, it probably wasn't pretty or even graceful, but he knew I was there.

After we laughed about it and rubbed our hurt knees and heads for a few minutes, and after I reminded him who I was, he told me he just flew back into town for a few days to spend Thanksgiving with his parents. But sadly, he told me his parents had decided to spend Thanksgiving in Florida. So, I got the brilliant idea to ask him to have dinner with me at my parents' house.

He arrived for dinner an hour late. Everybody just assumed that he had changed his mind, so by the time he came in, we had already started. And it was quite obvious that he was high and been smoking some kind of crack because when I tried to introduce him to my family he shook my mother's hand and grabbed my father and kissed him full on the mouth. He was strong so try as he might my father could not push him away. When Dean finally let my dad go, he looked around the table at my startled family and smiled.

"Got any pie?" he asked.

Well, I don't know what it's like at your house at holiday time, but at our house, dinner took two days to prepare and twenty minutes to eat – so, we were all but done. My mother didn't really think about it. She just went over to the counter where she had an array of pies and brought two over. Apple and pumpkin. Then, she went back to the counter to get a knife to cut the pie with.

"Apple or pumpkin?" she asked him.

"Yes," he said, bringing himself up to his full height of about five feet, ten inches. "I'd love some pie." He smiled and winked at her. Then, added, "Thank you."

He took the seat next to mine, never looking at me; but noticing my sisters, he began to blow kisses at them. I don't even think he saw the babies or Bob and Kris, Charlotte and Lucy's husbands.

He ate pie. He ate pie like he had never eaten pie before. But he didn't just have apple and pumpkin. He also had coconut custard, banana cream, and blueberry. He didn't talk while he ate pie, except for the occasional 'mmmm, mmmm, mmmm' and to ask for more pie. None of us said anything either. The whole time he was eating pie, my mother kept looking at him with a very weird look on her face.

Finally, when Dean got to the blueberry pie. my mother found her voice – and truly, *truly* I wish she hadn't; I wish she would have just let him eat his pie and leave – but, no, because this is my life we are talking about. My mother *had* to find her voice.

"Don't I know your mother?" she finally asked.

Dean just continued to eat his pie.

My mother's hand came up out of her apron pocket and pointed at him. "Yes," she said. "You're Carol's son, Carol Winchester. Isn't that right?"

He nodded his head, but didn't stop eating until the last of his blueberry pie was done. Then, he pushed himself away from the table. My sisters, of course, were looking at me like I was crazy.

"Aren't you married? To that charming Reilly girl? What's her name?" My mother continued.

*Oh, sweet mother of God,* I thought. *Please tell me I did not invite a married man to dinner.*

He nodded his head, "Yes, Donna – love that woman. She can't make pie," he said, as he stood up from the table and proceeded to throw up all the pie into a nice little mess on the floor.

Yes, you could say that none of my Thanksgiving guests worked out very well.

# CHAPTER FOURTEEN
## IT'S DELIGHTFUL

"I think this will be different." But even as I spoke the words, even as they came out of my mouth, I could see Sam eating, licking his fingers, smacking his lips, and doing the 'mmmm, mmmm, mmmm' song. Not to mention that I was bringing yet another married man to dinner and I could hear giggling in my head about it. "I said get out of my head."

Yes, that's right, said it right out loud – didn't have to, but it was what I was used to doing when I spoke to people. Been doing it since I was about eighteen months old – still don't know how to stop, not to this day, can't get the hang of talking in my head. Maybe I was worried about making dumb faces while talking to him.

"Are you okay?" Lucy asked.

"Yeah, sure," I said. "So, the guy I'm inviting is Sam. You know Sam, he's the guy from the mall the night of my birthday."

"Yes," Lucy remembered. Yeah, she'd remember, she thought she was going to have a heart attack.

"Well, we ran into each other again at Wal-Mart and he asked me out," I said, waiting for their reaction.

"He just asked you out at Wal-Mart?" Charlotte asked.

There it was.

"Yes, why? Is that so unbelievable? That a man would ask me out?"

"Of course, not," Charlotte said. "You're an attractive woman. Why wouldn't he ask you out?"

Now that was different. I was fifty years old and neither one of my sisters had ever used the term 'attractive' to describe me. *I* would never have used that word to describe me.

"Oh?" I asked. "I'm attractive all of a sudden?"

"Not all of a sudden," Lucy chirped in. "You've always been attractive – just look at you, you have great skin, you don't wear glasses, your hair doesn't even have a hint of grey in it. It's obvious you don't have arthritis in any part of your body yet."

In my head, I heard Sam say, *'Don't.'*

*Don't? Don't what?* I thought. *Don't get upset because my sisters don't even know me?*

"Look at you," Lucy continued. "You can see you still have great boobs from not nursing babies and you still have all your teeth."

At this point, I noticed that Jill had a queer look on her face, like she was trying to remember something.

"How could you not remember?" I asked. "How could you not remember that I weighed two hundred and fifty pounds on my birthday, and today I weigh about one hundred and seventy-two pounds? I stopped wearing my glasses the day after my birthday because I didn't need them any more. And, of course, my hair isn't grey – I colored it the night before my birthday, but in three weeks I don't have to color it again – ever. *And it's not even my real hair color!*" I was talking fast.

*'It's not?'*

"The arthritis in my knees is gone – oh, what a glorious feeling." I pointed to my face. "The age spots and brown patches on my face are gone, and look – no more dark circles under my eyes." I think I actually had tears in my eyes. "You wanna know why? You wanna know why there are no dark circles under my eyes?" I must have sounded like a crazy woman. "It's because I sleep all night. I sleep all night," I squeaked. "Do you wanna know what that's like? It's delightful! Yes, delightful not to have to get up and go to the bathroom all night." Then, I added, "Any more."

The three of them looked at me, speechless for about two minutes, then Charlotte said, "Don't be ridiculous, nobody loses seventy-five pounds in three weeks."

That's what Charlotte got out of all that?

"And if they could, the person who invented it should bottle it because people would buy it," Charlotte said, dumping all the chopped vegetables into a big sauté pan. "I know I would." She and Lucy bumped shoulders, and laughed at me.

I was hurt. How could they not know? How could they not realize all the changes I had been through in just three short weeks?

"And if I've always been attractive how come you have no pictures of me in your house?"

*'Don't get emotional!'* Sam said in my head. He seemed very adamant about it.

Charlotte and Lucy looked at me with their mouths open. Jill looked around the room looking for pictures, I suppose.

"How come at weddings – your kid's weddings, for instance – no one ever took any pictures of me with one of those disposable cameras?" They were still gaping at me. Jill had big, fat tears rolling down her cheeks.

"Yeah, that's right – check their wedding albums." By this time my voice had risen several octaves.

*'Please calm down,'* Sam pleaded with me.

"Well," I said. "Maybe Sam and I won't—"

Sam's voice in my head said, *'I need to meet your family.'*

So, I just growled and asked what time dinner was and what we could bring – and shouted, "Get out of my head!"

By the time I got home, Bandit was starving. I could tell he was starving because he was in and out of my legs, rubbing his head against me and squeaking nonstop.

"At least you know me, my little boy." That's when the tears started – and that's when the odd sensation in my 'vajayjay' started. Okay, it wasn't so much that it was an odd feeling, it was just odd because of the timing. There were times I would think about Sam and my body would tingle, and I would wish Sam were there to hold me and take our relationship to the next level.

But this was not the time and I wasn't even thinking about Sam. In fact, I was really pissed at him. He needed to stay out of my head. Just because he could be in there, didn't mean he should be in there.

So, I started thinking about something else, like feeding Bandit, which made him happy – he was hungry, after all. But when Bandit had been fed and watered, I was still hot to trot. In fact, I was getting hotter to trot all the time – and since I hadn't had a hot flash in such a long time, but could still remember the agony they caused – I can honestly tell you this was something else.

I began to be afraid that something was wrong, so I called to Sam.

# CHAPTER FIFTEEN
## LIGHT MY FIRE

*'Sam?'*

But I didn't hear him say anything back. I started to cry because I was afraid something was wrong and because Sam didn't answer me – and frankly, because the fire between my legs was getting worse and I had to put it out. I thought about masturbation, but this fire was too big for that. And with Sam not answering and his being determined that we had to wait until we got married to have sex, I had to think of something else and fast.

About forty-five minutes later, Sam found me in the tub with my head against my bent knees sobbing. The cold water had not helped and still didn't help the colder it got.

He kneeled by the tub and touched my shoulder. "What's wrong?" he asked.

"Don't you know?!" I almost screamed at him.

"No, you told me to get out of your head. What's wrong?"

"I don't know," I hiccupped. "I left Charlotte's house and all of a sudden my body." I breathed and took him in. "My body needed you more than ever." His hand was on my shoulder and the heat was stimulating, and I began to rise up onto my feet.

Sam said, "Uh, oh!"

And I said, "What's the matter? I thought you loved me."

"I do."

Sam started to back away and I stepped out of the tub one foot at a time, and walked toward him. He stepped back a few more steps and grabbed the towel that was hanging on the hook beside him, and tried to cover me.

"I need you, Sam."

"I know, but we can't."

"Don't you want me?" I asked.

"Oh, yeah, I do." By now, he was breathing hard. "But we can't, it's the law."

He looked seriously uncomfortable, but there was no denying my body knew him and meant to have him.

I continued to walk toward him, even though this was nothing like me. I had never thrown myself at a man before and, honestly, wasn't sure I could even pull it off – but I didn't stop; *couldn't* have stopped if I wanted to. Even my nipples were screaming for him. I thought they might bore holes in his chest.

I reached him and pushed him up against the wall in the hall between the bathroom and the bedroom.

"I asked you not to get emotional," he said just before my lips were on his. Despite what he had just said, it only took a few seconds before he was kissing me as hungrily as I was kissing him. He wrapped me up in his arms and his hands were on my back, lightly doing the finger boogie down my spine until they finally rested on my butt. I still had a one hundred and seventy-five pound butt, but his hands had no trouble cupping them and pulling me even closer to him. He gave them a gentle squeeze.

I could feel his desire for me, so I lifted my right leg and did my best to get it up and around him, so that I would be as exposed to him as I possibly could be.

But it was at this point that he stopped kissing me and took in a very deep breath. "I'm sorry, we really can't."

"But I really need—"

"I know and I did this to you," he confessed. "It's my fault. I had to speed things up a bit because we're on a schedule, but we can't make love." He really looked sorry, but I still had needs.

"*Please…*" It was not like me to beg, but I was in a bad way – I needed him *so bad*.

"I can help you through this, but you just have to let me."

"Oh, I'll let you."

"First, you have to put something on because the nudity is teasing me," he said, as he took me by my wrist into the bedroom.

That was new.

"Should I get on the bed?" I giggled. My heart was pounding like a drum in my chest. I never wanted anybody this bad before in my life. I thought, *yeah, we're gonna do it.*

"Yes, you get on the bed and I'll get your pajamas."

I couldn't figure out what I needed pajamas for if we were going to make love. Oh, hell, I didn't care if we were going to do the other thing – I just needed him.

He came back with a tank top and pair of flowered granny panties and tried to put them on me. "Touch me," I said. Okay, so I was actually begging him to touch me as he pulled my panties up my legs.

"You need to relax. I could really hurt you doing this to you."

"Oh, no, you aren't going to hurt me. I'm not a virgin." I smiled up at him.

"Yeah, that's fine," was the last thing I am sure he said; because, all of a sudden, I felt tipsy, like I had been drinking for three days in a row. But I hadn't been drinking. I had been drowning in Sam for weeks and I needed him to rescue me.

I had to ask Sam what happened next, I'm not even sure if it's true, but it's all I have to go on.

"Are you doing this to me?"

"I have to, you need to relax."

"What are you doing to me?"

"I am going to shut the fire down."

"Oh, thank God!"

But as soon as Sam took my wrists in his hands and closed his eyes, I was totally aware of everything that was happening. This is why I'm not sure what he told me we said to each other is true, because I wasn't relaxing. My body tensed up, my nipples hardened, and I was sure my crackerjack box no longer had a curse in it. My legs lifted, my knees bent, my butt was gently bouncing up and down on the bed, and my toes were wiggling.

Sam was completely in control and I wasn't. He was the drug they give you for twilight sleep for a small procedure – my senses weren't heightened, but I felt good. My orgasm came like an explosion – it was sweet, and it was rough, and tender all rolled into one. And it was my first.

And I'm pretty sure I heard Sam say, "Holy crap!"

# CHAPTER SIXTEEN
## THANKSGIVING MORNING

On Thanksgiving morning, I laid in bed for as long as I could, basking in the leftover tingles from Sam's quick and dirty – what was it? Intimacy? Foreplay? Whatever it was, it was wonderful and I was still feeling it. It was like a fantasy! The fire was now at a tolerable simmer.

That's when I heard a noise coming from the other side of the apartment. Not the racket of dishes crashing to the floor, just a soft *thump, thump.* I looked around for Bandit, but he wasn't on the bed. So, I got out of bed to go look for him and see what all the noise was.

I strolled into the kitchen in my tank top and panties and found Sam standing at the counter with a knife in his left hand chopping what appeared to be an avocado. He glanced at me and quickly turned back to the salad.

"Hey, baby, whatcha doing?" I asked in what I thought might be a seductive tone.

"Your sister said we should bring the salad today," he said.

"You look good," I said, leaning up against the arch separating the kitchen and dining room trying hard to look and sound sexy.

He was wearing jeans and a t-shirt, and had to be the sexiest man I had ever had the pleasure to know. He put the few other guys I had known in the biblical sense to shame in every way.

"We need to talk about what happened last night, Sam," I said as I moved into the kitchen. I looked down at his bare feet and was astonished at what I saw. As beautiful as he was, his feet looked as though he lived with no shoes on. His toenails were long and jagged, and looked a lot like talons.

"Oh, sweetie," I said. "But before that, we need to get you a pedicure." I was sincerely happy that we didn't end up between the sheets last night. I loved the sheets I had on my bed.

"I bathed," he said defensively. "And my clothes are clean."

To this day I still don't know what he thought I said.

"So?" I said, going back to the seduction in my voice. But then, I thought it might really get lost on him, so I stopped. "So, what would you like to do today?" I asked, hoping we could do that thing again. I still wasn't sure what to call it.

"It's Thanksgiving," he said, "We're going to your sisters for dinner, Jill will be there."

"Of course, Jill will be there, but what would you like to do before that?"

"Well," he said. "I thought I would make the salad."

"You cook?" I asked.

"Well, no," he said sheepishly. "But I put things together real well."

I looked on the counter and saw that he not only was chopping up avocados, he also had walnuts, cranberries, shredded coconut, and chocolate chips. I was amused, to say the least. I wasn't sure anybody would actually eat it, but you never knew.

"Need anything else?" I asked, trying not to sound amused.

"Um," he started. "Lettuce. I can make the dressing if you have a blender and some olive oil," he said, but continued chopping his avocado. "Cucumbers, tomatoes, cheese, and whatever else you like in a salad."

"You're not looking at me."

"Would you mind going and putting some clothes on?" he asked.

"Why?"

"Because you're distracting me."

"Like I did last night?" I giggled. "When I was naked? When we were kissing? Was that a rabbit in your pocket? Or were you just happy to see me?"

"Yes," he said, still not looking at me. If he did or didn't get the line from *Who Framed Roger Rabbit*, he didn't let on.

"Well, why don't you come into the bedroom with me and do that thing you do again for me. I promise I'll cooperate better this time." I smiled at him and nuzzled his ear.

He didn't exactly push me away, but I thought I felt a mental push, so I stepped away. "Did you do that?"

"Yes." He finally turned to me. "We can't do that again – at least, not right away," he said. "You got very emotional. The fire quickened because of your emotions. You are now way ahead of schedule and I like to keep a nice schedule."

I suddenly remembered those nights he stood over me in my room while I slept. He did mention that I was 'on schedule'.

"Those weren't dreams those nights I thought I was dreaming you were in my bedroom? You were really there?" I asked.

He nodded, still not looking at me.

"What schedule?" I asked.

"Please go get dressed, then I will tell you. I promise."

As I walked out of the kitchen, he asked when he would be pedicured and I yelled back, "As soon as possible."

On my way to the bedroom, I heard the all too familiar clatter of dishes, cans, and bottles crashing to the floor.

"Did you hear that?" I called to Sam.

"No," I heard him say. "What did you—*oh, no!*"

# CHAPTER SEVENTEEN
# THE RETURN OF THE HAPPY DAYS GANG

"They're back!" we almost said in unison.

Sam came out of the kitchen and we walked to the bedroom together. *'I really wish you had something else on,'* he said in my head.

When we got into the bedroom, I saw them in that same 'V' formation. The guy in the front was dark; his hair was greying, but originally it had been black. It was styled neatly around his neck with a dusting of grey here and there. He had a strong chin and high cheek bones. I could tell his eyelashes were long. He had a five o'clock shadow. I would categorized him as very good looking, but he was standing there, smiling like a lunatic. He looked slightly familiar.

He looked past me to Sam and I heard Sam take in some air and cry, "*NO!*" in agony.

I looked back at him and he looked like he was in pain. He was starring at Fonzie with tears in his eyes, his head was rocking back and forth.

"That's right, Sammy," Fonzie said. "That's right. Take it all in, get a good headful, you psychic dummy."

Now Sam was no dummy and I resented this clown calling him that.

I looked back at Sam again and I saw he had fallen up against the wall; the tears were now streaming down his face.

"What's wrong?" I asked. He just shook his head.

"Why are you here?" I asked to 'The Fonz'.

"Oh, don't you worry, sweetheart. You will find out in good time. All in good time." He smiled a very revolting smile.

"What do you want?" I asked.

"I said," His voice rose to just short of a shout. "Don't you worry your pretty little head about that."

"I said, *what do you want?*" I asked again, more forcefully this time.

"Oh, she's feisty, Sammy, just like Ariel. No wonder you love her so much," he said with a mocking tone in his voice.

I looked at Sam again and he was now holding his chest like he was having a heart attack, and he was sobbing.

"Sam, what's wrong?" I said, going to him.

"Oh, Sammy is just fine. I gave him a good picture of what Ariel and I have been doing. Now he knows the love of his life wants me and not him." A sick grin spread over his face.

"Highly doubtful," I said.

He looked at me and the grin disappeared.

Oh, it's true," Fonzie said. The gang behind him were laughing and nodding their heads at each other. *Buffoons.*

I looked at Sam. "Is he psychic?"

Sam shook his head and managed a very weak, "No."

"No, I'm a genius, not a dummy like Sammy here."

"That is highly doubtful, too."

His sick smile disappeared again.

"No, he is a genius." Sam found his voice and between sobs, he said, "He worked on the time travel project."

"So, he's smart. That doesn't mean you're dumb."

"Didn't Sammy tell you about me?" he asked.

"He said you're Ariel's ex and you hate him."

"That's right – he took my girl, that dummy took my girl. So, I took her back while Sammy was *soooo* busy getting all the artificial environments ready and delivering all the babies. He's been away a long time and Ariel got lonely."

I looked at Sam and he was shaking his head from side to side again.

"And I'm gonna take you, too," he said, and the clowns behind him stopped laughing as if that statement actually bothered them.

*Interesting,* I thought. That declaration was a problem for them.

I heard Sam behind me, crying, "No, no!" again.

"If Ariel is a genius and she's like me, she wouldn't give you the time of day," I said as his smile disappeared again. "And what do you mean, you're gonna take me, too?"

Sam just kept on with his chanting, "No, no." He was getting on my nerves, but I stepped closer to him anyway.

"It means that when you're ready, when the eggs are implanted, the baby will be yours and Ariel's." And he snickered, "And *mine.*"

The horror must have shone on my face because he threw his head back and laughed an actual maniacal laugh. It appeared that this statement did not make the gang behind him happy and they seemed to be murmuring to each other.

He was laughing so hard, he didn't see me grab the Louisville slugger and get into the batter's stance. It had been a long time since I had swung a bat, but I was pretty sure I could still do it – and make it count.

He stopped laughing when he noticed the bat in my hands. "Oh, look," he said, looking back at his gang. "The little girl has a bat."

"And I know what to do with it." I was tired of him calling me sweetheart and now little girl. "Get out of my apartment and don't come back."

"Or what?" he mocked. "You gonna hit me with that thing?"

When Charlotte, Lucy, and I were teenagers, the town we grew up in offered a recreation program during the summer at the school we lived across the street from. The program offered arts and crafts, movies, a bus to the beach a couple times a week, and sports. It kept us off the streets and out of trouble.

We loved going to the beach and watching the movies. Lucy was very good at arts and crafts, but Charlotte and I excelled at sports. Not all sports, just baseball. Charlotte was known as Choo Choo Charley in those days because when she hit the ball, it stayed on track all the way out to left field.

They called me the Louisville slugger because I would become one with the bat and I could hit any kind of ball the pitcher threw.

"Oh, yeah, I'm gonna hit you with it, and I'm gonna hurt you with it unless you get the hell out of my apartment."

"Okay, we'll go, but we'll be back," he said. "When you're ready." He winked. They vanished in that same clatter of dishes, cans, and bottles crashing to the floor.

I looked at Sam. He was now down on the floor, his hands over his eyes and he was sobbing.

"Sam? What is it?"

# CHAPTER EIGHTEEN
## THIS IS KIND OF AWKWARD

It was then that I heard a woman's voice calling to me from the living room.

Wait. What? There was someone else in my apartment?

"What? Another uninvited guest?" I said as I took Sam by the hand, lifted him up off the floor, and went toward the voice.

The TV was on – not that I remembered putting it on – and there was a woman's face in the center of the screen; a lady with stringy blonde hair, pale skin, hollow cheeks, and dark circles under her eyes. As I got closer, the picture changed and the camera moved back, so that I could see that she was in the center of the screen flanked by an older woman on her right and an older gentleman on her left, who didn't look much healthier than the first woman. They were practically emaciated and they were talking to me.

"Emily, what's going on? I sense that Sam is in distress."

Things started to go black, but I knew I had to be strong and to fight it because Sam was pretty close to being hysterical. But who was she and how did she know my name?

"Are you," I began. "Are you Ariel?"

"Yes, and these are Sam's parents, John and Alice."

"But how? How are you here? Are you here? Or are you still in the twenty-third century?" I asked tentatively.

"I see there's still a lot that Sam still hasn't told you."
She looked at Sam and asked, "What's wrong with him?"

He was not looking at the screen. In fact, he had his
back to the screen and looked like he was losing the
ability to stand on his own. So, I took a hold of him and
stood him up straight. He still wouldn't turn around and
look at the screen.

"Sam," I heard his mom call gently.

"Sam, what happened in there?" I asked softly.

"I saw," Sam said in between sobs. "He showed me."

"He showed you what?" his mom and I asked gently
at the same time.

Sam looked as if he were struggling to get the words
out. "He showed me what he and Ariel have been doing
behind my back."

Ariel looked confused. "What do you mean? He's
been a pest around the lab for months. I didn't tell you
because I knew it would upset you."

"Sam," his mom said calmly. "Sam, look at me."

Sam turned his head to her – she was after all, his
mom.

"Ariel hasn't done anything she needs to be ashamed
of. She's been telling us how Arthur has been hanging
around the lab. She would never hurt you. She loves
you." His mom paused for a few seconds, then asked,
"Besides, could she really keep that from you?"

I could feel Sam start to relax, but I still had to
support him.

"Come home, Sam," Ariel said. "Let me take care of
you. I love you."

I could hear her love for him in her voice. It was
strong and deep. I could tell that fooling around with

Arthur... *Arthur? Like Arthur Fonzarelli?* Well, in any case, cheating on Sam was not in her.

"I love you, too," I said, for emotional support, then asked, "Will you be able to travel?"

"But we have to go to dinner with your family."

I still couldn't figure out why that was so important, but said, "You need to go home and regroup. Can you travel?"

"Yes, but what about dinner?"

"Sweetie, you're a time traveler. Come back in a few hours, when you feel more like yourself."

He was gone in a rushing of air through a tube and I saw Ariel move away from the screen. She looked back at me and smiled. Sam's parents remained as they watched Ariel go to Sam.

"Hi," I said awkwardly. "I'm Emily."

"We had hoped we would meet you under better circumstances," Sam's dad said. His voice was gentle like Sam's and his eyes were a perfect match – blue and big and really cute. His mom is grey; she also has blue eyes with big dark circles under them.

"How come when Sam comes and goes, I hear air rushing through a tube, but when Arthur and his pals come and go, I hear dishes and cans and bottles crashing to the floor?" Of all the questions I could have asked, I have no idea why that was the first.

Sam's mom smiled. "We don't know. But you're not the first to report hearing noises associated with the travelers."

"I don't think Sam could hear their arrival, but I'm sure he still knew," I said.

"Sam can sense other travelers and other psychics, and he hears their thoughts," she continued. "He's known for awhile that another traveler had been in your apartment, so he created a barrier. He never had to do it before, maybe that's why it's not holding." She shook her head. "I honestly never thought it would be Arthur. It's been thirty-six years."

"And he never married?" I asked.

"No," was all she said about that.

"So, then, how does this work for him? Who was chosen for him?

"He wasn't alone? Was he?" she asked.

"No."

"He and a group of nine other singles went to live in the nineteen fifties to meet women who fit the proper criteria, to see if they could fall in love and have babies, too."

Sam's dad continued, "Eight of them met and married very sweet women, who like you, are willing to help us. And they found love; they are families now. Well, all but one."

"Who raises these children in the twenty-third century?"

"Surrogate moms – women who never married, but still wanted to have a part in raising the future," Sam's dad said.

"Did they use the single surrogate's DNA?"

"Yes," Sam's mom said. "It was necessary to have time travel built into their DNA."

"So, what about the 'all but one' and Arthur?"

"The ninth guy found a very nice woman and they fell in love," Sam's mom said with a smile. "But she never conceived. Her body absorbed the environment before she could conceive. I don't know if Sam has told you, but the artificial environment doesn't last very long.

There's only a short window of opportunity. Sam was dispatched to the fifties – the fifties are not his domain, as you can understand why not – to see if he could help." Sam's mom pursed her lips.

"Is Sam the best?"

"He was the best available at the time."

I thought that was a strange thing to say when they pretty much controlled time.

"Who is the best?" I asked, even though I thought Sam was the best. Sure, it's true, at the time I had only met a few people from the twenty-third century, but I knew Sam and he was the best.

Sam's dad spoke again, "Her name is Bonnie Olive Olsen. She was born a genius and a psychic healer. She likes to be called Boo and she is the best of both worlds." It sounded like he really admired her and I really had to wonder about this prejudice that existed in the twenty-third century.

Really? Two hundred years and there are still classes or stations? The geniuses and the psychics? Did I really want to bring a child into that world?

"Where was she?"

"She was here in the lab with Ariel trying to figure out a way to get Arthur's baby born in less than nine months and back here to the twenty-third century." Sam's mom sounded disgusted. Wow, her tone really changed.

Wait. What?

"Arthur's baby?"

"Yes," Sam's dad continued. "Arthur met a nice girl named Ruth. It wasn't long before we found out that she was pregnant... uh, the traditional way."

I was dumbfounded. But not really – this was Arthur we were talking about. He didn't really seem like the kind of guy who would follow the rules, even if they were laws.

"Did they figure it out?"

"No, they decided they need to leave Ruth alone and let her gestate normally – let her give birth, and then take the baby from her," Sam's mom said, never taking her eyes off of me.

Wait. What?

*Then, take the baby from her? What is she talking about? This woman never gets to know her baby? Is that what they were planning for me?*

"Are the babies usually just taken from the mothers?" I asked worriedly.

"Oh, no. As per the plan, the baby stays with the natural mother for a week, then the baby comes home, so the mother here can experience motherhood, too," Sam's mom explained.

# CHAPTER NINETEEN
## CHOCOLATE CHIPS AND CRUETS

It was while I was talking with Sam's parents that I realized I was still in just a pair of panties and a tank top. So, after talking for about a half hour, I made excuses and went to shower and to dress. I also went to Foodtown to get the lettuce and olive oil for the salad Sam was making; and I picked up more avocados and chocolate chips.

It would be time to leave soon if I was going to get to Lucy's just in time for dinner. Like our mom, Charlotte and Lucy – depending on whose house we were eating at – were determined to have dinner at three thirty sharp, and even though I was still mad at them, I didn't want to rock the boat. Just as I was about to call and tell her that Sam wasn't going to make it, I heard that familiar rushing of air through a tube coming from the kitchen.

I put the phone back on the base and ran in there. I know he had only been gone a few hours, and he was married, and I had briefly met his wife, but I still missed him and wanted to hold him.

I stopped in what is sometimes called, 'dead in my tracks'. Sam looked good, better than ever. He had a beard and a moustache, trimmed short and neat – and his hair was longer than it had been three hours ago. He was wearing the familiar jeans, a green sweater, and the navy sneakers. He looked good – *good enough to eat.*

Sam turned to me and opened his arms to me, and I ran into them. He wrapped me up in them and I felt at home.

"Oh, Sam," I said in between kisses. "I missed you so much."

"I missed you, too," he said, stepping away and turning to the counter. "But I need to finish the salad, so we can go."

"Oh, let's just go. Forget the salad," I said, waving my hand at it. "Or we can just stay here and do some really fun things," I said in a playful voice, because I wanted to touch his beard in the worst way.

"We have to go to dinner."

"Why is dinner with my family today so important?" I asked, exasperated. "And how did this happen?" I asked, rubbing my hand on his now hairy chin.

"Because today Jill is bringing someone special to dinner and I think we're both gonna want to meet him."

Jill was bringing someone to dinner? Shocker! No doubt he would be normal and everyone would love him.

"And what's so special about him?"

"He's Ariel's great, great, great grandfather Rick."

If my jaw could have literally hit the floor, it would have just then. Jill was only fifteen years old and she was bringing someone that important to dinner already.

And why did he have to say this kid was Ariel's third great grandfather? Why couldn't he just say Jill was bringing her future husband to dinner today?

"And about this," he said, tugging at his chin. "I didn't feel like shaving when Ariel and I were at the Falls." He grinned at me. "And I thought you would like it."

"The Falls?" I asked with some contempt in my voice.

"We decided to get away. So, we went up to Niagara and spent a wonderful week camping out. The weather was great, perfect for camping. It was like another honeymoon for me and Ariel. We love the Falls."

"Another honeymoon? How many have you had?" I asked.

"Six, I think. I'm not really sure, you'd have to ask Ariel."

*Yeah, why don't I do that,* I thought. *Because Ariel is just the person I want to talk to right now.*

"Oh, and we got pedicures while we were there," he said excitedly, slipping his right sneaker off and showing me his foot. His nails were nicely trimmed and shaped. Thankfully, there was no polish.

"You did?"

"Yes, one of our first generation females – her name is Mary – is a cosmetologist." He was so excited his eyes seemed to get bigger and bluer. "It was great!"

"And she lives in Niagara?" I asked weakly.

"Yeah, she has a little shop up there. She calls it a day spa. Ariel got her hair cut." *Ariel again.* "You don't know how long it's been since Ariel has had someone wash and cut her hair." *He was saying her name an awful lot. It was getting on my nerves.* "I hear women really like that."

The whole time he was telling me this story, he was chopping avocados. "It was good because we haven't been able to spend more than five or six hours together since this project began and I really needed to be with Ariel."

So, when did he have time to miss me?

I couldn't stand listening to him talk about Ariel any more. I know she's his wife, but her name was beginning to grind on me. I went into the living room and sat in my favorite chair.

"I'm feeling much better," he called from the kitchen. "I'm sorry I acted that way,' he continued. "But it would just kill me if Ariel and Arthur were…"

He stopped talking and I was, for the first time happy not to hear his voice. I heard the blender go in spurts and I assumed he had put chunks of avocados in there.

"You're going to love this dressing," he said over the noise of the blender. "It's my mother's recipe. I think I told you we have avocado trees in our backyard, so we eat a lot of them. Ariel loves them, too."

I heard the blender for a few more minutes, then nothing for a few more.

"You okay?" Sam asked.

"Yeah."

"What are you thinking about?"

"I'm thinking that I've lost twenty-eight more pounds, so I need new clothes again," I said distractedly.

"Really? That's what you're thinking?"

I conceded that I needed to tell him something. "I'm wondering why you're going to put chocolate chips in the salad."

"Oh, I'm not. I'm eating them."

I wasn't surprised.

"Do you have a container for the dressing?" Sam asked, poking his head out of the kitchen.

"You mean like a cruet?" I asked.

"Yeah, a cruet," he said with a grin.

*Yeah, sure I have cruets, for all those fancy dinner parties I have. Because I always have people over for salad and I make my own dressing because it's not just easier and more convenient to buy it in a bottle at the store. Especially for someone as lazy as me.*

"You have a funny look on your face," Sam said.

How come when you want him to be connected to you, so he can hear the sarcasm, he's not?

"Just use anything. I don't have cruets."

When we were finally in the car and on our way to Lucy's, I was regretting bringing Sam. For the first time since my birthday, I didn't want to be anywhere near him. I looked out the window.

"Ariel really loves you and is so happy with her choice."

I turned to look at him. "Was there another choice?"

"Yes, there was one other woman in the line, who was single, never been married, never gonna marry, but she was a mess. She was an addict, smoked, and drank a lot – cocaine was a big problem." He blew some air out of his mouth. "And I'm not sure I could have done what was needed for the artificial environment to develop in her body. Also, I don't think I would have fallen in love with her."

"So, what you're saying," I began, and what came out of my mouth next was a surprise even to me. I didn't even know I was thinking it. "So, what you're saying is she was too pathetic and too much of a loser?"

"What does that mean?" Sam asked. There was no malice or concern in his voice. It was a question, but an innocent question.

"What does what mean? Pathetic or loser?"

"I know what loser means – it means not a winner," he said simply. "I don't know what pathetic means."

"Really? You don't know what pathetic means?" I was really getting irritated now and not really sure why. "It means pitiful, a failure. It means I couldn't find someone to love me and have a family with, so Sam swoops in and changes all that for poor miserable, lonely, ugly Emily – and the rest of us who couldn't get someone to fall in love with us."

Sam pulled over and stared at me.

"It's not like that," he said with an untroubled voice. "We picked great women – women who were never given a chance for one reason or another. Why would you even think that?" he asked. "Did I ever give you a reason to think something so horrible about yourself? And you are absolutely beautiful to me," he said gently. "And like I said," he continued, as he pulled the car back on the road, "Ariel loves you."

He almost had me and I knew if I had to hear her name one more time, I would scream. But thankfully, we were at Lucy's house and I knew he would not talk about her while we were there.

# CHAPTER TWENTY
## IF I HEAR THAT NAME ONE MORE TIME

"Do you think I'm a combination of all your former dinner guests?" Sam asked with a chuckle as we approached the door.

"What do you mean?" I asked, glaring at him.

I think Sam wanted to say something, but was interrupted by the door opening and Charlotte reaching for me. I thought it must be a week for new things as Charlotte's arms went around me in a bear hug, almost cracking the salad bowl.

I pushed her away and looked at her. "What the hell was that?"

"I'm just so glad to see you – you must be Sam," she said in one breath, extending her hand to Sam, then pulling him into a hug.

She pulled Sam into the house and was just about to shut the door when she remembered I was there, too. I handed her the salad and walked into what looked like an intervention.

Lucy and Kris were standing in the left corner of her living room. Kris had a drink in his hand. Lynn and Annie were seated on the sofa with their husbands, Jerry and TC. Lynn had the baby in her arms and I could see she was nursing him. Annie's husband's name was Loren, but he thought that was a girly name, so he wanted to be called 'the champ'. But no one would, so we settled for TC.

Charlotte went over to where Bob was standing on the other side of the sofa. Eli and Brian were standing behind the loveseat their wives, Tammy and Chipee, were sitting on. Brian's wife's name is Maggie, but she's British and Brian always said she was the best looking Chipee he had ever seen. Jill and an unknown young man, presumably the future father of her children, were on the floor with Eli's twin boys, Evan and Ethan, who were four years old.

"Aren't you going to introduce us, Emily?" Bob was the first to say anything.

"Everybody – this is Sam. Sam – this is everybody. Let's eat." I clapped my hands and started for the dining room, and for a second, I was afraid the table hadn't been set yet and I would have do it.

Jill giggled, which started the boys giggling, which made me giggle, too. But Sam went up to Bob and introduced himself and went down the line until he got to Jill and her friend.

They got up and Jill introduced her friend as Derrick. I guessed Rick would probably come later, when they knew each other better. He was cute and seemed very nice. Sam took Derrick's hand in both of his hands and shook lightly, then pulled him into a full bear hug. Seemed about right, for one of my guests.

I looked at Kris to see what he thought of Derrick, but he was getting another drink. Great, just what I needed – Kris under the influence.

Over the years, Kris had gone from one beer before dinner, to a few drinks before dinner, to drinking all through dinner. Lucy seemed very happy and still very much in love, so I could never pinpoint the reason behind Kris' decline. Lucy assured me Kris was not an alcoholic and only drank when the family was together. Maybe it was Kris, maybe it was me, but he was never really nice to me.

And Kris was not a nice drunk. He embarrassed Lucy when he drank too much and he was a bad wisecracker when he wasn't drunk – he was worse when he was. But since I had decided in the car that Sam was never coming to dinner again, it really didn't matter what Kris would say about me.

Thankfully, the table was already set and dinner was ready, so we could sit down to dinner immediately. We sat down, with Jill and Derrick in charge at the 'kiddie' table. The boys adored Aunt Jill and didn't mind at all that they were shunned from the grown up table.

Lucky me, I was seated next to Sam, but right across from Kris. After Bob said grace and started to carve the turkey, Kris started.

"So, Sam, do you like pie?"

"I love pie," Sam said with a grin. "What kind do you have?"

Kris leaned forward in his chair and said, "Oh, we have all kinds, just for you."

"Why? Doesn't anyone else like pie?" Sam asked innocently, his eyes as big as saucers.

Kris smiled and looked over at Bob, who was still carving turkey and did not try to stop him.

"Have you robbed a jewelry store lately?" Kris chuckled.

"Really Kris? Is this necessary?" I asked, giving a look that said, *stop it or I will kill you.*

"Yes, it is."

I looked at my sisters for support, but there was none to be had. And they both pretended like they weren't even listening.

"Lucy?"

"What?" she asked shyly.

"A little help here ,please."

"With what? What's happening?" she asked, looking around.

"You're sitting right next to him and you can't hear him?" I asked with irritation in my voice.

"You see, Sam, Em's dinner guests before you haven't exactly been charming," Kris said to Sam. "So, we just want to know if you are going to be par for the course or, shall we say, *normal?*"

"Please stop?" I asked.

"Sam?" Bob asked, now that the carving was done. "What sort of work do you do?"

"I'm a doctor," Sam lied.

"Really?" Charlotte said. "Impressive." Funny how she heard that part.

"What's your specialty?" Lucy chimed in. Guess she was listening now, too.

"I'm in obstetrics and gynecology," Sam said with a big smile on his face.

"Ooh, tough break, Em." Kris said, taking another sip of his drink.

"Why do you say that?" I asked with a challenge in my voice. I just couldn't see what Kris could possibly make of that.

"Well, you see, Emily." He sat upright in his chair. *'Relax,'* I heard Sam say in my head. "And understand, I have the deepest sympathy for you," Kris continued. "A person who serves coffee all day doesn't want to come home to coffee."

I heard a chuckle go around the table. They were quicker than I was. It took several minutes for that to sink in, but I finally got it. A man who deals with a woman's sweet spot all day doesn't want to come home to another sweet spot.

I looked at Lucy and said, "Thanks for stopping him." And the tears started. I don't know why, especially since Sam wasn't a gynecologist. But I guess it had to do with everything about Sam.

I got up and started for the bathroom and I heard Kris say, "Oh, I see that's already started, poor Em."

In my head, Sam was trying to soothe me, but I didn't want any part of it.

"Get out of my head."

"Who are you talking to?" I heard Lucy ask from the other side of the door.

"What do you care?" I yelled back. "Your dumbass husband mocks me and you do nothing about it."

"We're just having fun," She told me.

"Does it look like I'm having fun?"

"Come on out, I promise I'll make him stop," She said.

I splashed some hot water on my face and dried off before opening the door. Lucy was still out there with a concerned look on her face.

"Really. We were just trying to have fun."

God, I really just wanted to punch her lights out at that moment.

I went back to the table and Kris' plate was still full, so I could see he was drinking his dinner. Everyone else, including Sam, was eating. But no one was enjoying it quite like Sam – oddly enough, no one thought it out of the ordinary.

I sat down in my chair and Bob said, "You're not a bigot or racist, are you, Sam?"

I guess it was Bob's turn to humiliate me. I looked at Charlotte and hoped she knew I wanted to punch her lights out, too.

"No," Sam said in between bites.

"How do you feel about God?"

Sam looked around the table and said, "He's the supreme being?"

By now, I wasn't hungry, but I felt it only right to have some of the salad we brought, so I stood up and leaned over Eli to get it. Then, I stood up and leaned over Eli again to get the dressing.

"Sorry, babe," I said with a forced smile. It wasn't Eli's fault, but he was in the middle of this and I was in a mood to spit nickels.

I filled my plate, and then I put some more on top of that and poured the dressing over it.

"Whoa, there, girl," Kris said from behind his glass. "Save some for the rest of us. Or at least me, I like a good salad."

"Oh, really? I figured since you work in the produce department at ShopRite you wouldn't want to look at produce at home."

The kids all burst out laughing, my sisters were horrified, and Bob was shaking his head appreciatively. In my head, Sam said, *'Nice one,'* and smiled at me. After that, dinner seemed to go smoothly until Charlotte asked Tammy what the boys wanted for Christmas.

"We've been watching Disney films with them – you know, to see what they like," she started. "Twins take a long time to form attachments to anything outside themselves," she informed us.

Before the twins were born, Eli and Tammy had joined a support group for parents of multiple births, so they would know what to expect and how to handle it. I thought it a good move.

"You know," I piped up. "Sam is a twin."

"Booyah!" Kris said drunkenly, pointing a finger at me like a gun. "I'll bet he's not a gyno and he wouldn't mind coming home to your vagina every day." He whispered the last part – only, he didn't say 'vagina' and everybody heard it. He winked at me.

"Gee, Dad," Annie said in disgust. "Have another drink, why don't cha?"

"Yeah, Dad," Lynn added. "There are children in the room."

Lucy got up and helped Kris up out of his chair.

"Where're we going?" he asked.

"You're going to watch the football game in our room," she said to him, but to us she mouthed, "He'll fall asleep."

I realized that sometimes the most innocent of comments have almost always come back to bite me in the butt.

After a few more minutes of stunned silence, Sam broke it. "My brother, Seth died when we were three," Sam said. I guess to shift the focus back to the twins.

"Oh," Charlotte said, surprised. "Sorry to hear that. Was it just recently?"

"No, when we were three." Was she even really listening?

"So, as I was saying," Tammy continued, trying to lighten the subject now. "We've been watching Disney movies and it seems like *The Little Mermaid* is their favorite. They just love Ariel."

"*Ahhhhhhhhhhhhhhhhhhhhhhhhhhhhh!!!*" I couldn't help it and I couldn't stop it. After about thirty or forty seconds of this, Sam put his hand on the back of my neck and like a light switch being flipped, my scream ended.

"What was that about?" Charlotte asked.

I chuckled and said, "Well, who doesn't love Ariel?" I stood up so abruptly, my chair fell backwards. "Oh, that's right. I don't." I walked out the front door and sat on Lucy's porch swing.

About three minutes later, Sam came out and put his jacket over my shoulders. I didn't look up, even as he sat down with me and we began to swing.

"I didn't know you felt that way about Ariel," Sam said, after about five minutes.

I didn't say anything and I still didn't lift my head. I couldn't look at him. From the corner of my eye, I saw Sam's hand move towards me and I slid away from him. I wasn't sure exactly how I felt. I didn't hate her, but I knew I didn't love her either. She was Sam's wife and I was in love with him. I didn't want to believe it, but I was jealous.

"Don't you want to talk about it?" he asked, and when I didn't answer, he said, "You do realize I can still connect with you without touching you."

"Then, why do you do it?" I asked, looking at him now.

"Because I like touching you," he said with a grin.

The truth is I wanted to talk about it, but I couldn't talk about it at Lucy's house, not even on her front porch. Sam had already warned me that they couldn't know anything about him.

"I don't hate her," I whispered. "She just seems to get so much more of you."

"That will change after we get married," Sam began.

"I don't want to talk about it here." I said, feeling very strongly that a marriage between Sam and me was never going to happen.

"We should go back in and finish dinner," Sam said.

"I'm not hungry."

"You really need to eat. After last night, you need to take in a lot of calories."

"Why?"

"Didn't you notice how your pants are hanging on you?"

"Yes, I told you I've lost another twenty-eight pounds and I need to buy new clothes."

"Is that as of this morning?"

"No, that's as of yesterday morning," I told him.

"Well, I'm sure after last night the number is now larger."

"Are you surprised my sisters didn't notice it?"

At that moment, the door opened and Lucy asked if everything was okay. I had to concede that the sooner I went back in, the sooner I could go home. We went back to the table, and I piled turkey and stuffing on my plate and drowned it all in gravy.

Charlotte gave a look like I was crazy.

"What? I'm hungry now." I wasn't really, but after all, after last night, I needed to take in a lot of calories. Because last night was pretty dynamic.

"You know, Sam," Lucy began. "We're going to have a lot of leftovers. You can take some home if you want."

Wait. What?

"What?" I asked.

"We have leftovers," she said. "I'm asking Sam if he wants to take some home."

"Yeah," I said. "I got that part. In all the years since I moved into my own apartment, leftovers have never been offered to me."

"Oh, Emily," she said, her face showing perplexity. "Sweetie, nothing's changed. I offered leftovers to Sam, not you."

"Yeah, that was rude."

# CHAPTER TWENTY-ONE
## LEFTOVERS

The ride home was quiet. I don't know why Sam was so quiet and I was quiet because I wasn't ready to tell Sam that it wasn't going to work out. I wasn't good at sharing and even though I didn't hate Ariel, I was jealous of her and all the time she got to spend with Sam.

And did I mention I'm not good at sharing?

I wondered why Sam didn't know this or maybe he just wasn't saying anything about it. But it had to be said. The longer I put it off, the worse it was going to be. For me.

I started to cry.

"Why? Why couldn't you come to me when I was in my twenties? You have the power to go anywhere in time and you come to me when I'm a fifty year old lady," I sobbed. "An old lady with no uterus and you already have a wife."

Sam was being very quiet and that made me even madder.

"*And you have a wife!*" My voice began to rise. "And you spend a lot of time with her. You made me love you – and Bandit doesn't love me any more and I have never been offered leftovers. My sisters like you better than me."

My voice was really up there now and Sam said, "Please relax."

"*RELAX?!*" I practically screamed.

"Yes," he said calmly. "We don't want a repeat of last night."

"You're damn right we don't," I shouted at him. "I don't want it, you don't want me. Why should anyone want poor, poor, pitiful Emily? You do know they only invite me over out of a sense of duty, because we're 'family'." I used the air quotes and said the word mockingly.

"No, they don't," he said calmly. "They love you."

"Oh, yeah, they love me," I continued shouting. "And the evidence of that is the friggin' half turkey sitting in the back seat that Charlotte sent home with *you* – plus, the mashed potatoes and the green beans. Oh, and let's not forget an entire apple pie."

At this point, I felt a mental slap in the face. I don't know how else to explain it. All of a sudden, I felt a slight burning sensation on my cheek and my head jerked to the side. The tears were flowing now. *HE HIT ME!*

I looked over at him, and he was combing his fingers through his hair and blowing air out of his mouth.

"Stop the car!"

"Settle down," he said as calmly as ever. "I only did that because I thought it would help."

I was quiet – I was *insane* with quiet.

Sam pulled the car into the spot next to my car and we were quiet. We walked up to my apartment in silence. I had nothing to say to him and I could tell he had nothing to say to me. If he was in my head, he was quiet for once. And I was happy about it.

I went into my bedroom and shut the door. I sat on my bed and tried hard to stop the tears from gushing. Bandit had been sitting on his window seat, then made the leap onto the bed to try and comfort me.

"You would never hurt me like that? Would you, boy?" I asked.

At that moment, I remembered Sam saying something about him and Bandit catching up. What exactly did that mean? I thought I might regret it, but I had to know what that meant. I scratched Bandit under his chin the way he liked and I said, "What exactly do you and Sam need to catch up on?"

Bandit buried his face in his paws and refused to reveal his secrets. I wondered if Sam could actually talk to Bandit. I couldn't remember if he had ever said that he could, but I was almost sure he never said he couldn't.

"Sam?" I called to him. "Are you still here?"

'Yes.'

"Could you come in here, please?" I called through the door. Sam opened the door and peeked in.

"I'm sorry," he said with a sheepish look on his face. "I promise I'll never do that again."

I knew he wouldn't, but someday I would get him back. I swore it to myself.

"Have you been listening to my thoughts?" I wondered.

"No," he said, walking to the bed.

I moved over a bit on the bed and pointed to the spot next to me, so he would sit down next to me. He sat down and I gathered my thoughts.

I took a deep breath and as I let it out, I asked, "The other day when I found you sleeping on my couch, you said you and Bandit were catching up... What did you mean?"

Bandit took his paws away from his face and laid them on my leg, and looked up at me with eyes as big as saucers. I wondered if he could possibly know what I was talking about.

Sam got fidgety – which was weird because normally Sam is very self assured. It was one of the things I loved the most about him. I assumed he was gathering his thoughts.

"A couple of days before I began to 'scout' you out... You know, just to see if you were really the author of that book everybody was reading at home."

That wasn't really saying much since apparently there's not that many people left.

"And?"

"Well, you didn't have a cat."

I was stunned. "I didn't have a cat? What are you saying?"

"Bandit wasn't living here when I dropped in the first time," Sam said sheepishly. His cheeks actually turned a very pale shade of pink.

"The first time you dropped by? When was that?"

"The real first time I checked in on you was about three days before your birthday. You were at work and I walked through the apartment and there was no sign of a cat," he explained.

I sat there on the bed in silence, just looking at him. I didn't know what to say and I was sure that whatever I said was going to be the wrong thing.

Finally, I said, "So, what makes you think I wrote the book? Maybe your real twenty-first century wife is still out there waiting for you to sweep her off her feet."

"You're my real twenty-first century wife," he said boldly.

I stood up and took a deep breath. I couldn't be near him or Bandit, so I walked out of the room and into the living room. Did Bandit really belong to me? Does he really love me or was he a spy? I opened the sliding glass door and went out on the balcony. Sam was right behind me.

"What's wrong?"

"Was I happy without Bandit?" I couldn't imagine that I was. I loved him so much.

"I don't know. I don't think so."

"So, how did he come to be outside my door that night?" I probed. "Maybe he belonged to someone else." But even as the words were coming out of my mouth, I knew that wherever he was from, he was probably going to die – and even though I knew that part of my life had been manipulated, I still loved Bandit and I still wanted him to greet me at the door every day.

"If you promise to relax, I will tell you... But you have to relax," Sam began. I did make an honest effort to relax.

"You mean, you won't give me another mental slap if I relax."

He promised, but he wasn't off the hook.

"Your friend, Dolly, is married to my good buddy, Kurt Wilson." He stopped to get my reaction.

"Dolly from work?" Dolly had been the only black girl on our team, and she was what kept us all awake and raring to go every day. She was smart and funny, and – like me – in her fifties and overweight. But about six or seven weeks before she found a box and gathered all that was hers on her desk and left the company, she'd lost a lot of weight. Like me, she had lost that weight in a very short amount of time. It was all beginning to make sense to me now. But why didn't I worry about her? Probably for the same reason no one was worried about me. Life.

"Yep! She's going to deliver soon. But when we first met and I asked her about you, she told me something and I couldn't forget it."

"What did she tell you?" I really could not imagine what Dolly would tell him that had to do with Bandit.

"She said that sometimes you dreaded going home to an empty apartment. That you'd go shopping, out to dinner, or to the movies just so you wouldn't have to go right home – and that stayed with me as I traveled because I knew you were supposed to have a cat." Sam took a breath and continued. "So, not long after Dolly conceived, another couple in the nineteen nineties had a son two months ago. Well, anyway, they found a box of kittens. There were three in the box – they were cold, wet, and near death, and I figured I should bring you one. So, I asked her if I could have one to give to you."

Sam stopped again and looked at me with a smile. I did not smile back, so he continued.

"She handed Bandit to me because she thought he was ugly… How surprised do you think I was when I saw he had the markings you wrote about, so I left him on your doorstep five years ago and I watched you find him and fall in love with him." Sam smiled when he thought about this, but then his smile turned into a frown.

"What?" I asked.

"He's been telling me about life with you. He loves you and he is very happy. But it's taking forever for him to tell me about five years with you because he gets distracted easily. He'll be in the middle of a thought and a piece of dust will fly by and he'd rather chase that. And headlights on the wall… Oh, forget about it. But when he gets on a roll—"

"*STOP!*" I screamed. "I don't want to know. I'm tired. Because of you, I now have a cat – albeit a cat that I love – who, as it turns out, has been spying on me for the last five years. You gave me a new uterus. Why would you do that?" My voice began to rise.

"Please relax."

"Don't you know how wonderful the last few years have been without a uterus? It's been great! Then, you go and harvest my eggs – you harvest my eggs right in front of the surgeon when he's taking my appendix out. Nobody asked you to do that. Nobody gave you permission to do that. And whether or not I was going to be using them is neither here nor there."

"Please relax."

"Then, you go to the Falls with Ariel for a whole week. You were only supposed to be gone for a few hours, and then – *and then!* – you get all the leftovers."

"You know I don't have a problem sharing with you."

"That's not the point!"

"You promised to relax."

"You've been in my life almost a whole month and in that time, you have manipulated every part of my life – from my health to my cat." At that moment, I knew what it was to love and hate someone at the same time. I really could not talk about it any more. "I really want you to go."

# CHAPTER TWENTY-TWO
## AN IDIOT FAR FROM HIS VILLAGE

In the time it took me to make less than a quarter turn, I saw the rose and a note. I knew it had to be from Sam, most likely placed there in travel time, but I was not interested in reading it.

It was at the moment that I heard the all too familiar sound of glasses and dishes crashing to the floor, coming from the direction of the bedroom. That was all I needed.

"Ah, poor Sammy," I heard that horrible person say. "Nobody seems to want him." Arthur walked out of the bedroom into the living room.

"What?" I asked, still annoyed at Sam.

"Ariel doesn't want him," Arthur said. "And now you don't want him."

This man had to be the biggest idiot in the world – twenty-first and twenty-third century.

"So, you're assuming that I don't know they spent time at the Falls together?" I jeered at him.

"Oh, he told you that, huh," he said.

"You're an idiot," I said to him. "And your village is looking for you," I said, walking past him toward the bedroom.

"I am a genius, in case you forgot," he said, following me into the bedroom. "And I know exactly what you want; what Sammy isn't willing to give you."

I turned around to face him and I saw a big goofy grin on his face.

"And what is that?"

He looked over at my bed and back at me.

"What is wrong with you?" I asked, irritation in my voice.

"Not a thing," he said, that goofy grin still on his face. "As you will soon find out."

To my horror, he was starting to unzip his pants. So, when I tell you that to this day I feel no remorse, have never felt ashamed, nor did I ever shed a tear for what I was about to do, you will understand exactly why I did it. The world leadership held me accountable, but what could they do? They were two centuries in the future.

I picked up the Louisville slugger and took the batter's stance.

"Oh, sweetheart, what are you doing?" he asked in that greasy voice that I hated. "You're going to hurt yourself with that thing."

"It's late and I'm tired – and I am really tired of you," I told him. "And I am going to hurt you."

"You know," he said, pulling his zipper back up. "The girls in the fifties do exactly what they are told to do."

I stood up to my full height and said, "I'm sure that's not entirely true, but you're not in the fifties now, are you? And we've come a long way, baby," I told him. "I am a twenty-first century girl, but not just any twenty-first century girl."

I could see he was becoming agitated with me. Just as it should be. As I spoke, I proceeded to get back into the batter's stance. "I am, and proud to be, a twenty-first century—" I paused for effect. "—*Jersey girl*."

And I swung.

As I swung, I heard air rushing through a tube and saw Sam from the corner of my eye appearing at the door of the bedroom. But I didn't stop; couldn't if I wanted to – and I didn't want to.

The bat made contact the first time just below his left elbow. I heard the crack and saw the shock on his face. The first scream didn't escape his lips until the bat hit his left leg above the knee. By this time, he knew that Sam had returned.

"Sammy!" he cried out.

"What?" Sam asked, unconcerned.

By this time, I had swung a third time and hit him in his 'special' place.

And he finally went down. As he hit the floor, knees first, he said in an unfamiliar soprano voice, "*Help.*"

"I don't think she needs any help," Sam said with a bit of mockery in his voice.

I brought the bat back up to swing again, but Sam grabbed it and smiled at me. "I think he's had enough, don't you?"

At that moment, I heard bells – like jingle bells – and a woman appeared in my bedroom. She was tall, thin, and very beautiful with long, wavy black hair. She could have been Oriental, but clearly only half, which made her the most exquisite and exotic woman I had ever seen in my life.

She was wearing a pair of jean capris, with a form fitting pink shirt that said 'NY Yankees' on it. She had a pair of pink canvas sneakers with white bobby socks on her feet. She was absolutely perfect. She's the kind of woman that makes straight women like me want to see how the other side lives. She looked vaguely familiar.

"Emily, this is Boo," Sam said.

On the floor, Arthur was wriggling with his hands over his crotch, but managed to say, "*Oh, no.*"

"I had hoped we could meet under better circumstances," she said, extending her hand. "But it seems my presence is necessary today," she said, glancing at Arthur. Her hand was soft and her grip was strong. I kind of felt like I knew her.

I looked at Sam who was now holding the bat and nodding his head in agreement with Boo. She walked over to Arthur, stood looking down at him for a few seconds, then walked around to his other side. He did not look happy for something more than just a wallop to his manhood.

"He seems to be afraid of you," I said to Boo.

"Oh, he is," she said, not taking her eyes off of him. She squatted down beside him on those magnificent thighs, and to Arthur, said, "This could all have been avoided if you could have just loved me."

I looked at Sam and in my head, I heard him say, *'They date on and off,'* and nodded his head.

Wait. What?

I looked back at Arthur and Boo and said out loud, "He really is a fool."

"Is he the fool or am I?" Boo asked, bringing herself up to her feet effortlessly. *Wow, those are strong legs,* I thought.

She looked at me and I had that feeling again, Sam put his hand on the small of my back. But she was just about perfect – how could anyone not fall in love with her? I wondered how come Sam didn't fall for her.

"I'll take him with me. I'll heal him and have a nice long talk with him," she said, squatting down beside him again. "You want to come with me?" she asked him.

And like a child, he said, "Okay." Then, they were gone in a clatter of plates and glasses crashing to the floor to the tune of jingle bells, but not before she gave me a sly wink. Kind of funny if you think about it.

And I felt a slight twinge of depression that she was gone. I wondered if I'd ever see her again.

"Tell me about them," I said to Sam, pulling him over to the bed and sitting us both down. "Tell me their story. Was she the rebound girl after Ariel dumped him?"

"Ah, no," he said. "They didn't go out for years after Ariel broke up with him. In fact, they started dating seriously about two years after Ariel and I got married."

"That was years after the breakup?" I asked. "When did Ariel and Arthur date? When they were teenagers?"

"Yes," was all Sam wanted to say, I could tell. His lips stopped moving and there wasn't any conversation going on in my head either.

"And?"

I could tell Sam really didn't want to talk about it, but I really wanted to know. So, I looked directly into his eyes and told him in my head – I may have moved my lips; remember, I'm not good at this – *'Just spill it.'*

"Spill what?" he asked out loud.

He was so cute, being coy like this. I almost changed my mind and was going to marry him and have a baby with him. But at this point, I hadn't.

"Tell me their story," I said, exasperated. "Or I will go turn the TV on and talk to Ariel about it," I said, getting up. "She'll tell me," I said on my way out of the bedroom.

"Hmmm," I heard him say.

"What?" I asked, backing into the room.

"I'll tell you," he said, but clearly he didn't want to. "Ariel doesn't like to talk about it either."

So, we went out to the living room to take seats on the loveseat. Sam still wasn't comfortable alone in the bedroom with me. But once we got settled in, he couldn't stop.

"We were all friends at the Center for Developing Abilities. Boo, Ariel, and Arthur are all about a year older than me, so they already knew each other when I got there right after my eleventh birthday. They were in the genius class together, because it was already asserted that they were of the genius crowd. I would see them every day in the lunchroom sitting together with other friends, who were also from the genius class," Sam began.

All I could think of was, *what genius decided to keep these kids apart?*

"Our dorms weren't in the same buildings, because they felt it would be best if the geniuses were apart from the rest of us, because after all, they would eventually save the world." Sam's lips were tight and his face was strained, but he continued. "I fell in love with Ariel the first time I saw her. I had never met her, and by this time, my – let's say, my talents – weren't able to reach that far, so I couldn't connect with her mind. But I wanted to meet her... *had* to meet her. So, I broke some rules..." Sam said, a smile beginning to form on his face. *Really? My Sam broke rules?*

"Yes, one night, I left my room and walked over to the genius dorm building. There were no guards. They just assumed we would follow the rules and stay in our own place. But they didn't count on me." He let out a small guffaw. "But when I got to their dorm, I heard something weird in my head, not just the usual chatter that I normally hear all the time." *How sad that there's never any silence for him.* "So, when I looked around to see what I heard I saw Ariel and Arthur sitting in the backseat of a car." He grimaced at this thought. "They were making out."

"Excuse me," I said. "They were twelve and they were making out in the backseat of a car?"

Sam looked at me like I had two heads. "Yeah – the car probably belonged to one of the professors. And yeah, I was appalled, too," he said.

"They were *twelve!*"

"What? You never kissed anyone when you were twelve?"

I hate those questions. "Of course, I didn't kiss anyone when I was twelve. I was a *kid*. Kids do not make out."

"Don't they?"

"*Ewwww!*"

"So, I saw them kissing and I guess I got mad... or jealous, or something, so I found a rock and threw it at the windshield," Sam went on.

"Okay, so, you threw a rock and the windshield cracks, or breaks or shatters..."

"No, you could throw a boulder at glass in the future and it would just bounce off," Sam said, nodding his head.

"So, the rock bounced off and?" I asked. I really needed to know what happened next.

"Well, I assume it hit me in the head because I woke up about a half hour later in the hospital." He looked at me, presumably waiting for me to laugh.

"Did you get a concussion?" I asked instead.

"Yes, but one of the psychic healers had to heal me and my parents were called. They arrived about two hours later and I could hear them discussing whether or not I should be taken home with the administrators of the center." Sam must have really liked this part because he was grinning from ear to ear.

"Why are you smiling?" I asked, confused. "I thought you hated talking about this."

"I do." He grinned even wider – if that was possible. "But this is the part where I meet Ariel."

Of course, that would make him smile. I wondered if he smiled like this when he was thinking about me around her.

"Go on," I said dryly.

"While the adults were in the other room arguing about me, Ariel came into my room," Sam said, nodding happily.

"Was that against the rules, too?"

"Yep, she broke the rules to come and meet the boy who had thrown a rock at her and her boyfriend."

"Was she impressed?" I wanted to know.

"She was impressed," he said proudly. "Ariel broke up with Arthur the next morning and he has hated me ever since." He paused to take a sip of his soda. "Boo told me later how happy she was that they broke up because she had been in love with Arthur since they met."

Kids falling in love? What did the twenty-third century raise? And what did they intend to raise? I really had to think about this. Because kids should be doing kid things, playing ball, learning how to swim, and drive. What happened to puppy love? When did learning how to deal with each other as friends become unimportant?

"Okay," I said, blowing air out of my mouth through a big sigh. "So, here was this love rectangle…" I was still trying to wrap my mind around all of it. "Did you get any work done? Did you have regular classes? Like math and science and Phys Ed?" My voice was reaching that aggravated pitch again.

"Oh, sure, and world history, but the genius and psychic classes were separate. They felt they needed to keep us apart, so we didn't mix. So, Ariel and I had to keep our relationship a secret."

Wait. What?

I thought I might vomit.

"Relationship? You were *twelve*."

"Yeah?" Sam said, still not getting it. "So, all through school, Arthur did everything he could to break us up... but it didn't happen. He tried to get me in trouble so many times by telling the professors where Ariel and I were going to meet. But what he didn't know is that my abilities were getting stronger and I knew what he was thinking almost all the time." Sam chuckled at this. "He just kept getting himself in trouble and the more trouble he got into, the more he hated me."

Yeah, I could understand that. He was a guy who blamed everyone else for his mistakes.

"So, you're telling me that all through school he didn't even try to date Boo?" I asked, having a hard time believing this. I would have tried to date Boo.

"Nope, but she still tried. She has never fallen out of love with him. I think they could have made each other happy if he had just accepted her. I mean, she's not a bad person. She's a bit high strung at times. But nobody's perfect," he said, shrugging his shoulders.

"After school, we went our separate ways. I'm from outside of what you call Philadelphia. Ariel and Boo are Jersey girls, as you put it, and Arthur is from Canada. Of course, Ariel and I stayed in touch because we wanted to get married."

"Of course, you did."

Sam decided to ignore my sarcasm and go on. "Ariel and I got married in a private ceremony by the justice of the peace; just my parents and Ariel's father on their boat on the Delaware river. It was nice. Ariel was happy with it. I was just happy we were married."

"Why wasn't Ariel's mother there?" I asked.

"Oh, I thought I told you," Sam said, scrunching up his face. "Ariel's mother died the same night Seth died."

Wait. What?

My heart stopped beating for a few seconds. That poor girl had to grow up without her mother. I wondered what it would have been like if my mother hadn't been there while I was growing up. She was my rock and a shoulder to cry on. Every girl needed her mom to kiss all the little hurts away when she's a child, go with her to buy her first bra, explain sex to her after her and her friends giggled about it for weeks. A girl needed her mom to help her mend her first broken heart.

Right up until the day I turned eighteen years old, my mother had been that for me. After that, I was pretty much on my own. But Ariel hadn't had that. You just couldn't hate a girl who didn't have her mom around to help her grow up.

Sam looked at me, waiting for me to complete my thoughts. "That night when she was tucked in was the last time Ariel saw her mother."

My heart ached for Ariel. Not sarcasm this time.

"Around our second anniversary, Arthur called Ariel and asked her if he and Boo could take us out to dinner. Well, Ariel thought that was strange because we hadn't seen either of them since we heard they were dating." He paused to see if I was still with him. He hadn't gone very far. Where did he think I would go?

"Back then, we still had a few restaurants and few 'date spots' to go to." He did the air quotes for me. "So, even though she thought it was out of the ordinary for him to invite us out on our anniversary, Ariel said yes. Without even consulting me."

"Would you have said no?" I asked

"Yes, I think so," he said distractedly. "When Ariel told me about the dinner invitation, I wasn't happy. I wanted to spend my anniversary with my wife – *alone* with my wife."

"Sure," I said. Because surely after only two years of marriage, you are still very much in love and want to be with just your spouse. I knew that – because when Charlotte and Lucy were both first married, I hardly ever saw them.

"We had a very brief, but very nasty argument – the first one of our marriage. That is, as you can imagine, exactly what Arthur wanted. So, when we got to the restaurant, we were just slightly on speaking terms and they both could tell."

Sam got up and went into the kitchen, and opened the refrigerator. From where I was sitting, I could see him bend over into it, most likely searching for something good to eat. He came back with some string cheese and offered me one. I smiled and said no.

"You know," he said. "You've stopped eating… well, as much as you used to."

"Yeah?" I asked. "What's your point?"

"Remember when we first started going out?" I nodded. "We always went out to eat… That was so I could make sure you were taking in enough food, so your weight loss wasn't that noticeable. And because I was hungry and wanted to try all the different kinds of food."

"What are you talking about? I lost four to five pounds a day. That's a lot," I told him.

"Yes, but if you hadn't been taking in that many calories, you would have lost ten to fifteen pounds a day. You had a bag of chips for lunch one day. That would have resulted in the artificial environment completing sooner, but not being able to sustain life," he said. "Another reason why I stayed here every night... just to make sure you were still healthy."

"And on schedule," I said, remembering what I thought were dreams of Sam kneeling at my bedside with his hand on my belly.

"Yes," he said, nodding his head. "And I knew Arthur was sniffing around."

I had to admit that I was beginning to have a better understanding of what was going on in my life. I think I was starting to soften up to the idea of sharing Sam with Ariel. But not completely at this point. But I was ready to hear more about Boo and Arthur.

"Okay... continue. Tell me about your double date."

"Um, where was I?" he asked.

"They knew you had been fighting."

"Oh, yeah, right. So, yes, they were already there when we walked in and Arthur had this nasty grin on his face. And Boo was looking at him like he was dog poo."

"Which he is," I interjected.

"Remember, Boo is not just a genius. She's a psychic, too," Sam reminded me. "So, she knew what he was thinking. I had been forbidden to connect with anyone's mind when I left school, so even though I wasn't sure, I was really just guessing."

"Hello, Ariel, you're looking very beautiful tonight," Arthur had said, standing up and trying to give her a kiss.

Ariel pulled away from him, and Boo and Sam looked at each other.

*'I'm going to kill him,'* Sam heard Boo say in his head. *'He is such a jackass.'*

Sam wanted to kill him, too. But Sam didn't really want to be there.

They all sat down and awkwardly opened their menus. All were quiet, until Arthur said, "Who'd have guessed you'd still look this good after two years of marriage to Sammy."

Boo rolled her eyes. Ariel put her arm in front of Sam to keep him from getting up and hitting Arthur. But Sam had no intentions of hitting Arthur. Sam is a lover, not a fighter.

"Yes, she does look great," Sam said, looking lovingly at his wife. Ariel looked at him and they kissed, bringing a sneer to Arthur's lips.

Boo turned to him and said, "Have you forgotten you are here with me?"

"No!"

Sam and Ariel's kiss ended with a pop and Ariel said, "I think I'll have the chicken parm."

"Sounds good, "Arthur said. "I'll have the same."

"You're allergic to cheese," Boo told him.

"I'll have it without the cheese," Arthur said, teeth clenched, eyes on Ariel.

"Then, it won't be chicken parm," Boo said with a slight giggle to her voice. "It'll just be chicken and tomato sauce."

Sam wished he could get into Boo's head to know what she was thinking, but legally he couldn't and she would know if he did – her abilities were much more powerful than his.

"I'm going to have the broiled salmon with a baked potato and the salad bar," Sam said, closing his menu.

"That sounds good, I'll have that, too," Boo said, putting her menu back on the table and as she did that, she noticed Arthur was still looking at Ariel. "Don't you ever get tired of that?"

"No."

Boo blew out a sigh and at that moment, Arthur's head went back like he had been slapped hard on his cheek. Boo smiled, unconcerned. Ariel was surprised and gave Boo a suspicious look. Sam chuckled and told Boo in her head, *'Good one.'*

"So, did you hear about the new plural marriage law?" Arthur asked, when he had recovered from Boo's mental slap to his face.

"We have heard about it," Sam said. "And we aren't interested."

"It wouldn't be you I'd be marrying," Arthur said to Sam with a sneer.

At this point, Boo couldn't take any more. "All right, that's it!" she shouted and she body slammed him into the wall about two feet above their table. Ariel let out a surprised, "Oh!" and Sam clapped.

Boo looked up at him. "You are such an idiot. Plural marriage will not and cannot take effect until all males are married. For the first time." She shook her head in disgust. "So, you may as well marry me."

"I don't love you," Arthur managed to say. "I love Ariel."

"You will never have Ariel." Sam and Ariel felt like they were eavesdropping. "I can make you love me – I have that ability – and I can make you happy." She seemed to be waiting for an answer, but Arthur didn't say anything.

Boo picked up her stuff, said goodbye, and walked out of the restaurant. At which time, Arthur crashed to the floor, knocking his head on the corner of the table; taking the table cloth with him and causing all the water glasses and the small vase of flowers – which were sitting in the middle of the table – to hit the floor with him.

"Sam, who categorized Arthur as a genius?" I asked.

"I suppose it's his IQ score, why?" Sam asked so innocently.

"What do you mean? He took an IQ test?"

"Yes, it's a mandatory test for all children who exhibit those tendencies."

"Did you take it?" I asked Sam.

"NO!" he said shortly. "I refused to take it."

Wait. What?

"Well, Arthur must have cheated. If he was a genius, he wouldn't have spent his whole life alone when he could have had a beautiful wife. And why does she look so familiar to me?" I pressed.

"I guess the heart wants what the heart wants," he said.

That wasn't the answer to my question, but maybe only because I was tired.

"Thanks for coming back. I might have killed him." I said sleepily. "But you really need to go. I have go to get some rest. Good bye, Sam."

# CHAPTER TWENTY-THREE
## TAKING INVENTORY

Getting a few things off my chest and learning about Boo and Arthur left me weak. I finally met the man of my dreams and I couldn't do it. I couldn't make the commitment that he wanted from me.

I wanted to be part of something big, but he already had a wife – a wife he loved and who was undoubtedly a nice person. I hadn't known him long, but I knew him well enough to know he'd be married to a good person.

My life would just have to go on the way it always did. I dragged my body out of bed and into the bathroom. I did my business and washed my hands. I went back to the bedroom and looked at the calendar I kept on the wall to keep track of my weight loss. I noticed that I had lost a total of sixty-eight pounds in twenty-six days.

I stood in front of the full length mirror on the wall and took a good look. I took my pajamas off, so I could take a full inventory.

Starting from the top, I saw that my hair was full, and in the time since Sam laid his hand on my back, my hair hadn't needed to be colored. I had colored my hair the night before my birthday as I did every year before my birthday and the color stuck. It wasn't even my real hair color. How did Sam do that?

My face was a beautiful shade of beige with a healthy pink glow and with just the few freckles that I had loved my whole life. My chin was tight and there was just one. There was no droopiness in my chin area and the little hairs I used to have to pull out because they drove me nuts weren't there any more. My lips were full and, even I had to admit, kissable.

My vision was a perfect 20/20 just like before my glasses. My eyes were open wide, thriving with life, somehow bigger, and my lashes were getting long again.

My shoulders no longer looked as if they were padded and my breasts would be envied by a porn star. Really, not kidding. And I had a waist again. My belly was pretty flat. Well, flatter than it was three and a half weeks ago. And my belly button looked as though it was closing up. Weird, right?

My butt no longer looked like a shelf. It was a lot tighter than it had been on my birthday and my hips were obviously slimmer and my legs were honestly toner. No wonder my pants didn't fit any more. With a real waist, slimmer hips, and toner legs, my pants never had a chance.

Walking was now a lot easier because arthritis was nowhere in my body. I didn't have x-rays to confirm that. I just knew because bending my knees was not a problem any more.

And my ugly toe was now beautiful. Together with my other toes and a pedicure, my feet were gorgeous. I even had nail art done on the big toes.

The age spots on my hands were gone, leaving only healthy, glowing, and younger looking skin. My fingers were svelte and slender, and my nails were hard and shiny without help from the Vietnamese girls at the salon.

I no longer had to take blood pressure or thyroid meds, or any of my over the counter supplements. After my blood work came back normal and Sam explained about his gift to me, I stopped taking everything cold turkey. I had expected to start feeling sluggish and have heart palpitations, but they never came.

What a wonderful gift Sam had given me. Was it fair of me to accept and use this gift and not do anything for Sam? Well, to be honest, he did give it to me without asking first, so by law I could keep it and use it and not have to give anything in return.

# CHAPTER TWENTY-FOUR
## DOLLY

"Dolly is going to deliver today," Sam said, taking me in his arms. "They actually live just around the corner. Why don't you come with me? So, you can see how easy it is and talk to someone who is involved – who isn't Arthur."

Like taking the fabric of time between my fingers, this also scared me. But I knew that since there was just a short window of time that the artificial environment could be used, I really was going to have to make a final decision on marrying Sam and having his baby.

And soon.

So, maybe going over to the house and witnessing the birth, and talk to the woman would help me make that decision. Who would know better about the situation than someone who was already involved and actually having a baby? I was in!

It was now the fourth day of December and it was quite chilly out, so I had to reach far into the back of my closet to find my winter jacket. I put my right arm into the sleeve and I already knew it was too big. How could I forget to buy a new jacket? So, I grabbed the heaviest sweater I had and we were on our way.

As soon as Sam turned the car on, that same black face with the trim goatee filled the screen, "Sam, it's time. Dolly is really scared and refuses to dilate without you." He sounded very anxious and moved his eyes to me. "Oh, hi, Emily. Are you coming with Sam?"

"Yes," I said timidly. "I hope that's okay."

"Oh, yes, that's wonderful." He smiled. "Dolly will be happy to see you." And with that, he was gone.

"I can't believe Dolly is going to have a baby. I guess that's why she left her job? Because she married a time traveler from the twenty-third century and now she's having his baby?"

"Yep, all in a nutshell."

Sam pulled the car over to a home just around the corner from me. I love Dolly, so why didn't I know she lived so close to me?

We got out of the car just as the front door opened and a very tall black man came out to meet us. He took Sam's hand and shook it vigorously, but then took him in his massive arms to give him a big hug.

"It's happening, it's really happening. Me and Dolly and Tina are gonna be a family," he said with tears in his eyes. "A real family."

He turned his attention to me and a big smile spread across his face. He came toward me with arms wide open.

"Kurt Wilson, this is Emily," Sam said as the big man took me in his arms.

There must be something really special about twenty-third century men, cause they've got it going on. When you're hugged by one of them, you're *hugged*. Sam had hugged me and I felt secure for the first time in my life. And up until now, I had never been bear hugged by a big black man before, but I now knew what all the fuss was about.

"Emily, this is my good buddy Kurt."

"Dolly is so glad you're here," he said as he led me into the house. To Sam, he said, "Dr. Clarke is already here."

Sam clapped his hands together and said, "Let's do this."

I walked through the door and I heard Dolly's voice rushing though her words, "I changed my mind. I don't want to do this any more."

And Dr. Clarke's soothing voice was saying, "Sam is coming and the whole thing will go exactly how we practiced."

And a female voice I didn't know was saying as I reached them, "You are doing a wonderful, beautiful thing for all of us."

That voice came out of a TV screen about the size of a smart car and I surmised the women with the front row seat was Tina, Kurt's wife in the twenty-third century. The eight or ten people behind her included Ariel and Sam's mom sitting next to Boo, who was looking a bit peaked. I noticed that all but Boo were emaciated and I wondered why that was.

Besides the big screen TV, I saw that Dolly's living room set of a couch and a loveseat had been pushed against the far wall. There was a well used recliner chair in the corner near an end table, holding a lamp with a bear hugging a tree base. I thought that might be Kurt's touch in the room because it didn't match the beach themed art on the wall. There was a fireplace and the mantle showcased what looked like a wedding photo and a short version of a grandfather clock. Dolly was situated right in full view of the spectators.

*Oh, sweet mother of God,* I thought, looking back at Dolly. *Please tell me she is not going to give birth in front of a live studio audience.*

Ariel gave me a wave and a smile. Sam's mom smiled warmly and Boo continued to look peaked. I had only met them once before, but I wasn't sure Sam's mom was really on board with me.

"Emily!" I heard Dolly screech.

Although she was in agony, Dolly looked a lot healthier than she did the last time I saw her about five weeks ago. Like me, she had lost a fair amount of weight and I remembered she had been losing weight just before she left the company. Now I knew why.

The dark spots on her face were gone, replaced by a milk chocolate glow and freckles under her eyes that I had never seen before. The glow was what women sought after by years of using expensive skin care products.

Her hair was fuller, wavy and all hers. And it appeared that Dolly, who – in all the six years I had worked with her – had never had her nails done had gotten a manicure. A French manicure. Since she was barefoot, I could see she had also gotten a pedicure, too. Nice!

Dolly had received a scar that ran down her hairline from her forehead to her right ear in a car accident on the way to work one morning in two thousand and six, but it was gone now. Sam had probably thrown that in for giggles, too.

He was like magic, but he wasn't Harry Potter. He is just a man. My man and I love him. Okay, so, he's Ariel's too, but I still love him.

"Hello, Dolly!" She always loved it when I greeted her this way. I rushed to her and gave her as big a hug as I could, bearing in mind her belly was considerable.

She was breathing hard, but managed to say, "I'm so glad you're here. I think I may have made a mistake, I don't think I can do this."

"You can do it," I told her. "You are Dolly the magnificent. But are you sure you want all these people watching?"

"Oh, it's okay. They're going to move my chair, so I'm sideways. I wouldn't want them to look right into the eye of the storm, if you know what I mean."

Of course, I knew what she meant. After all, I had a curse stuck in the eye of my storm for a very long time.

*'I love you,'* I heard Sam say in my head. I almost forgot he was there. I turned around and he was smiling at me. I was about to say something back to him, but Dr. Clarke came back into the room and I forgot what it was.

"Hi, Emily," Dr. Clarke said to me and gave me a peck on my cheek – something he'd never done before. He chuckled and said, "Well, I am going to deliver your baby, it's only right."

I had been going to Dr. Clarke once a year for a very long time, before he did my hysterectomy. I really thought he would deliver a baby for me. Things were different now.

I backed away and watched as Sam and Dr. Clarke moved Dolly's chair just as she said they would. Kurt was standing practically right up against the TV, talking to Tina softly. He had his hand up on the screen and Tina was doing the same on her end. Dolly was looking up at Sam expectantly. I felt like I was in the way.

Sam took Dolly's hand in his and smiled at her. When their eyes met, I could see Dolly's body immediately relaxing and a smile spread across her face, and she said, "Let's do this."

I went over to sit in a chair, but Sam and Dr. Clarke both said I should pull it over and sit next to Dolly.

"You will have the rare opportunity to see Sam in action," Dr. Clarke said as he pulled up the sheet and exposed the storm of the century. "I wish all of my patients could be anesthetized by Sam."

I looked up at the screen and all but Boo were standing with Tina, practically right up against the screen. Kurt was now on Dolly's other side, holding her hand and cooing at her. She was doing great and I was happy there was going to be no screaming involved.

Softly, Sam said, "Dolly, the baby is crowning, so I need you to push gently, just like we practiced."

Dolly nodded her head and began to gently push, once, twice, three times and she looked up at Sam.

"Good girl," he said to her. "His head is out, now one more push and his shoulders will be out. A little bit stronger push, just like we practiced."

Dolly did just as Sam encouraged. There was just the slightest of uncomfortable looks on her face and it was over. The baby was here – it was a boy. He was bald and he was the color of weak tea. At least, that's the color I saw with all the birthing stuff all over him.

Dr. Clarke held him up and presented him to the viewers in the twenty-third century. Hmmm, before his mother, I found that to be a bit odd. Tina was being hugged by Ariel and Sam's mom and the others took their turns. Boo looked shell shocked. I wondered what was going through her head.

Then, Dr. Clarke placed the baby on Dolly's chest and the baby found her exposed nipple and was already a pro sucking at her breast. She had the biggest smile I had ever seen on her face.

Sam was watching as Dr. Clarke massaged Dolly's belly – I assumed coaxing the afterbirth out; if there was an afterbirth. Was there afterbirth in an artificial environment? *'Yes,'* I heard Sam say in my head.

Dolly looked exhilarated and in her element. *She was beautiful.*

I wanted that.

But I was curious. My sisters had both said that the pain of childbirth was a pain you forget right after the baby is born. But there was still pain. I saw no pain in Dolly since Sam took her hand the first time after we got there.

Dr. Clarke tied off the cord close to the baby's belly, then slowly and gently pulled the umbilical cord from Dolly's ying yang until he had the end. Dr. Clarke handed Kurt the scissors and showed him where to cut the cord just about an inch from the tie.

The baby continued sucking and had a tight grip on Dolly's thumb in his chubby little fist. His eyes moved to me and he appeared to be smiling as he sucked. He let go of Dolly's nipple and giggled at me. That was weird. Babies don't normally giggle before they've even been cleaned off. He had no trouble finding her nipple again and resumed his first meal.

I leaned over to Dolly. "What's the baby's name?"

"Praxeda."

When I looked confused, Dolly went onto explain that Praxeda was her great grandfather's name and Kurt's mother's name. I thought it was perfect.

When all was said and done and the people from the twenty-third century went back to their real lives, Dolly asked me if I wanted to hold the baby. I wasn't sure. The baby at three minutes old had giggled at me. That was kind of spooky. But I didn't want to hurt her feelings, so I took the baby in my arms.

"Doesn't Kurt want to hold him?" I asked.

"Kurt isn't ready."

"Why not?" I asked and quickly said, "Oh, duh."

The poor guy probably didn't even remember ever seeing a baby, let alone holding one. So, I brought the baby over to him and held the baby out to him. The look on Kurt's face was one of total trepidation.

"Just make sure his head is stable," I said, handing Praxeda over to his father. Although, I wasn't sure that was going to be a problem. If the baby could giggle for the crowd, his neck was probably not as fragile as an ordinary hour old infant.

Kurt took the baby, but held him like he was a bomb.

"Oh, don't drop him," I said with fear in my voice and Kurt instinctively pulled the baby close. "There you go," I said in a sing-song voice and the baby giggled. Weird!

Kurt's eyes were wide as Dolly was being helped up off of the birthing chair and into a robe. She chortled at her husband.

"See," I said to Kurt. "Already you're a pro."

Kurt smiled and looked down into his son's eyes, and he began to weep. Sam walked over to his friend and embraced them. Dolly motioned me into the next room. On the way, I looked back and the baby was being gently laid on a scale and weighed, then measured. Sam gave Kurt the numbers and wrote them down, taking a quick glance at the clock on the mantle.

In the kitchen, she asked me if I wanted a cup of tea. Before I could answer, she put the kettle on and motioned me into a chair. She got two cups out of her cabinets and set them on the table, followed by a small bowl of Splenda packets and some Coffee-Mate out of the fridge.

When she finally took the chair next to me, she took my hand and said, "It is so good to see you and I am so glad you were here to witness Praxeda's birth."

I didn't know what to say. I had so many questions for her, but didn't know where to begin. But by now, the kettle began to whistle and Dolly got up to pour the water.

"Dolly, are you sure you're ready to be up and around?" I asked. "Shouldn't you be laying down, complaining that your wazoo hurts or at least nursing the baby?"

"Ah, I'm fine and I'll nurse again later," she said, waving the question away with her hand. "Kurt and Tina need time alone with the baby while he's still an infant."

"Wait. He's not bringing the baby to the twenty-third century right now, is he?" I was confused. I was sure Sam told me it wouldn't be until the baby was a week old.

"No, no. The baby can't travel for a whole week. Kurt's going to hold the baby up to the screen of the tele-communicator and they will bond as best as they can. You know, until the baby can travel," she explained while she made her tea. "I'm so glad you and Sam are going to do this, too."

I wasn't even sure I was going to do this with Sam, but now was not the time.

"Dolly, how long have you known Kurt? When did you meet him?"

"I met Kurt about five months ago. I think we would have met before that, but he stalked me for almost a month," she said, shaking her head and blowing on her tea.

"He stalked you?" I said indignantly.

"Yes," she continued. "I saw him all over the place. I saw him when I picked up my dry cleaning, I saw him when I put gas in my car, but mostly I would see him at Foodtown. And after about three weeks of this, I decided it was time to find out what his problem was." She giggled and sipped her tea. "So, I turned a corner and bumped his cart with mine." She gave me a sly wink. "After that, it was like magic."

"Magic?"

"Yeah, he liked me and that made it easier for me to like him. You know how I was with guys. I never trusted our boss as far as I could throw him in the ocean." She gave a snort.

It was true. Dolly and I had both given up on men long ago and trust was one of our issues.

"How long was it before you knew he had a wife?" I wanted to know.

"Oh, maybe three weeks. By then, I was so deep in like and lust with him, he could have asked me to kill somebody for him and I probably would have done it."

That did sound like magic. But there was no timetable for falling in love – it could take years or it could take a minute. Or it could just take Sam.

"When did you meet Sam? Did he ambush you at the mall and force a new uterus to grow in your body?" I asked cynically.

"Ambush me? No. Is that what you think happened to you?" she asked me with a sly smile. "When Kurt and I went into New York City to take a horse and carriage ride through the park, he told me who he was."

"When was that?" I asked.

"In the summer. It was nice. The weather was perfect and so was he." She got a far away, dreamy look in her eyes. "He made me feel special. And I love when he looks in my eyes, I know he loves me. And I know he loves Tina, too. But this is a really good thing we're doing."

So far, she hadn't said anything about her being in love with Kurt. And this troubled me. Should it matter? Of course, it should!

"Is that when you met Sam?"

"Yes, he came from the nineteen nineties where I think he delivered a male with Dr. Clarke," she said, getting up to offer me cookies.

Wait. What?

Sam knew Dr. Clarke in the nineties? I wondered how long they had known each other and how did they meet.

"No, thank you."

"You should still be eating," she said in a motherly tone.

"I haven't stopped altogether." I snorted. "Why would I?"

We laughed together and she sat again, putting the cookies onto the table.

"Kurt and Sam told me they were time travelers," she continued. "And there was something about the way they were talking about it that I just knew it had to be true. It explained a lot."

"Like what?"

"Like why Kurt was just always there. I mean, he never really followed me, he was just always suddenly there." A tiny giggle escaped her lips at this thought. "Like he appeared from nowhere."

"Did you hear anything when he did appear?"

"No, I don't think so. Nothing out of the ordinary."

"So, when they told you what they wanted, you were okay with it?" I asked unevenly.

"Well, to be honest, I wasn't thrilled at the idea of having a baby. I was okay with sharing Kurt," she told me. "He really is too much man for just one woman."

I had been hugged by Kurt, so I had no choice but to agree.

"So?" I asked. "How did Sam do it?"

"Well, we were sitting at a little table at the deli, Kurt and I on one side, Sam on the other, and he took my hand and looked into my eyes." She had that far away look in her eyes again. "At first, I didn't believe he could do what he said he was gonna do. So, we made a bet that if he couldn't tell me everything I was 'ailing' from—" Her fingers went up with air quotes. "—We could forget all about it." She took a breath and continued. "But, Emily, he took my hand and I swear to God I felt something leave my body." She was shaking her head vigorously.

I remembered I had that feeling, too.

"Well, he told me everything I was taking medication for – you know, he really is something." I had to agree, he is really something.

"Sam told me everything I wasn't taking medication for. He told me how I felt when my mother and father died. He told me about my first time." She gave me a wink on her last words.

Really? My Sam talked about her first time? I was going to have to have a *long* talk with him.

"He told me things that I had forgotten, happy things, sad things, things I never told Kurt." She was very excited now.

I was about to tell her that Sam could connect with her mind and could have dug all that out, but the point was moot. That's exactly what he did.

"So, you agreed." It wasn't a question, just a fact.

"Yes, I agreed and now look at me. I'm a mom and I have a superman of a husband – and at fifty-four years old, I have a killer body."

Okay, Kurt was cool, real cool, and he gave great hugs, but a superman? The killer body I wasn't so sure about as she just gave birth to a baby.

"Did they tell you about the possibility of a second pregnancy?"

"*A WHAT!*" Dolly banged her cup on the table as she stood and knocked her chair back.

Kurt came running in, the baby still in his arms – Sam right behind him with Dr. Clarke bringing up the rear.

"What happened?" Kurt asked.

Sam came to my side and Dr. Clarke stood close by. I looked at the baby and almost wet myself. The baby was all of what? Twenty minutes old and he already had a dark tuft of hair on his head, resembling a Mohawk. His weak tea colored skin was getting to be more milk chocolate and he had freckles on his cheeks. His eyes were a beautiful brown and huge like his father's, and he was hanging off of Kurt's arms like he had grown a few inches in the short time it took me to upset his mother.

"I might get pregnant again?" Dolly didn't shout this. I assumed so she didn't upset the baby.

Sam began to laugh and Kurt relaxed. Dr. Clarke had a bewildered look on his face. The look on my face probably matched his. Because Sam wasn't laughing at what Dolly said. He saw me looking at the baby and knew what I was thinking.

*'The baby will be five years old in a week, what did you expect?'* he said in my head.

"It has happened, but it's very rare," Kurt said calmly, handing the baby over to Dolly. "You should probably nurse him again and Tina would like to talk to you." Dolly left the room, but not before looking back at me with apprehension in her eyes.

I was left alone in the kitchen with Kurt, Sam, and Dr. Clarke, who were all looking at me like I was delirious.

"What?" I asked innocently.

# CHAPTER TWENTY-FIVE
## EMACIATED

When Sam and I got back into the car after settling Dolly and her little family in, I decided it was time to ask Sam about the health issues in the twenty-third century.

"Sam?" I asked timidly.

"That was fun, wasn't it?" he asked, before I could bring myself to ask to talk about Ariel's emaciation with him. "Well, right up until you told her she could have another baby."

"Yes, that was a very different experience for me," I told him. "The baby giggled at me."

"Yes," he said with a chuckle. "Babies giggle."

"Usually not quite so soon," I informed him.

"Really? When do they giggle?"

"Well," I started. "They tend to wait until long after they've been cleaned up."

"How long is that?" He sounded a little frustrated.

"Well, babies are different. Some take longer than others," I told him. "But it usually takes months. I mean, babies don't even really smile for a long time. Oh, sure, they look like they're smiling, but that's because of gas when they attempt to push it out."

Sam looked like he was turning green.

"Well, our baby won't have to wait that long – and besides, the new generation doesn't get gas," he enlightened me.

"Great!" I said. "So, no one will know how to deal with it when the second generation babies come along."

Sam seemed to be thinking about this when I saw Arthur's face appear on the information screen. He was there just for a second and the screen went black. He didn't look like he was in pain, so I supposed Boo had healed him and he was pretty much back to normal. I saw Sam roll his eyes. He had to be fed up with Arthur's juvenile behavior.

"Sam?" I began. "Why does Ariel and your mom and those other people look so...?" Now that I had started I didn't know how to continue.

"Look so... What?" he asked.

"Why do they look so unhealthy?"

"They're pretty healthy, but you have to remember we haven't had any real food for a long time, except for some fruits, and avocados, walnuts, apricots, some grapes, and a few figs we get off of the few remaining trees," he told me. "They may get an orange once in a while from a visitor who has an orange tree."

"So, how are they surviving? And how come you, Boo, Kurt, and Arthur look so good?" I wondered.

"We survived on protein pills that were mass produced about forty-five years ago when the world leadership realized that our food supply was dwindling," He divulged to me.

"Can't you do something?" I probed. "Look what you did for me and all the other women."

"I can only do so much with the material I have to work with," he told me. "You and the women of your century already have a decent immune system and your metabolism isn't... Well, hasn't been damaged from years with no real food. Ariel and my parents are actually very healthy compared to most people, because I do what

I can. Boo's mom is much healthier than most, because of who she is. The World Leadership doesn't exploit us."

I thought about this and my heart ached for them. Sometimes when I would be looking for something to eat in my apartment and couldn't find anything to satisfy me, I would get in my car and go get something. But these people had nothing to chew on, no hard candy, no cheese fries.

"So, you and Boo, Kurt and Arthur look this good because you've been eating real food here in the twenty-first century and Arthur in the twentieth century?"

Sam pulled into the empty parking space at my apartment and frowned at me.

"To be fair, that's why Kurt and Arthur are healthy. Boo and I are healthy because we have this internal thing that does it for us. The other healers are the same. A healer has never died because of the virus. Healers usually live a very long and healthy life."

We walked upstairs together and I pondered this.

Sam went right for the fridge to get a wild cherry Pepsi. "Since the project started, all the other guys have been eating real food, so they all got real healthy, too," Sam said, opening up a box of Entenmann's chocolate covered donuts and added, "Food is good."

I remembered the way he ate the first few times we went out and I remembered what he said. He said our food was good here. He's not an alien from another planet, just from another time – and he was making himself at home. He was born to do this.

Ideas began to roll around in my mind, people needed to eat – and I could feed them.

A couple days later, I went back over to see Dolly, just to see how things were progressing. I was not prepared for what I saw. In fact, for a moment, I thought I was dreaming.

Dolly, looking like she had entered a wet t-shirt contest, had just finished bathing her son. She was watching her naked son run around the room and I have to admit, she really did have a killer body. Tina was watching from the tele-communicator and the look on her faced a very proud mama. I gave her a finger wave.

In just two days, Praxeda had changed a lot. He was about two and a half feet tall. He had a full head of springy hair, his skin was the color of a dark chocolate Hersey bar, and he was proud of his junk. I know this because each time he ran past me, he would stop long enough in front of me to do a little dance and giggle. I think he actually remembered me.

"Hello, Praxeda," I said to him, when I found my voice.

"Hi," he said on the run, but I distracted him long enough for Dolly to catch him.

She gestured to me to follow her to the bedroom and now that she had him in her arms, he had settled down and was inundating her with kisses.

"Oh, my God, Dolly. He's so big," I told her.

"Yeah, tell me about it." She dumped him on the bed and he laid back, so Dolly could dress him.

"I love you, Mommy," Praxeda said in his sweet, little toddler voice.

"Was he outside playing? Is that why you bathed him this early in the afternoon?" I asked as I watched Dolly put a pair of huge big boy underwear on him and an oversized t-shirt.

Praxeda yawned as Dolly pulled him back into her arms. "No, my little man has to go to bed. He's exhausted." I followed Dolly into another room that had to be Praxeda's room.

There was a dark wood crib in the corner, but also a toddler bed on the floor with Sponge Bob sheets. Dolly gave him a kiss and pushed him into my face, so I could kiss him. She laid him down on the yellow sheets and as soon as his head hit the pillow, he was asleep. Wow, that was amazing.

We went into her kitchen, where Dolly took two martini glasses from the freezer and set them on the counter. She went into the fridge and removed the half and half, and a squeeze bottle of chocolate syrup. From the cabinet over her stove, she brought out a martini shaker, a bottle of vodka, and chocolate liqueur. Without measuring, she filled the shaker, took some ice cubes out of the freezer, and began to shake it. I never knew Dolly to be a big drinker and I had never mixed a martini myself, so this was fun for me to watch.

She squeezed about a tablespoon of the chocolate into the bottom of each glass and topped it with the martini mixture. She took one in her hand and pushed the other toward me. I took it and we clinked them together. Dolly never said a word throughout the whole process. She threw back her head and tossed the whole thing down her throat.

Dolly sighed and said, "I really needed that."

"Why? What's going on?" I asked.

"My child sleeps fourteen hours a day. The other ten hours, he eats and poops – and while he sleeps, he matures a whole year. My two day old son eats with a fork, uses the potty on his own, and holds real conversations with his dad." She commenced to fill the shaker again.

"But you're happy, right?" I inquired.

"Oh, yeah, but I miss the little things I always imagined would come with motherhood. His first words should have been Mama or Dada. Praxeda's first words were 'Mama, I'm hungry'. And he didn't just take a few steps and fall, he got up off the floor and just kept going." She took the martini glass in hand again and tossed it down her throat again.

# CHAPTER TWENTY-SIX
## A LESSON IN GESTATION

"Okay, here's a question. I don't know why I didn't think to ask this before. But really? You say you don't want to change anything too drastically, but people who were never meant to have babies are having babies?" I pointed out to Sam. "I mean, most of the people I know, know that I had a hysterectomy. I think some questions will be asked.

"I mean, sure, they barely noticed that I lost weight. People don't want to know that you're losing weight, especially when they're trying, but can't lose weight. But people always notice when you gain weight. Really, Sam, women tend to put on weight during pregnancy," I was babbling. "How are we supposed to hide my belly from my sisters? And how does this happen in so short a time?"

"We have this under control. Ariel studied animal gestation for a whole year." Sam sounded very delighted to tell me this and if I still hated Ariel, I might just hate her more after this revelation.

"A year, Sam? A *whole* year?" I challenged. "People go to school and study animal biology for *years* to become veterinarians." There were so many questions going through my mind, but so far I wasn't liking any of the answers.

Sam was very patient and let me speak. The truth is he could have went right into my brain and saved us a whole lot of time. But out of respect, he waited for me to actually articulate my thoughts.

"You have to remember that Ariel is one of the smartest people on the planet right now in my time," Sam said.

"What could Ariel have possibly figured out in just one year?"

"She figured out why some species gestate longer than others.," Sam explained. "First, she found out that elephants gestate for three years, horses gestate for a little under a year. Camels go about fourteen months, that's weird, huh? And cats gestate sixty to sixty-seven days. While hamsters go sixteen to twenty-eight days and chipmunks gestate thirty-one days. A mouse will gestate nineteen to twenty-one days, while an opossum will gestate just twelve to thirteen days." He looked right into my eyes and said, "Get it so far?"

"Get *what?*"

"Large animals tend to gestate longer than smaller animals."

"Okay," I said a bit hesitantly. "I still don't get it."

"So, because human beings are large animals they gestate for thirty-six to forty weeks or nine to ten months," Sam went on. I already knew this part, but Sam was on a roll. "Ariel had to figure out why, and then she had to figure out how to get humans to gestate for the same amount of time as a small animal."

"Okay," I said. "So, obviously she must have figured it out and that's a good thing, if I were to become pregnant," I said, because there was a chance I wouldn't conceive. "And to be pregnant even for just a few weeks people will notice that my belly is getting bigger." Which was my major concern.

"And your boobs, too. Don't forget them." He smiled when he said the word 'boobs'. Sam's a breast man.

"Why would that be important?" I asked.

"You will have to nurse for two days."

"Two days? Two *whole* days?" He missed the sarcasm. "Sam, get on with it."

"Emily, we were almost out of time. We needed to come up with a plan where everything had to come together as soon as possible. So, nine months to gestate would just be too long."

I really wish I could tell you about Ariel's discovery, but to do that I would be letting out a twenty-third century secret – And plus, my head would explode, because it almost exploded while Sam was explaining it to me. Also, it only works in the artificial environment anyway.

"I think I understand. But still four weeks is four weeks and I have to assume that my body will show signs of a baby growing inside me. So, again, don't you think my sisters will notice my belly getting bigger? Jill is a very smart girl, she will definitely notice," I pointed out. "And what about the people I work with? I really think they will notice that kind of change in my body."

Sam took in a very deep breath and said, "You won't even show for the first two weeks." He took another deep breath. "And you won't be able to see your sisters or Jill until after the baby goes to Ariel and you'll have to quit your job."

Wait. What?

I wanted to come back with some quick retort, but it made sense. Dolly left right after she and Kurt got married.

But before I could stop myself, I blurted out, "Quit my job?" My voice cracked. I mean, I didn't love my job any more, but it gave me something to do every day. "What will I do?"

"You'll write a book."

Okay, that was fair. But I still had questions.

"Okay, that's all well and good, but still it takes eighteen years to raise a child. How many children can be birthed by then? Will it even be enough to repopulate and keep the world going?"

Sam smiled that wonderful, beautiful smile that I love so much. "As of yesterday afternoon there are nine hundred and sixty-one first generation babies. Five hundred and thirty-one females, four hundred and thirty males – with twenty-one more within the next three weeks." He sounded humble, but proud. And then added, "Fourteen males and seven females. Ours will be the last. I had to modify the schedule after I agreed to be a part of all this."

I was impressed, not just because of the numbers, but also because Sam could remember all the numbers. He really is pretty perfect. Something about that was nagging me somewhere right on the edge of my thoughts.

"That is an awesome number and how long has this project been going on?" I really felt he should know just how impressed I was.

"Just about a year. The first child, a male, was born about seven and half months ago," Sam said humbly. He really should have taken a bit more pride in the accomplishment.

"So, in a year there have been nine hundred and sixty-one births? Impressive."

"Well, you know what they say about the best laid plans? And in the beginning, we still had to get the bugs out, as you like to say here in the twenty-first century," Sam snickered.

"And Ben, he was the first to meet with his girl, he was just a little shy," Sam chortled. "He was that way with Gina, too – his twenty-third century wife. They would have been married a long time before they actually were, if he weren't so timid."

"Sam, how do you expect to get the world going again? I mean, it will be years before these children can do anything more than have a few hundred play dates."

"Sweetie, you will gestate for just twenty-eight to thirty days. That in itself will speed up the momentum of the ongoing maturation process, until such time it will slow to a more normal maturing pace." He stopped and took a breath. "The baby will stay with you for another seven days, at which time the baby will mature and resemble, and be like any other five year old. Only, of course, the baby will be in no way average. Then, I will take the baby to Ariel and she will be able to experience motherhood and raise the baby in the twenty-third century."

Wait. What?

"Will I ever get to hold my baby again?" I asked anxiously.

"I'll bring the child to visit you once a week for another month. In between, you have the tele-communicator to watch Ariel and the baby, and she will watch you when the baby is with you."

I remembered the size of Dolly and Kurt's TV and assumed that's what he was talking about.

"Then, what happens after that?"

"Remember how Dolly's little boy aged in just the few minutes the two of you were talking in the kitchen?"

"Yeah?"

"After four weeks, the baby will mature to be about sixteen years old and basically be on his own."

"*His* own? We're going to have a boy?" I asked at that special volume that happened when I couldn't wrap my head around something.

How manipulative could these people from the twenty-third century be? Couldn't anything just happen normally and in its own time?

Sam looked over at me. "We don't choose the babies genders. That does happen naturally."

"Sam, how long have you been working with Dr. Clarke and how did you get him to work with you at all?" I wondered.

"Family history was done on my side, too. In fact, all the healers had their family history done – to find someone in our lines who was also a healer or an obstetrician. Austin is my great, great Uncle." Sam flashed a very pleased smile again. "Getting him to come on board wasn't that simple."

# CHAPTER TWENTY-SEVEN
## FOOD FOR THOUGHT

Ever since that day at Wal-Mart when Sam finally came into my life, there was just so much to think about. I had just about decided to marry Sam and have a baby with him, when other things began to creep into my mind. I couldn't stop thinking about them and I couldn't sleep.

Sam needed to go to 1974 to help Boo with a delivery. The woman was a bit older than me and according to Boo, she was very nervous and she was afraid there might be complications. That was fine. It would gave me the opportunity I needed to go take a walk on the boardwalk, so I could be alone with my thoughts.

We said our goodbyes – he headed to the 70s and I headed to West Long Branch.

My whole life had been spent planning everything about my wedding – most girls do. I had always wanted to get married outside; a small wedding for just the immediate family. I had chosen a spot in West Long Branch at the lake. There was a gazebo there and it was my dream to say my vows there.

I parked my car and walked up to the gazebo, stepped up and looked around. I took a long, deep lungful of the lake water. I looked out over the water to see that a few of the Canadian geese had stayed behind to make this a picture perfect scene for me. My wedding would have been lovely – *perfect,* in fact. Because it would have been exactly what I wanted.

But before that, my sisters would have thrown a very lavish shower for me – or, at least, I thought they would – and all my friends from work would have come and maybe some of the people from church would have stopped by. And all the guests would buy everything on my bridal registry at Bed Bath & Beyond and the Cellar at Macy's. And I would write my thank you cards six months after the wedding because we'd be too busy loving each other to even think about them before that. Now there probably wouldn't be time for them to properly plan one.

Charlotte and Lucy both got married when our mother was still alive. Our mom, although a seamstress by trade, loved throwing big parties. So, I was not needed nor was I consulted on any of the details. I guess I was lucky I got a verbal invitation. It was then that I found out that moving into my own apartment before getting married was the worst possible thing I could have done to my parents. Feelings were hurt and grudges were held.

And speaking of plans, I had always planned two years alone with my husband, traveling, eating out, and sowing our oats before even thinking about having a child. Our life together would have been right out of a romance novel. A good life where there are no fights and no current wife in another century and everything is just perfect.

Then, we'd plan a baby and I'd get pregnant and my sisters would throw me another lavish shower – okay, maybe they wouldn't – and all my guests would buy me everything on my baby registry at Babies "R" Us. And I would love everything and write my thank you cards right away, so they all would know how much I appreciated them taking a part in welcoming my baby into the world. Now my sisters wouldn't even know that I was having a baby.

Our mother was still alive when Eli and Lynn were born, so I was left out of the planning of those showers, too. But I love my sisters. They are my family, so just being with them was important and special, and I love my nieces and nephews.

So, my baby was just one more thing I wouldn't be able to share with my only family. I sat in the gazebo, and cried and mourned the loss of my beautiful day. I mourned the loss of the beautiful white gown I would have worn and my guests at a great reception that would have proved to be awesome. And let's not forget the gifts and the well wishes. I wept because I would never get to be the center of attention like all brides. Then, I would at least know what it was like to be at the center of it all.

And I mourned the proposal... Sam had said it so many times. *We're gonna get married... After we get married...* And the ever popular, *not until we get married.* In our very short courtship, I wondered if he'd even bother or even if they did that in the twenty-third century.

There were people taking a walk around the lake, but no one noticed me.

When I was finished lamenting, I wiped my face off and went back to my car. I drove down to the beach and parked in a spot by Pier Village. I love walking around Pier Village, but today I just needed to walk and think. So, I turned and walked the other way.

I was not only going to be cheated out of my showers and all the gifts, my baby's infancy was going to be cut short. I was only going to nurse him or her for two days. How crazy is that? Isn't that the period of continual bonding between mother and baby, and isn't it healthy for both?

I was going to miss the terrible twos. Okay, I wasn't so upset about that. I could live with that.

Sam told me that the babies are genetically engineered to not only mature at an alarming rate, but also to have the intelligence of much older children. Reading and writing, even math would come easy to my baby and I was not sure I was unhappy about that. Don't all mothers want math geniuses? My baby will be a potential genius with Ariel for a mom, too. What would I be bringing to this genetically engineered would-be genius? Was I just the vessel?

My baby would grow to be five years old in just one week. My child would not have to hug the furniture for weeks before taking his or her first real steps. Would he or she even crawl first, or roll around as some babies do? The baby would be walking and talking by the third day. Momma or Dada might not even be the baby's first words. Wouldn't I miss all that?

*'Emily?'* I heard Sam's voice in my head interrupting my thoughts. *'Are you all right? I sense confusion.'*

At that moment, I didn't care what anybody said. Sam had to be a genius.

I really didn't want Sam to know exactly what I was thinking, so I said, "I'm taking a walk on the boardwalk, and I'm confused as to why there are only a few other people here with me."

*'Oh, okay, as long as you're sure you're okay,'* he said. *'Do you need me to come back right now? I thought I might go home and see Ariel for a few days.'*

I guess I was going to have to get used to that. Ariel was home and I was back. "No, I'm okay. Tell Ariel I said hi." I thought maybe I should start using my cell phone as a prop, so when I spoke out loud even the few people around me didn't start thinking I escaped from the mental ward at the hospital.

But then, I had a thought and I grabbed my cell out of my pocket and put it up to my ear, "Sam, before you ran out of food, what did Ariel eat? What did she like?"

*'Um,'* I heard Sam say, *'Oh, yeah, when we were up at the falls Ariel said it would have been really perfect if she had a cheeseburger. She even said—'* Sam chuckled at this. *'—she'd kill for some chocolate. She wanted me to tell her how the cheese fries tasted.'*

"Tell me again why the women don't travel?"

*'It didn't seem prudent to the World Leadership to waste the chips on those who didn't really need to be in the past. Boo is the only female traveler.'*

"Why don't you ever bring Ariel food?" I asked.

*'I have brought her food in the past.'* He chuckled again at this. *'But she has to share it with the others in the lab and I'm not that imaginative, so I really never bring that much and she feels bad.'*

"How much longer will she need to be in the lab?"

*'Actually, that's over. Yours were the last eggs to be inseminated, so she's not there a lot any more.'*

"So, she'll only need to share with your mom and dad now, right?"

*'I guess so.'*

"When do you think you'll be back?" I needed to know.

*'I'll be back tonight. I want to have dinner with you at Chili's tonight, if that's okay.'*

"Have a good visit," I said, putting my phone back in my pocket and getting back in my car. I knew that whatever my problems, what Sam was offering me was far better.

First, I drove out to Eatontown to AC Moore. I bought the biggest and prettiest basket with a handle, and some pretty Christmas wired ribbon. Because I was already there, I went into Acme to pick up a couple of frozen pies, some peanut butter cups, and Hersey kisses. And while I was at it, I picked up some peanut butter, jelly, and Wonder bread – because everybody knows Wonder bread is the best thing since... sliced bread.

I drove down to West End to the Windmill to get an order of cheese fries and some cheese on the side. The cheese fries were for me. I'd make some fresh fries for Ariel later. On the way home, I picked up cheeseburgers at McDonald's, Burger King, and Wendy's. I also stopped at the 7-Eleven to get some whipped cream in a can, because you can't have pie without whipped cream from a can.

At home, I put the pies in the oven, wrapped the burgers in foil, started the fries frying, and made peanut butter and jelly sandwiches. When the sandwiches and fries were done and the pies were cooling, I fixed up the basket. I laid one of my better tablecloths on the bottom and let some of it hang out the sides, and made bows with the ribbon and attached them to the handle.

When all was said and done, there was one apple pie, one pumpkin pie, ten peanut butter cups; three of each of McDonald's quarter pounders, Burger King's Whoppers with cheese, and Wendy's bacon cheeseburgers; about a pound of fries, which I poured the cheese on; nine peanut butter and jelly sandwiches; *and* a can of whipped cream.

It just didn't seem like enough, so I took a two liter bottle of wild cherry Pepsi out of the fridge and placed it in the basket. I stood back, but it still didn't seem like enough, so I went into the bathroom and chose a headband and some barrettes that I don't use and – just for giggles – I took my brand new bottle of hand lotion off the shelf and placed them in the basket.

Just then, I heard the rushing of air through a tube and knew that it was time. Sam came into the kitchen and looked at the basket.

"What's all this?" he asked.

"It's a basket of food and I want you to take it to Ariel and your parents," I said proudly. "And there's some other stuff in there for Ariel."

At first, he looked perplexed, then a smile began to grow on his face and there was tenderness in his eyes. He put his arms around me and pulled me close. He didn't say anything for a few moments, then he let me go, took the basket, and he was gone. I found it funny that I never saw him reach up and pull the fabric of time apart.

In my head, I heard Sam's voice say, *'Put the TV on.'* Holy crap, I heard that all the way from the twenty-third century in my head?

I went into the living room and turned the set on, Bandit strolled in and took a front row seat.

Sam was standing right up to the set and he said, "You are crazy beautiful!" He stepped away and I saw three very happy people. But it was not and I can't stress this enough: it was not a pretty sight.

Ariel had a quarter pounder in one hand and a peanut butter cup in the other, and she was alternating taking bites until her mouth was full and her cheeks were puffed out. Sam's mom was holding a peanut butter and jelly sandwich up to her eyes. I could see she had tears in her eyes. I also saw that it was dripping with whipped cream.

Sam's dad was eating the apple pie with his hands. "I'm coming back," Sam said, and a moment later, he was back in my apartment.

He turned the TV off and asked, "Why did you do that? Have your feelings for Ariel changed?"

"I'm going to share motherhood with her. I'd like her to be around long enough to enjoy it with me," I told him.

# CHAPTER TWENTY-EIGHT
## THE APPETIZERS

I had been out almost all day and had still forgotten to buy a new jacket, so I put my heaviest sweater back on and we drove to Chili's. Sam was very quiet on the way. I thought he might be a little bit upset about the reason I told him I bought all the food. But, in all honesty, Sam seemed very nervous to be with me for the first time ever.

We were barely shown to our table when Sam slid out of the booth, looked around to see if anyone was coming, and got down on one knee. My heart began to flutter. This was it. He was actually going to propose. *I must be ready,* I thought and that thought made my heart flutter even more.

We had been talking about getting married almost from the beginning and what I thought should have been eventual, Sam didn't. He raised a small box toward me and said, "Emily Leigh Ann Gibbons, I love you. You are so special. Only you can do the things for me that need to be done. Please complete me and become my wife."

He was about to open the box, but I clasped both my hands around it. Diamonds had no value in the twenty-third century. I couldn't even imagine what he would think was appropriate for our engagement.

"What?" he asked.

The fact is, I didn't really need an engagement ring and there was just so much about my marriage to Sam that wasn't going to be traditional. A ring wasn't really necessary, but as long as I was going to get one, I really wanted it to be a great one. Does that seem selfish?

"You don't really have to give me a ring," I told him.

Sam got up and slid back into the booth. "But I want to give you a ring. It goes with the band." The smile on his face was so sweet and reminded me of those paintings of the puppies with the big, puppy dog eyes. "It's a set."

He put the box on the table and pushed it over to me. I decided it was now or never, and took the box and opened it.

I'm not really sure what I expected, but it was perfect. Not too big, certainly not too small – and in what I have found out is the marquise shape. The band was in two pieces and was meant to wrap around the stone, which I saw was pink – but it was *beautiful*. I couldn't wait to be wearing it.

I put my left hand out, extending my ring finger, and gestured for Sam to put it on. He carefully took the diamond out of the box and slid it onto my finger. It fit! I was really surprised that it fit. But who knew what he did at night in my apartment when I was sleeping. He could have measured my finger.

"I can show my sisters? Right?" I asked.

"Yes, you can show your sisters. They have to know we're going to be married."

"They do?"

I couldn't stop looking at my new diamond engagement ring. It was so pretty. I didn't even care any more that I wasn't going to get a big, extravagant wedding and a magnificent reception. I was just happy to have the ring – and Sam, too.

"So, I'm ready, then?" I said to Sam.

"Well, you will be, just before Christmas."

It was then the waitress came by, introduced herself as Hannah, and said she would be our server. In all honestly, she would just take our order and some underling would actually bring us the food. After scanning the menus, Sam was excited to try all the appetizers, so we ordered them all to be brought out at different intervals of the meal. I was learning from the best how to order food.

"You mean I have to wait three more weeks before we can get married?" I asked with disappointment in my voice. Now that I knew I was going to marry Sam, I wanted to do it now. *Right now*. Get *married* right now – get your mind out of the gutter!

"Well, there's still some last minute things that need to be done," Sam said, clapping his hands because the Texas cheese fries, and the artichoke dip and chips arrived.

"Like what?" I asked, taking a chip, filling it with dip, and stuffing it in my mouth.

"First, you need to give notice at your job."

"I do? Can't I just quit? Dolly did."

"And you have to give your sisters enough time," he said with a smile.

"Enough time for what?" I watched Sam put fries in his mouth, close his eyes, and chew like he was in heaven.

When he had swallowed, he said, "You know."

I didn't know – well, at least, not for sure. My big exquisite bridal shower would be iffy once the ball was in my sister's court.

While I was thinking about the shower my sisters might or might not throw for me, the server brought out potato skins and the nachos. Sam's face lit up and I was almost sure his very recent proposal and the thought of my shower just fell out of his head.

Almost immediately, the southwestern eggrolls and the cheese dip came out. Sam ordered more chips and another round of sodas – and he was happy. By the time the hot spinach and artichoke dip and the Buffalo wings came, I was sure Sam couldn't eat any more. I was wrong. I really couldn't figure out where he put it all.

"Can we show them tonight?" I asked anxiously.

"Yes! The more time they have the better," Sam said, dipping a wing in the dip and placing it in his mouth. "And we have to implant the eggs."

I couldn't eat. I was just too excited. So, I just sat there and watched Sam enjoy his food – and enjoy he did, until there were no appetizers left. I was ready to go see my sisters.

We stopped at Lucy's first because we both wanted Jill to know first. Sam knocked on the door and I was giggling. I have no idea where that came from, but there it is. I was giggling.

Jill answered the door and I wrapped my arms around her, and said, "Thank you, thank you, thank you!"

"What for?" she asked.

I was thanking her for marrying Derrick and having the children, who would eventually give birth to Ariel – who, in turn, would do family history and send her husband into the past to find me. But I couldn't tell her that.

So, I said, "Thank you for answering the door. We have something to tell you."

I led Sam by the hand past Jill into Lucy's house. Lucy was sitting on her loveseat with Kris watching TV. I really think I hate that man. Neither of them looked up when I entered the room, but as soon as Sam entered the room, Lucy was up and Kris feigned interest.

Lucy's arms went around Sam and she said with enthusiasm, "It's so nice to see you again."

I stuck my hand out to her and she took it… and offered me some tea.

I was hurt – how could she miss it? It had be at least a carat, but I'm almost sure it's a bit bigger.

"Lucy, look!" I squealed.

Lucy took a look and grabbed my hand to get a closer look. "Oh, my God, Kris look at this."

*Oh, why did she have to get Kris involved?* He got up out of his seat slowly, as if to show he really didn't want to be involved. He looked at me and sighed – a *big* sigh. He looked at Sam and said, "Are you sure about this, man?"

*Oh, where is a Louisville slugger when you need one?*

"Yes," was all Sam had to say.

Kris shook his head and took my hand from Lucy, and brought it up to his face, so he could get a better look. The grimace on his face slowly turned into a smile and I really thought that for once he was going to be nice and be happy for me. But it's *Kris* and the smile became more of a grin and the maniacal laughter that came out of his mouth was clearly Kris being a jackass.

Lucy gave me a 'so sorry' look. Kris looked over at Sam and said, "Really, man?"

At this moment, Jill walked in and saw the ring, and she began to squeal. She turned to Sam and gave him a hug, then grabbed me and hugged me.

It was then that Kris showed his true colors and said, "Jill, sweetie, just relax. Aunt Emily is not engaged. Sam is playing a trick on us all."

"Why would you say that?" Sam asked, aghast.

"Because," Kris said to the room in general. "Everyone knows that real diamonds are colorless, clear or white. Emily's 'diamond' as you can see has a pinkish tint. It's not real. He says he's a doctor, but he buys her a cheap knock off." He gave me the same look Lucy gave me and snorted.

"Please tell me he's not really the father of your children," I pleaded with Lucy.

"I am a healer and I thought you worked in the produce department over at the ShopRite," Sam said calmly. "How could you possibly know anything about diamond colors?"

"I do know they're white," Kris jeered, rolling his eyes at my sister, who cocked her head at me in concern.

Jill was becoming agitated. "So, what do you care?!" she screamed at her father. "Why are you always so mean to Aunt Emily? Can't she just be happy? Can't you just stop being nasty to her?"

"Jill, baby, I'm only looking out for her because I know you love her so much."

Jill stopped as abruptly as she had started her rant. I found that to be curious, but because Sam began to talk at that moment. I knew he did it and I was about to find out why.

"Well, Kris I guess you haven't heard about fancy color diamonds. No, you haven't."

Kris was abnormally quiet. Sam's doing again, I supposed.

"I deal with diamonds almost on a daily basis. There really are fancy color diamonds. You see, Kris, only one in ten thousand diamonds possesses natural color and is referred to as a fancy color diamond. The more intense the color, the rarer and more valuable the diamond. Because you can actually see the tint it proves the value of the diamond." Sam smiled. "The fancy color grid goes from faint to vivid. Emily's diamond is intense, one step below vivid. I bought this particular diamond because I love her so much."

Kris was not convinced nor was he amused. "Sorry, I don't believe you, and I don't believe that you could love—"

Kris didn't finish his thought. At that moment, his head jerked to one side and he fell backwards onto the loveseat, but rolled off onto the floor. He lay there for awhile until Lucy ran to him to be sure he was okay. I looked over at Sam, who was looking down at them with trepidation on his face.

Jill came running into the living room and before she saw her parents on the floor, she said, "It's true, it's all true."

She had a print out in her hand, but she then saw her parents on the floor and seeing that they were both alert and breathing, she handed the paper to her father and said, "Here ya go, Dad. Read up on fancy color diamonds. So, you won't have to work yourself up into a seizure again." She gave me another hug and to Sam, said, "You better make her happy."

Sam smiled and took my hand to lead me out of the house.

In the car, on the way to Charlotte's, I asked Sam if he did that to Kris.

"Some people can't see past their own noses and how *dare* he try to tell me how I feel about you." He never admitted to giving Kris a mental slap in the face, but I know he did it. I don't believe it was his intention to hurt Kris, but to just snap him out of his own stupidity and although Sam is not in any way a failure, Kris is still a jackass.

Sam drove over to Charlotte's house; but, in all honesty, I did not want to go in and see what the next installment of the 'Emily Show' would bring. We sat together in the car in front of the house because I just could not bring myself to go in. I really wanted to cry – then again, I really wanted to be strong, too. *But whatever.* There was a rapping on the window and Charlotte was outside the car, and beckoned me out of the car.

I opened the window and Charlotte said, "Come on in the house, it's freezing out here."

Inside, the four of us sat at the dining room table in awkward silence. Charlotte paid very little attention to my ring, but focused on Sam.

"Sam, if we had known you wanted to marry our little Emily, we would have spent more time with you to get to know you better." Charlotte had that same look on her face that Lucy had been sporting at her house just before Kris went tumbling to the floor.

"You want a drink, Sam?" Bob said, getting up to go to the bar. "I need one."

*Oh, dear Lord, kill me now.*

"No," Sam told him. "I'm fine."

Like me, Sam isn't a big drinker.

Bob poured himself something amber in color into a tumbler I recognized as my wedding gift to them. He sat back down and said, "You do know it's customary to ask the girl's father for her hand in marriage?" Bob asked, after taking a swallow of his drink.

"I was under the impression that Mr. Gibbons passed away a few years ago," Sam informed Bob.

Our parents had been away on a second or third honeymoon – maybe their fourth, I had lost count – in Europe. They had been on their way to the Vatican when the train they were riding collided with an eighteen wheeler truck that had gotten stuck on the tracks. Exactly where they had been in the train was never known, but we were told that they didn't suffer.

My parents and my sisters were all I had. After the accident, Charlotte and Lucy had their husbands and children, and all I had was them. But their lives were full, there was no room for me. I became an afterthought – not that I was thought about much before that by any of them. My dad never forgave me for moving out of the house when I was eighteen. That's when I went to Montclair instead of Monmouth College.

"Yes, Charlotte's father is dead." So, now he was 'Charlotte's' father. "So, being the oldest male in the family—" *He was my father, too!*

"You're *not* my father," I interrupted him. "And for your information, we didn't come here to get your permission."

"Now, Emily, Bob is just trying to do what's right by you," Charlotte interjected.

Wait. What?

"I am fifty years old. I don't need him to do what's right by me." My voice was slowly rising. "Sam is a great guy and I am going to marry him."

*'Please relax.'*

"We came over here, so I could share something really special with you. Something I've always wanted to share with you." I really tried to be calm.

"Emily, you've only known this man for a few months. I'm just looking out for you," Bob said, with the same pathetic look on his face that Kris had. "Shall I remind you that your choices in the past have not always turned out very well?"

"This is the first time I've chosen to marry!"

I stood up at the same time Sam did. He took my hand and led me out of the house. I tried hard not to start crying until I was in the car.

Once in the car, I said, "Just *once* I really wanted it to be about me." Then, I couldn't help myself. The flood gates were opened.

# CHAPTER TWENTY-NINE
## PLANNING MY ESCAPE

Sam gave me the option of getting married in Las Vegas, the Bahamas, or the court house. I chose Vegas because at least one of the chapels there would be better than the court house. Sure, the Bahamas would have been nicer than Las Vegas. We could have gotten married on the beach at sunset or sunrise, but I wanted to stay in the country. I was afraid if I chose the Bahamas, Charlotte and Lucy would have both changed 'their plans' and come along. After the fiasco their husbands created on the night Sam and I became engaged, I was pretty much *done* with them.

The only bad thing about flying to Sin City was that Sam couldn't fly with me, so Dolly was going to fly with me. Kurt would already be there with Sam, so he could modify the rental car for us. Kurt, I found out, was on the crew that modified all the vehicles and the tele-communicators.

I spent the next three weeks getting ready for my wedding. Sure, I was going to elope, but that didn't mean that there weren't plans to be made and it wouldn't be nice. Every day, I would either shop at Wal-Mart or Foodtown and bought all different kinds of food for Sam to bring to Ariel and my future in laws. I also sent skin care products and vitamins. I just didn't think the protein pills were doing the job they were designed for.

I also took a trip to Freehold to visit David's Bridal, just to see if I could find anything that I would be interested in wearing at the Chapel of Love in Las Vegas.

As it happened, I found many gowns I was interested in. Now that my body was back to being as healthy as any twenty-five year old, everything I tried on looked absolutely great on me.

However, I ultimately chose a satin gown – ivory in color – with a halter bodice, champagne colored sash, and chapel length train covered in Chantilly lace. I chose a veil of matching lace and a short sleeved satin jacket. It was winter, after all. The beading on this gown was like a fantasy. In the right light, the beads shimmered in multi colors. I would only wear it once, because I was only getting married once, but once would be enough.

At work, I slowly gave my accounts away to my colleagues. Because, well, I didn't want to work anyway. I had so many other things on my mind.

Sam had given my sisters too much credit. In the three weeks I planned my wedding, neither of my sisters called me once. Jill called a couple of times just to be sure I was okay and that I was going ahead with the wedding. She wanted to come with us and be my maid of honor, but her mother wouldn't let her. Which, under the circumstances, was a good thing. I told her when I saw her again, I would be an old married lady.

The day before my wedding day, Sam came into my room and woke me up. I no longer had a job and my weight loss had pretty much come to a standstill, and I was determined to do something I used to enjoy. *Sleep in.*

"Unless you're getting into this bed with me, get out." I said, putting the pillow over my head.

"I want you to go to Austin's office today around four. I'll meet you there," Sam told me.

"Why? Where will you be that you have to meet me there?" I asked, confused.

Since leaving my job, we had spent almost all day every day together, talking, eating out at restaurants I had ever wanted to try and we got food baskets ready for Sam to take to Ariel. Afterwards, Ariel and I would talk for hours via my tele-communicator.

"I'll be bringing the last food basket home and you'll be sleeping."

Wait. What?

"You're going to let me sleep? And it won't be the last basket."

"I'm going to help you sleep." He chuckled. "After this, you won't be able to sleep in for weeks."

"I love you." I smiled at him. He took my hand up to his smile and kissed it lightly.

The next thing I remember, I woke up to Bandit doing the kneading thing on my back. I rolled over to see it was three o'clock. Sam is a great man!

I got up and took a quick shower, wondering what I needed to go see Dr. Clarke for. As I dressed, I speculated that he was going to give me 'the talk'. I guess I was just too happy to really give it any real deliberation.

When I arrived at the office, I noticed there was just one girl at the front desk. Normally, there is a lot of hustle and bustle at this office, since Dr. Clarke is in practice with four other doctors and a midwife.

He was waiting for me and gestured me into the back, telling the receptionist that she could go as we were just going to talk in his office. But he escorted me to one of the exam rooms and asked me to get up on the table.

What? No gown?

I got up on the table and laid back as I lifted my legs, and Dr. Clarke pulled out the leg rest. Sam came in, gave me a quick kiss on the forehead, and shook Austin's hand.

"So?" I asked. "Why have we all gathered here this fine afternoon?"

"I'm going to implant the eggs," Sam said with a smile.

"Oh. Will it hurt?"

"You won't feel a thing. I'm going to do it in travel time. No fuss, no blood, and no scar."

I looked around and wondered where he had the eggs. There was no cooler with a big red tag boldly stating: HUMAN EGGS FOR IMPLANT ONLY.

"Why couldn't we just do this at my apartment?"

"Because, unfortunately, Arthur is still hanging around." Sam's voice confirmed his disgust. Does that man never learn?

"We don't think he'll bother coming over here, since it will only be a few minutes," Sam said, pulling my shirt up and unzipping my pants.

"Should we ask Dr. Clarke to leave?" I asked devilishly.

Sam and Dr. Clarke both found this funny and chuckled. Then, Dr. Clarke walked out of the room.

Sam said, "Are you ready?"

"Sure, let's do this," I said, but in the time it took me to finish my sentence, Sam was zipping my pants back up and pulling my shirt down. "What? It's over already?"

Sam nodded his head as Dr. Clarke reappeared, bearing a cup of what turned out to be orange juice.

"Drink up, we're getting married tomorrow," Sam said, helping me to a sitting position. What orange juice had to do with implanting eggs or getting married, I don't know. But it was good.

The next morning, Sam and I loaded his car with my suitcase and my gown. We went over to Kurt and Dolly's and loaded her suitcases in the trunk. I wasn't happy about flying without Sam and he hadn't as yet told me why. So, I asked.

"Sam? Why can't you and Kurt fly with us?"

Sam and Kurt were sitting in the front seat and they turned to look at each other, which made me think neither one would tell us.

But then, Sam cleared his throat and began, "It's really very simple. The World Leadership has forbid us to travel in any vehicle that hasn't been modified with some Helenspew."

"One of our friends, Erik Weiss, one of the first travelers," Kurt continued. "After he met and married a nice woman named Ivy and she became pregnant, Erik was in a car accident. At least, we think he was in a car accident."

"Our cars had not been modified at this point because we didn't know that they needed to be," Sam said.

"What did you mean you think he had a car accident?" Dolly asked.

Sam and Kurt looked at each other again.

"His car was found after it was hit by another car, a minivan, but he wasn't in the car," Kurt told us. "There was blood and other human tissue in it that later was determined to be his. His chip was also found in the car."

Dolly and I were appalled.

"So, what do you think happened? Did you ever find a body?" I asked.

"First, you should probably know that we all have a homing beacon of sorts injected into our brains with the chip, so if we were to die somewhere in time, our bodies would return home, where we belong," Sam informed us.

"We think that on impact, he hit his head and died, and his homing beacon attempted to bring him home, but instead he got ripped apart as he was thrown through time," Kurt continued.

"We came to the conclusion that we needed to be protected and the Helenspew had to be the answer, but we don't take chances," Sam finished.

Ever since then, the travelers never traveled in any vehicle that had not been modified with a piece of the Helenspew, the material that the last Mount St. Helens eruption created. Each of the travelers, who had his car brought into the past as Sam had, had a small piece of the concoction somewhere on the vehicle. The cars belonging to the new spouse also had to be modified and a piece of the spew had to be attached to the TV to qualify it to be a tele-communicator. It seemed that stuff was very necessary in so many ways.

# CHAPTER THIRTY
## A STORM IN THE BRIDAL SUITE

"Honey," I heard Sam calling from the other side of the bathroom door. "I need you to stay in there a little bit longer."

"What?" I said, opening the door and going into the suite. Sam was standing close to the door like a force field. He didn't even notice that I had a short black teddy on.

"Really, please go back in the bathroom."

Or maybe he did.

Now I understand being nervous. I was a little nervous myself, but Sam had been married for thirty-six years. I had been led to believe that sex was an ongoing routine with them and he was pretty much a champ at it. My experience with him said all that was true.

He tried to push me back in the bathroom, when I heard the familiar crashing of dishes and glasses to the floor. Sam pushed a little harder, but I got away from him.

"What do you think you're doing here?" I shouted over Sam at him indignantly.

"Hello, little girl," Arthur said, with that creepy sneer on his face. "Sammy." He did not look at Sam when he said his name. His eyes were only for me. "I'm here to take what's mine. You look good."

The look on Sam's face was not what you are thinking. I looked at Sam and there wasn't disgust on his face – he was genuinely dismayed.

"You should leave... *now*," Sam said to him. "Before—"

"Don't tell me what to do," Arthur said, sounding a lot like a defiant child. "Her baby will be mine. Now implant the eggs. You can stay and watch if you want, but the baby will be mine."

At this, I burst out laughing. Both Sam and Arthur looked at me, stunned.

"Oh, don't I have anything to say about this?" I asked between snickers.

Oddly enough, neither of them had anything to say until Arthur got cocky.

"Of course, you can say 'thank you' for the best sex you'll ever have," he sneered.

"Sam," I said. Now I was livid. "Go back to my apartment and get the bat. I thought he learned his lesson the first time I beat the shit out of him. I see he's going to need another beating."

"I can't," Sam said from the corner of his mouth.

"Why not?" I asked, my voice going up an octave or two, as it always does when I don't understand something.

"Sammy? You haven't told her yet?" Arthur said with contempt. I hated when he talked to Sam that way.

"Told me what?"

"You would have been mine if Boo and I had been married," he said. "So, essentially, you are mine and I will have what's *mine*."

I looked at Sam. He was still looking at Arthur with a sort of sadness on his face. I didn't understand it then, but now that I know why. I love Sam even more.

"Ariel and Boo are cousins," Sam said, shaking his head. "Boo is in Jill's direct line, too. That's why she looks so familiar to you. She's Jill in about thirty-five years."

"And we would have had you first, since Sammy took so long to make up his mind." Arthur finally looked at Sam. "So, I'm taking what's rightfully mine."

"So, what? Sam and I are just supposed to let you rape me?" I asked curiously.

"Oh, *rape* is such an offensive word," he jeered. "Especially when what I'm going to do to you is going to be so—"

At that moment, I saw something happen that I never would have believed if I hadn't seen it myself – and in the past few weeks I had seen some very strange things. That was when Arthur was lifted up off the floor and body slammed up against the wall. I jumped back and let out an involuntary, "Oh."

I looked over at Sam, who now looked like he'd had enough of Arthur and said, "Shut up."

"Sam? Did you do that?" I asked weakly.

"I had to. He wouldn't leave. He just kept talking and making things worse for himself." Sam was shaking his head from side to side. "He just doesn't know when to shut up. He should have learned his lesson when—"

He was interrupted by the sound of jingle bells. She was here – *here* in the bridal suite. That beautiful, exquisite woman was here on my wedding night. She was wearing black leggings on those legs that went on forever, with a really nice pair of black heals with purple glittery flowers on them. She had a form fitting grey shirt on, showing a pencil drawing of Tinkerbell. Her sleek black hair was pulled back in a pony tail. She's fabulous, there are no other words to describe her – except that she really did look like an older version of Jill.

I heard Arthur blow out some air and say, "Oh, crap!"

That's when I noticed the single, fat tear sliding down the left side of Boo's face. She looked so sad. There was another tear welling up in the corner of her right eye.

"Let him down," she said calmly.

Arthur crashed to the floor as Sam reluctantly released him. He got himself up off the floor and faced Boo. That second tear rolled down her face.

"I'm sorry," Arthur pleaded. "I just want what's mine. Don't you think I—"

He was interrupted by the appearance of two men accompanied by the sounds of thunder and lightning. I wondered which one was thunder and which one was lightning. They both kind of teetered on entry and they both put their hands out straight in front to them for balance. I found out later it was their first time traveling experience.

There was a storm in my bridal suite. Nobody told me there was a storm coming.

But I knew that a storm could not be good. They were both older gentlemen, probably in their early seventies – evident by the graying in both their hairlines, even though one of them was practically bald. I did not have a good feeling about this.

"Oh, my God!" Arthur said with a crack in his voice.

"Emily," Sam said, turning to me. "This is Ben Weaver and Charlie Schultz of the World Leadership committee."

*Oh, my God,* I thought. *The World Leadership Committee is here, in my bridal suite.* Now I knew this wasn't going to be good and it was then that I remembered I was in a short, black teddy. Could things get any worse?

"Arthur, it has been brought to the attention of the WLC that, after many conversations with Miss Olsen, you still find a need to interfere with the program." Let's say 'Ben' said this.

"And because you refuse to leave Sam and Emily alone, you will need to be destroyed," said Charlie.

Arthur's eyes went wide. I was stunned. *Destroyed? Like, killed? Dead?!* I hoped he was kidding.

*'It's not what you're thinking,'* Sam said in my head. I looked over at him and he was visibly sad about this. What I didn't understand was why Arthur didn't try to escape now that he was back on the floor. I mean, he was a time traveler. Why didn't he just disappear in a clatter of dishes and bottles crashing to the floor like he always did?

*'He can't leave,'* Sam said in my head. *'He's being held against his will by Boo and me, because basically this is his trial.'*

Sure, Arthur was a pain in the rear end, but he was still a human being. I don't care how far in the future these people are from, you don't just destroy another human being. You put him in a jail cell, a rehab hospital, Fort Knox, but you don't just kill them.

*'Relax,'* Sam said in my mind.

"Miss Olsen? Will you do the honors?" Ben asked.

Boo's face showed the heartbreak. Those beautiful eyes were wet with pain. I could tell she had discussed this with Arthur and the village idiot had not listened. He was a man who wanted what he wanted when he wanted it. His jealousy over losing Ariel to Sam had not only festered over the years, it had developed into a full blown canker sore – and it was not going to end well for him.

It was about to end right here; right now in the worst possible way.

"No! Wait!" I yelled. Sam moved to my side and put his hands up to quiet me down.

"You shouldn't interfere with the World Leadership Committee," he said. "This has been discussed at great length, Emily. He knew it would come to this if he didn't stop."

Wait. What?

"You knew?" I asked him incredulously. "You knew? How stupid are you?"

"I'm not stupid, I'm a—"

"So far, I see no evidence that you are a genius." My voice was up an octave.

"SILENCE!"

"Excuse me?!"

"Mrs. Malone." That was the first time I had been called 'Mrs. Malone' and it threw me for a minute. "From the time it was obvious that you and Sam would meet, he has been doing his best to interfere. The time has come for his reign of terror to end.

"Reign of terror?"

Sam tried to get me to go back in the bathroom.

"This has gone on much too long. Miss Olsen, do it." Charlie was fed up.

Boo had not said a word this whole time because it was obvious her heart was breaking. She truly loved him and it was now her responsibility to 'destroy' him because he had been stubborn and had not listened to her or anyone else when told to step back.

She closed her eyes and took a deep breath. I held my breath, too.

"Miss Olsen? Are you up to this?" Charlie asked, like a concerned father asking if his daughter was up to her coming out party. "Should we have Sam do it?"

*NO!* I thought. *Not my Sam, please not Sam.*

"No," she said softly. "I can do this."

And true to her word, Arthur was lifted off of his feet once more and brutally thrown against the wall. But he didn't hit the wall, he disappeared through it in a clatter of dishes and glasses crashing to the floor. His scream – which started out as loud as an air raid horn and decreased in volume as he apparently got further and further away – made my head want to explode. As the world got dimmer and dimmer, I felt Sam's hands on me and everything went black.

When I came to, Boo and two of the world leaders of the twenty-third century had left Sam and me alone. I was on the bed and Sam was on his knees watching me. There was concern on his face and it just made sense. There had been three too many people in my bridal suite. There had been violence where there should been love – *lots of hot, sweaty love* – and now all I wanted was an annulment.

"I'm sorry, but I did ask you to stay in the bathroom," Sam said.

"Would that have made a difference, Sam?"

"I think it would have made this all a lot easier for you."

"You mean, if I didn't know what was happening?" I asked calmly. "Don't you think I would have still heard him dying?"

"He's not dead. Boo would never have agreed to throw him to his death," Sam told me. "But if it makes you feel any better, the laws of execution have changed enormously in the last two hundred years. We lose people from natural causes and the ongoing effects of the virus much too often these days. Intentionally killing someone for being, as you've thought, annoying would be sinful."

Oh, my Lord, then what did 'destroy' mean? I didn't want to know and you shouldn't either.

"Then, why was she so upset? And you—even you were sad about it." My voice raised an octave, but I really was trying to stay calm.

"Because what happened to Arthur didn't need to happen. But he's just so stubborn and he doesn't listen. He's so damned smart—"

"He's not *that* smart," I said with disgust. "A smart person would have listened and stayed away from us."

Sam nodded his head at this. "Yeah, I have to agree with you."

"So, what did happen to Arthur. Where is he?"

Sam was reluctant to tell me, I could tell, but he knew I would pester him until he told me. As I listened to Sam explain the Leadership's actions, I felt like I was in a dream. Where did they have the right to treat another human being that way?

"Boo pitched him through time, pulling the chip out his head. I felt bad because I knew what kind of pain that would produce, knowing what kind of pain putting it in generates and I didn't think he deserved that." Sam truly was upset about this.

I was appalled and I really couldn't understand the purpose of all it.

"Arthur always felt like he was alone and ignored and no one really knew or cared about him, so it was decided that his punishment would be that he would know how that really felt." Sam got up off his knees and began to pace around the room. "He was just annoying. He hadn't – and I don't believe that he would have – really hurt you. He just wanted to hurt me."

My heart began to ache and break for him.

"Where is he?" I asked.

"I don't know," Sam said, "Without the chip, I can't sense him. But when he's found, he will probably be taken somewhere and given a bed to sleep in, and maybe some food."

"What happens when he tells them he's from the twenty-third century?" I wondered.

"He won't be able to tell anybody anything. He's lost all of his motor functions." Sam winced as he said this. "He won't even be able to control his digestion functions."

"Why couldn't they just put him in a jail cell?" I wondered.

"We don't use that form of punishment any more. We actually have very little crime, so we have no need for a jail cell."

I had made a vow to Sam and I still wanted to be married to him and have his baby. I so wanted to be a part of repopulating the world and I didn't think it would hurt if, at the moment I gave birth, I was glowing the way Dolly glowed.

I had waited long enough. It was time to get the party started. But I was still a little emotional about what happened to Arthur and I thought I would need help getting over it.

"Sam, I need help to get over what happened to Arthur. I won't be able to do anything tonight unless you suppress the memories." I looked right into his eyes. "You can do that, right?"

Sam smiled that smile I'd walk a million miles for and stepped closer to me. He placed his hands on my waist. I took a deep breath. Sam brought his lips to mine and barely brushed them, moving his lips lightly over my chin and down to the hollow of my throat. I closed my eyes and the horses were chomping at the bit.

I woke up to the smell of bacon and breakfast sausage. I rolled over in bed, hoping to see my husband lying next to me, but he was at the table starting without me. After the night we had, I just didn't have the heart to be upset with him. He was also masterful when he got 'physical'.

But I'd be lying if I said I didn't want him back in bed, so in my most seductive voice, I said, "Whatcha thinking about?"

Now the right answer here would have been something to the effect of, *"I'm thinking about jumping back in bed with you and making love again."*

But what he actually said was, "Boo and I are planning a time when we're going to go take the baby."

Wait. What?

# CHAPTER THIRTY-ONE
## BLACKMAIL

"What do you mean, you're going to 'take' the baby?" I asked, my voice becoming shrill. I got out of bed and looked for the white fluffy robe they leave in the room for you.

"Emily, please relax." I was actually starting to hate it when he told me to relax.

"Relax?" I asked. "How am I supposed to relax? Last night, I watched as your World Leadership commanded Boo to 'destroy' a man. And for what? For being an abominable pain in the ass."

"I don't know why you're having a problem with that? Did you have feelings for Arthur?"

Now if this was a movie, this is where I would turn to the camera and show the audience a very baffled look on my face.

"It's a matter of *respect*, Sam. He is a human being – albeit a flawed human being. I don't understand why he couldn't just have been brought back to the twenty-third century and put in a jail cell for a few weeks. Instead, he was not just thrown though time, he was thrown through time pulling the chip out of his head; causing more pain than even you can imagine." I was furious.

"We had no choice, Arthur had been spoken to. He wouldn't listen – you heard him. He really feels that you belong to him." I rolled my eyes at him. "It was the decision of the World Leadership. Boo had to do it."

"And the decision to 'just take' the baby? Is that their decision, too, Sam? Then, what makes them better than the government who murdered sixty billion people? Give or take a few hundred million."

"I can't go against their decision."

"But you can go against me?"

Sam had a puzzled look on his face and said, "I don't really see what this even has to do with you."

I was outraged.

"As a member of the human race and a woman who was ambushed into doing your bidding, I think I can relate to how she'd feel if her baby was just ripped out of her arms," I explained through clenched teeth.

"We would do the humane thing and wipe her memory," Sam said.

"You do that and I will make you regret it."

Sam looked confused.

"Sam, I love you. But if you don't do what's right—" I thought a little bit and said, "I'll change history."

"What? How? Why?"

"Who and where?" I asked, mocking him.

"What?"

"Well, I haven't written the book yet," I whispered. "I'll change everything in it. Maybe I'll marry Arthur in this version. I'll write everything exactly how you explained it to me."

"Why would you do that?" Sam really was innocent.

"Are you not familiar with the term *'blackmail'?*" I asked with a big grin.

Sam sighed – a big sigh – and blew out a lot of air, and said, "What is it that you think can come of this?"

"Sam, all I want is for mankind to do the right thing, treat this woman with respect, at least *talk* to her about it. Who knows? Maybe Arthur actually told her who he is and where he's from."

I walked away from him and went into the bathroom. While I was in there, I heard jingle bells. I gave them a few minutes to discuss my terms, then joined them back in the room. She was wearing the same clothes she had on the night before and she looked like she'd been crying all night.

"Boo? Are you all right?" I asked sympathetically.

"I destroyed the man I *loooooovvvvve!*" She drew out the word so long, I really had to think fast to figure out it was 'love'.

"Come with me," I said, taking her hand and taking her into the bathroom.

In my head, I heard Sam say, *'So much for our honeymoon.'*

I yelled back – because I am really bad at the head talking thing. "Do what I want and we'll have a great honeymoon." I wet a wash cloth with cool water and wiped Boo's face. "I'm sorry you had to do that."

"I'm sorry you had to watch that – nice teddy, by the way."

I almost forgot I had been wearing a short, black teddy last night when the number of people in bridal suite far exceeded the room's occupancy. But Boo was in a bad way and I was just the woman to help her. Yes, I know what it sounds like, but remember – I had a wonderful night with my husband.

"Forgive me, Boo, but can I ask you why and how you can be in love with him?" I asked, knowing full well what she could do to me if I made her mad.

"Arthur isn't always a self centered jerk," she began. "Sometimes he's sweet and loving and quite normal. We've dated on and off, mostly when he's normal. We've even broken the law and have been, well…

*intimate.*" She actually blushed. "I was the aggressor."
She smiled. "I had hoped – because I am a genius, you
know, and a psychic healer – I could become pregnant.
But, well…"

Wait. What?

She tried to get pregnant with Arthur's baby?

"Once, before all the time traveling, he drove up the
coast to a place you call New England and brought me
back fall leaves. They were beautiful, all red and gold
and orange. There were some that were multi colored."
She had a far off look in her eyes. "He also picked pink
and white dogwood flowers. It was all *sooooo* beautiful."
She wailed.

Wow. My only conclusion to that was that because
there were so few people in the world, activities had to be
limited. So, I had to concede that this was a very sweet
gesture – and it was Arthur, and he was a man, and he
probably wanted intimacy.

"When Ariel and Sam got together at school, you
know Ariel and I are cousins, we're very close, so I
always hung out with her and it just seemed like the
normal thing to happen. You know, Sam and Ariel, me
and Arthur." She wiped a tear from her cheek, so I wiped
her face with the cool cloth again. "And deep down, he
really just wants what everybody wants."

"And what's that?" I know, an obvious question, but
I wanted her take on it.

"Oh, you know, love and family, a baby," she said.
"You know he never would have hurt you. I think that's
why it hurts so much that I had to do it."

"Why did you have to do it?" I don't know why I
asked that. If not her, would it not have been Sam?

"I told the World Leadership I would take responsibility for Arthur. I promised I could get him to leave you alone, so that he and I and Ruth could have a baby together. You know, he really does like her. I'm not sure he's in love with her so much, but he does like her. So, I thought I could get him to want that, too." She sat down on the toilet and began to sob. "Her baby doesn't belong, you know."

"Accidents happen all the time," I said softly.

"No, what you're thinking of as accidents are really 'meant to be's'. Arthur didn't belong in the fifties, so having a baby with Ruth is a catastrophic event. If we allow the baby to stay there, we may as well go back and stop the Japanese from bombing Pearl Harbor and prevent the planes from flying into the World Trade Center. We could stop the Titanic from hitting that ice berg and sinking, and replace the O-ring that caused the Challenger to explode. But we can't do that. There are rules to time travel. Are you shocked that Arthur was the one to break them?" She giggled at this.

I wasn't shocked. But I understood.

"I get that. But don't you think this woman deserves a little respect? She didn't know that Arthur was the court jester of time travel," I said. "You know, there's a very good chance that he told her who he is and maybe she even agreed to give him the baby."

"You think?"

"It could happen."

"So, you think she'll let me have the baby and raise her as my own?" She was crying hard again.

"It's a girl?" I asked.

"Yes." She had the hiccups now.

How sweet, a little girl. You couldn't blame the baby for what the adults did foolishly. A baby is a gift from God and should be treated as such. Poor Ruth, she was going to miss out of this little girl's life.

"But Arthur should have a part in raising his little girl, too." I told her.

"That won't happeeeeeeen," she wailed again. "I don't even know where he is. I pulled the chip out, so we can't sense him.

"Have you read the book?" I asked her.

"Yes," she said, taking a piece of toilet paper and blowing her nose. "Twice."

"Well, let me just say this." And yes, I was fully aware of the fact that I was tempting fate, but it had to be said. "If Arthur is not found and brought home, you'll be reading another version of the story."

"It's not up to us." She was still visibly upset. "I would love to go find him and bring him home to his mom."

"You will find him and bring him home to his mom... Where's his dad?" Very dumb question. In fifty years, sixty billion people died. Odds are Arthur's dad may have been one of them.

"Dead."

"Did he die that night?"

"No. But it would have been better if he had."

I wasn't sure what that meant, but I wanted to get back to Sam, so I wiped her face one more time and was amazed to see she wasn't wearing any make up. Wow, she was lucky. I hoped that Jill's skin was this perfect when she was Boo's age.

I took her hand and we left the bathroom. Sam was sitting on the bed, waiting for us to come out of the bathroom.

"Were you listening?"

"Yes, and I think I have a solution." He looked at Boo.

"Yeah!" she said, snapping her fingers and she was gone.

Wait. What?

"What was that all about?"

"She went to find Arthur," he said, smiling at me. "It's what you want, right?"

"The point is it's the *right* thing to do. How is she going to find him?"

"I relayed the plan to her and if it takes her more than a few days, I'll find him myself."

And that's when I knew.

"You know where he is? Don't you?"

"I have a feeling I know where he is," Sam said, scooting up on the bed.

"Did you think of this plan on your own? Or did you go home and discuss it with Ariel?" I asked without malevolence.

"I've been here the whole time," he said, patting the spot next to him.

"How do you think the World Leadership will handle this?" I asked him, putting one knee on the bed.

"When Arthur is found we'll have to talk to them together." Sam said, reaching for me. I stepped off the bed.

"What will you say?"

"Exactly what you told me. They aren't going to want any of this to change. It would be catastrophic." He scooted down to the edge of the bed again.

"Sam? Remember that night you kissed me the first time?" I asked.

He smiled and said, "Yeah?"

"You were hesitant at first, so I asked you if you had done this before. What did you mean when you said yes and no?"

"I meant that, yes, I had kissed before; but, no, I had never kissed anyone but Ariel," he said, trying to get me back on the bed.

"Sam? Who raised Ariel?" I asked.

He had a puzzled look on his face and asked, "Are you sure you want to know that right now?"

"Yes." I'm not sure why, but I really wanted to know.

"Boo's mom, Megan," he told me, getting off the bed and moving toward me. "Megan and Ariel's mom, Erin, were sisters. In fact, they were twins."

At Sam's last words, my head began to swim and my body began to sway. I felt dizzy and my heart began to beat really fast.

"Twins?" I asked faintly. I didn't know why at the time, but the truth is, that no matter what Dolly and Sam told me about how I would give birth, I was still afraid for the pain. The thought that I might do something permanently detrimental to the development of our child scared me to death – and now that there was the possibility of me screwing up two little lives was almost too much for me.

"What's wrong?" Sam asked.

I was floating in blackness and my legs seemed to be weak to hold my now one hundred and thirty-two pound body. Sam reached out to catch me before I fell. As the room began to fill with light again, I saw a big goofy grin on Sam's face.

"What?" I asked weakly.

"You're pregnant!"

# CHAPTER THIRTY-TWO
## BABIES "R" US

One week to the day Sam and I got married in Las Vegas, I was at the Babies "R" Us in Eatontown, looking at cribs, strollers, blankets, and other stuff. Since I no longer had a job and had two babies coming, I was going to need some of that stuff and there wasn't going to be a baby shower. Boo was going to need stuff, too.

Yes, my fear that I would conceive twins had come true. I asked Sam if they were identical or fraternal twins, but he didn't know. He said that by the time he knew I was pregnant, that part of it had already happened, so he couldn't be sure. There had been multiple births before, but they had been one at a time to the same parents. The important thing about my pregnancy was obvious. I was going to deliver both of our children at the same time. I was somewhat of a celebrity in the twenty-third century for more than one reason.

But even though I was a celebrity and my girls were only going to be with me for a very short seven days, they were still going to need a place to sleep, clothes, diapers, and other baby paraphernalia.

*'Where are you?'* I heard Sam's voice in my head.

"I'm at Babies "R" Us." I said out loud. As I've said before, I'm not good at talking in my head and the red headed woman looking at the crib next to me looked over and nodded her head.

*'Without me?'*

"I got anxious," I told him, as I moved away from the red head. "And we don't have much time. Three weeks is not a long time."

'I know,' Sam told me as he stepped through the front door.

I went to him and threw my arms around him the best I could with a bulky coat on. I kissed him hard – what can I say? I love him. I took him by the hand and led him over to the cribs, and showed him the one I wanted.

"How much money do you have on you?" I asked exuberantly, but immediately felt flustered. I had never asked him for money before and wasn't sure if it would be acceptable.

"How much do you need?" Sam asked without blinking an eye.

"Baby stuff is expensive . Look at this crib. It's over five hundred dollars and we need two. Boo is going to need some stuff, too – a lot of stuff. Unless you've got someone building baby furniture and manufacturing diapers and baby clothes, Arthur's baby isn't going to have a place to sleep, have diapers changed, and clothes put on," I told Sam. "She's also gonna need some lessons in baby care."

"Why? She's a baby."

"Well, how often did Boo babysit when she was a teenager?" I asked.

'Never,' I heard in my head.

Wait. What?

That wasn't Sam's voice I heard, it was Boo's. She was now talking to me in my head, too – and I wasn't sure I wanted that, no matter who she was. I looked at Sam to see if she had spoken to him, too, but he seemed to be fascinated with the monkey mobile attached to the crib I had been looking at.

"What's this?" he asked, like he had never seen one before. I knew he had. He just couldn't remember, since he had been a baby the last time one rotated over his head.

"It's called a mobile," I told him as I found the switch to turn it on. It began to turn slowly as it played a lullaby. Sam smiled.

"What's it playing? I'm not familiar with the tune." My heart always broke when he said something like this. I found it to be sad that he had lived all these years and couldn't remember a lullaby.

"It's a lullaby, music to lull the baby to sleep."

"Why would they make the monkey's different colors? Monkeys are brown, aren't they? At least, they are in the books I've read and the movies I've seen," he asked curiously.

"Babies love the colors. As the colors move, the baby learns to focus."

"How do you know all this?" I heard Boo's voice from behind us.

"Experience is the best teacher," I said, as Sam and I both looked at her. "I have three nieces and two nephews, and I babysat a lot over the years."

I noticed that Boo looked a bit better than she had the last time I saw her. She must have come from visiting Arthur.

"How is he?" I asked.

Her face lit up – it always did when she talked about Arthur.

Boo found Arthur just where Sam thought he'd be. Boo had been covering the guys in the 1970s and she really loved that decade. She loved the clothes, the people, and TV shows. It just made sense that she would pitch him to a place that she loved and was comfortable in.

She and Sam checked him out of the nursing home that he had been brought to after he was found. A couple of kids playing by a stream in 1974 Florida, somewhere near Disney World, found him lying in the sand. They thought he was sleeping off a hangover, so they called the police, who put him in lockup overnight. When they discovered that he couldn't talk and had no control over any of his bodily functions, he was transported to the nearest ER, and because there wasn't anything they could do for him, he was brought to a state run nursing home.

He was not happy when Sam came with Boo to bring him home. Sam told me his hatred had grown in the few days that had passed since his judgment day. But he was happy to know he was going home to his mother's house. Amelia, Arthur's mom, was happy to have him.

"He's about the same. He's letting his mom bathe him now, and he sits on her sun deck and enjoys the warmth of the sun." This looked like it made her happy. "We sometimes sat on her deck together and talked about the future. Once he started working on the time project, he told me all about how the male healers were going to oversee the health issues and it was on that deck that I decided I would be the only woman on the project."

This was something new to me. I guess I had just assumed that anyone who was able would be part of it. I never questioned why Ariel did not travel back in time.

"I won't be needing a crib. Amelia still has Arthur's crib. She packed it away after she knew there would not be any more children because…" she said, running her hand over the bumpers in the crib and without finishing her sentence, moved on with, "We took it out yesterday and put it back together, and it's still good. Ali said it's still perfect. We just need a mattress and these things." She was pointing to the bumpers.

"What about a changing table?" I asked. "She still have one of those?"

"What do I need a changing table for?"

"To change the diapers."

"Change diapers?" Boo asked.

"Yes. You do know what diapers are, right?"

Sam stood by with a befuddled look on his face. Clearly, neither one of them had given this a second thought.

I walked over to the back wall and showed them the diapers.

"These are diapers. Notice how the numbers change on the packs. That means they are getting bigger. They start with newborns. You're going to need tons of these." I stopped because they both seemed to be oblivious to the purpose of diapers. So, I took a deep breath and smiled – this was going to be *fun*. I threw a couple of packs of newborns in the cart.

"Diapers go around the baby's butt and peepee area," I moved my hands down to my hips. "And every once in awhile, you're going to have to change them and you're not gonna want to do it on the dinner table."

"Why not?"

"Because what you're gonna find won't be the prize at the bottom of a Cracker Jack's box or even a cereal box." I smiled. Over the years, I had changed at least what seemed like a million diapers, especially when the kids were newborns and it was never pretty. I threw a couple of more packs in the cart. I'd just take what I needed for the twins from these.

"What will it be?" Boo asked, as both of them seemed frightened to know the answer.

"Diapers catch everything." I hoped by now they would see what I was getting at. But just for giggles, I pulled in a memory of what was probably the worst diaper change I ever had to be a part of.

At this, Boo's face took on a greenish tinge and she looked like she wanted to throw up. Sam grimaced.

"How long does that last?" Boo asked, sounding like she was going to cry.

"Well, for genetically engineered babies about two days. For normal babies, like Arthur's, about three years."

"Three years?" She looked like she couldn't decide whether to faint or throw up.

Sometimes, it really did seem like they were from another planet.

"You could get lucky." I tried to sound encouraging. "She is Arthur's child and he is a genius – even though I never saw any evidence to that fact. Some babies, especially females—" Now Sam had me doing it. "— have been known to potty train in nine or ten months. So, you could get lucky."

"Couldn't I fix that?" Boo asked.

"Yeah," Sam said. "Heal her, so it's not so disgusting,"

"NO! Really, no. Try really hard not to heal that, it's not a disease." My voice almost rose an octave. "It would be like helping a butterfly out of its cocoon."

They both looked at me blankly – just like they were from another planet.

"If you help a butterfly get out of its cocoon, the wings won't be strong enough to get it off the ground."

"Oh, poor butterfly," Boo winced.

"Besides, once she starts eating table food, it will look more like human poopies."

"That's pretty gross," Boo said, dismay all over her face. "I'll never be able to do this – I want to, I really do – but I can't. She'll be better off with her mother." Tears began to roll down her cheeks.

"You know, babies don't come with instruction manuals," I told her. "New moms learn from their mothers, older sisters, aunts, grandmothers, best friends – after the first week or two, you'll be a pro."

That news really didn't seem to help her.

"Let's do this. Once the baby is born, bring her to my apartment." Then, I remembered that I was married now and said, "Our apartment. You'll stay a week or two, then you'll bring her to Arthur's mom, who has to remember him as a baby. It'll all work out – and I'll give you lessons in bathing." I started over to where the bath supplies were.

"Bathing? I'll have to bathe her?" she asked anxiously.

"Well, yeah, after eating, playing, and especially after explosions."

"She's going to explode? Why? Will it hurt her?"

"Yes, possibly, but butt explosions happen fairly often."

For a few seconds, Boo looked positively paralyzed, then she looked toward the front doors and made a mad dash – I assumed to throw up.

"You did that on purpose, didn't you?" I had almost forgotten that Sam was there.

"It's fun messing with geniuses," I said with a big smile on my face.

Boo came back in, wiping her mouth with the back of her hand. She was still looking a bit green, but she had to know because the baby belonged to the twenty-third century.

"Butt explosions," she said. Letting all the air out of her lungs, she asked, "Anything else I need to know about?"

"Well," I said, as I dropped bottles and pacifiers in the cart, then turned to go back to the diapers. "There's also projectile vomiting."

Sam closed his eyes and shook his head. Boo looked like she wasn't sure what that was, so I explained it.

"It's vomit that flies across the room." I pointed to the other side of the room.

Poor Boo, she did not look well. Even the two girls at the registry desk noticed and came running over. I told them she was expecting and what I just explained to her, and they helped her to a chair. One of them ran to the restroom to get a cool cloth.

"When is your baby due?" the remaining employee asked.

Boo, in her nauseous state, said weakly, "In just a couple of days."

"Wow," the young girl said. "You look great!"

The other girl returned, and I took the wet paper towel from her and wiped Boo's face. She bent over and I feared she was going to vomit. I can only suppose that Sam thought so, too – because he put a hand on Boo's shoulder and she sat upright, looking better than before.

"I'm okay," she said, getting up. "Let's just get what we need. We will certainly need to talk more about this," she said, leaning on the cart.

Boo asked me to just help her choose all the purchases she would need to make with no immediate explanations. I could do that.

We went to the other side of the store, so we could get the new crib mattress Amelia needed. While there, we picked up a couple of pink laundry baskets and some pink and white hangers. Boo noticed the Minnie Mouse blankets and sheets, and threw them in the cart. She smiled – Boo is a big Disney fan and felt like Minnie was an old friend.

I sent Sam to the front of the store to retrieve a couple more carts because we had a lot more shopping to do. We moved over to the cribs and I chose an espresso colored crib with delicate curves and two toddler beds. My daughters would not be with me very long, but for the short time they would be with me, I would make sure they were comfortable.

We moved onto bedding and Boo spotted the Minnie Mouse layette with a matching blanket, and threw it into one of the carts. On our way over to the strollers and car seats, we picked up more diapers. Boo nearly wet herself when she caught sight of the Minnie Mouse car seat. We found the matching stroller, swing, pack and play, and Boo was just about beside herself with giddiness.

On our way to the bathing and infant care department, I heard Sam on the phone and stopped because I couldn't even imagine who he'd be talking to.

"It looks like we're going to need your truck, buddy. We need to take all this baby stuff to Emily's apartment."

He hung up and smiled. "Well, we're not going to bring it home from here."

By the time Kurt got there, we had twenty-five packs of diapers in different sizes because my girls would grow faster than Boo's. There were three cradles, two cribs, one crib mattress, three layette sets, the matching Minnie Mouse stroller, car seat, pack and play, the swing, and the highchair, little girl dresses, baby jeans, baby shirts, infant clothing, a waterfall bathtub, tub toys, gift sets of bath accessories, binkies, bottles, bibs, and finally, a breast pump.

We went to two registers, so as not to raise any suspicion because of how much cash they had between them. I had no fears that there wouldn't be enough money, because I knew they could go into travel time and go get more if they needed it – and to be honest, I can't say that they didn't.

Kurt and Sam had everything packed in the back of the truck in very little time and had no problem bringing it up to my apartment.

# CHAPTER THIRTHY-THREE
# BRINGING HOME BABY

When Sam and I were married for ten days, the apartment looked a lot like Babies "R" Us. We had gone back a few more times just to get more of the little things that babies and toddlers need. We got more diapers, wipes, formula, hooded towels, wash rags, and Dreft, the baby clothes detergent. I was pretty sure they didn't have any in the twenty-third century, so we stocked up. We bought monitors, more infant clothes, booties, more diapers, and a rocker Boo spotted when a pregnant customer was sitting in it.

There was just too much baby stuff in the apartment and I had to put my foot down – some of it had to go. My tele-communicator was now connected to Amelia's, so I informed her that some of my stock was now going to her house. She was actually excited and more than ready for it. Then, there were people in my apartment – more than Bandit and I have ever had. They were other travelers and two more healers. I don't know what made me think Sam and Boo were the only healers in time. They were older, probably in their seventies, but pretty healthy for their age. But, soon, all the stuff that wasn't needed right away were gifted away.

It was on that day, I felt the babies move. At first, it felt like a little more than butterflies, but soon got much stronger. It scared me. I thought they might be trying to get out too soon. I had at least eighteen more days.

"Sam, I think something's wrong," I said out loud.

*'What's going on? Ruth's baby is almost here.'*

"It feels like the babies are trying to get out."
*'They're fine.'*
"How do you know? You're in the nineteen fifties."
*'Because they told me.'*
Wait. What?
"What does that mean?"
*'They're both psychics. I promise you they're fine.'*
I took a deep breath. I wasn't so sure about that. My kids, psychics? I had hoped they would take after Ariel and be geniuses. Now some smartass like Arthur would come into their lives and make fun of them. Well, I wouldn't have it. I would teach my girls how to swing a bat.

*'Why don't you sit down and rest? Rub your belly in circles and they'll go to sleep. You've been busy, so they got restless.'* He chuckled at this. *'Boo and I will be back with the baby real soon.'*

I sat down and did as Sam suggested. Soon, the babies were calm. Bandit got up on the arm of the chair and put his front paws on my belly, yawned, and fell asleep. Soon, I fell asleep, too. Right up until I heard the jingle bells, I opened my eyes, and Sam and Boo were standing in front of us with the baby wrapped in a Minnie Mouse blanket.

"How's Ruth?" I asked, hoisting myself up out of my chair.

Sam handed the baby to me. I noticed a fresh boomerang shaped scar on her right temple and wondered how they did it without killing her. I looked at Boo and I saw she was a bit green, but there was happiness, too.

"I think she'll be fine. I had to help her… just a little. Boo is going to go back and visit her in a few days to be sure she's still okay," Sam said in the calm, soothing voice. I expected that was more for Boo than for me or the baby.

I handed the baby to Boo, who took her reluctantly. I sat her down in my chair, so she could get more comfortable holding her.

"What's her name?" I asked.

"Ruth said she and Arthur decided on Abby for a girl," Boo said, as she slowly began to rock the baby. I knew it wouldn't take long. She is a genius.

# CHAPTER THIRTY-FOUR
## THE CHILDREN SAVE THE WORLD

When I was in my third week of pregnancy, I finally knew what pregnant women meant when they said they loved being pregnant and I was sad that it wasn't going to last. Boo was out taking a walk with the baby. She had taken to motherhood like a fish takes to water. Diaper changes were the biggest problem, but she stopped vomiting after the first week.

For me, it was very different having Sam and Boo around almost all the time every day, but I was getting used to it. I also noticed that I wasn't having any trouble finding things to talk about. Soon, it would be just me and Sam. Boo had announced earlier that she felt she was ready to take the baby home to meet her father and grandmother. Ever since my tele-communication station was connected to Amelia's, she was able to be a part of her granddaughter's life. Arthur was there a lot and I could see in his eyes that he was happy to see her. I had to agree with her – it was time for them to be a family.

So, Sam and I finally had a few minutes alone.

"Tell me about the babies, the children," I asked. "What are they doing now? How are they saving the world?"

Sam and I got comfortable on my love seat – well, as comfortable as I could get. I could tell this was going to be a very long and interesting conversation. Maybe even an eye opener.

Sam sat back and I leaned back against him, and he began.

"The first male, born about seven and a half months ago – they named him Richard – he's a farmer. He took a large piece of land in northwest New Jersey and he planted corn, potatoes, green beans, carrots, peas, and tomatoes."

My first thought on that was that a seven and a half month old was a farmer. Was he wearing OshKosh B'gosh overalls? Was he driving a tractor? How many acres does he have?

"All the children have met each other except for the last few who are still aging. The world leadership threw a party, so they could meet and get acquainted and maybe pair off. Richard, for example, met one of the females. Her name is Tricia and she is younger by three and a half months. They fell in love and were married a couple months ago. Their first child is due in about eight weeks," Sam said – he was all fired up now.

Wait. What?

"How can that be? Eight weeks? I'm only gonna be pregnant for four weeks."

"Oh," Sam said. "The second generation will gestate for about sixteen weeks and maturation will take one third longer then the first generation took. Ariel feels that normal thirty-six to forty weeks gestation will be back to normal in about four generations."

"Will they still have time travel in their DNA?" I asked.

"Well, they're thinking by the fourth or fifth generation time travel won't be necessary any more, but it will still be in their DNA."

"What do you mean, it won't be necessary any more?" I asked. But then, I knew the answer. "Oh, by that time you think we'll all be dead, don't you?"

I looked back at Sam and the smile had disappeared. I felt him shift behind me. He was not comfortable with the way the conversation was going.

"You know, don't you? You already know we'll all be dead?"

Sam's eyes were wet and I could see the pain in them.

"I know I'm gonna die someday, Sam. And I know you'll go home to the twenty-third century with your family. I'm okay with that," I told him. "I'm just grateful for the time we have together. I have more than I would have had if you had not come to save my life." I smiled back at him, but his eyes were still moist. "It's okay, Sam. You need to be okay with it, too."

He wiped his eyes and continued, "The first female, born around the same time as Richard, became an actress here in the twenty-first century."

Sam told me her name. She was in the movie *Twilight* and had a pretty decent part. I saw no reason to put her name in the book.

"A four month old male named Teddy is our first veterinarian in about forty years. His dad, a friend of mine named Randy, decided he wanted to go on a safari of sorts and, while he was in the Serengeti in Africa, came upon a pack of lions killing a baby elephant. Well, Randy just couldn't allow that, so he went into travel time and took that poor creature to the twenty-third century." I could tell Sam was smiling.

"But?" I asked. "Wouldn't that change things? What about the food it was going to be?" And even as the words were coming out of my mouth, I was repulsed.

"Well, of course, that was a possibility, but I haven't heard that anything was changed because of it," he told me. "So, Teddy became a vet so someone could look after Jumbo. Teddy found him a mate – her name is Sofia, born to a circus mom. Sadly, they never even knew she was having a baby because the circus only has female elephants."

"So, then how did she get that way?" I asked.

Sam chuckled. "Artificial insemination."

"But not Jumbo's stuff, right?"

"Right."

"And I've already told you about Mary. She's the cosmetologist who lives up by the Falls. She's the one who gave Ariel and me our pedicures and cut Ariel's hair. She's three and a half months old and she is busy," Sam continued. "She added facials to her menu and something called waxing." Sam made a horrified face. "Do you know what that is?"

I nodded my head.

"Do I want to know?"

I shook my head. I knew Ariel would tell him if she had been getting that service.

"A five month old female named Alice went to culinary school and is going to open our first restaurant – in I don't know how many years – to serve maybe two meals a day, maybe three times a week." Sam was really thrilled to tell me this.

"In order to do this, she has made deals with Ricky – who is five months old; he has a chicken ranch – and Richard." I could tell he was smiling. "You know, the farmer in his OshKosh B'gosh overalls."

"There's prostitution now in the twenty-third century?" I asked, trying to bring some humor to our evening.

"*Nooooo*." He drew out the word to let me know he got the reference to the movie *The Best Little Whorehouse in Texas*. "Ricky started out with about twenty laying chickens and a rooster. He calls the rooster Barney – don't know why."

"That's sweet."

"He now has over one thousand chickens. Sixty-five percent lay eggs and the rest are for eating. Ricky doesn't like killing them, pulling the feathers out, and preparing them for roasting, so Alice helps with that." Sam blew air out of his mouth.

"What, no turkey?"

"No, not yet," he said. "So, Alice serves chicken and vegetables for lunch, and eggs for breakfast. Alice's restaurant is a big hit."

Yes, I see what happened there.

"A seven month old male named Leo and his six month old sister named Lacey want to be entertainers, so they are trying out for the X-Factor. A rare multiple birth – their parents are so proud. A two month old male named Clyde wants to be a doctor. A two and half month old female named Kathy wants to be a singer. She's decided on the fifties because she just loves the music."

Sam continued, "Four males ranging in age from seven months to two months are in construction and they've already started to restore a lot of the old buildings. We really needed that; it's probably the biggest reason Ariel and I live with my parents. The structures are all solar powered, but the buildings themselves are falling apart."

He continued, "A four month old female named Sandy wants to be a marine biologist, but we have little more than a few species of fish in the ocean. The only species that survived the virus are sharks and guppies. Of course, if there's anything else, there's still not enough people to know if that's true."

"Okay. You said that once before. You didn't become a surfer because the water was dangerous because of the sharks and guppies," I said, turning to him.

"Yeah, so?"

"Sam. Guppies are little fish you put in a fish tank in your home," I told him.

"Oh, you wouldn't want these in your house."

I thought about all this and decided I didn't want to know. I was certain that even though it wasn't what I was thinking about when Sam first talked about saving the world, I guess these children are exactly what the world needs. These progenies are saving the world by settling into real lives that are comfortable for each of them. Sam assured me that they were not forced into anything. They chose their own lives.

# CHAPTER THIRTY-FIVE
## SOLO FLIGHT

Four weeks after the twins were born, they were allowed to come visit me on their own. I was very nervous – after all, my four week olds were time traveling without Sam to escort them, as he had been doing since they were two weeks old.

Ariel was joking that she was 'pushing them out of the nest'. She had all the confidence in the world – both worlds – that they would be just fine. Sam was okay with it, too, but this was my first time seeing a first generation do it and I was duly nervous.

Sam was coming, too, but not holding their hands. He hadn't been home with me in a week and we missed each other. By the way, I highly recommend getting married for the first time in your fifties to a man who already has a wife in another century. By the time you wish he'd leave and go somewhere far away, he does – and when you miss him so much that cold showers or baths just aren't enough to get you through the day, he comes back. Perfect!

This is part of the reason why I love him so much and made the decision to marry a man who already had a wife and give them a baby in good conscience. Or, in my case, two babies – two females.

It was on this day of days that I decided to start this manuscript. It had to be done at some point. Ariel has been telling me how much she has enjoyed all my books. She won't tell me how many or even what they are about, except to say they are all related to love of God, family, and the home. She also says that they just seem to appear in the Entertainment Center at different times.

So, on this day of days, three months after I passed out in Sam's arms at the lottery kiosk in the mall, I was standing in front of my new sixty-two inch TV, watching my daughters and waiting for them to make their first solo time traveling jaunt.

Ariel was kissing them and hugging them tight with the biggest smile I've ever seen on her face. Motherhood really agrees with her. My daughters appeared to have aged about sixteen years in the four weeks since their birth and Ariel had regained much of her health.

The world leadership has deemed that four weeks biologically and sixteen years physically to be the age of solo time traveling back to their birth mothers. They got to visit once a week since they were a week old, or physically five years old, and went to live in the twenty-third century with Ariel and Sam. I cherished those days.

I was amazed not only by their physical growth, but their emotional and intellectual growth as well. Ariel got to spend all two days of puberty with them and she thought she might pull her hair out. I was glad I was spared – there are two of them.

It was decided that Samantha would come first. She came into the world first, so it just made sense. She gave Ariel one last hug, squeezed her sister's hand for a second, blew a kiss to Sam who would follow, and said, "Here I come." And with the sound of a pop, pop, pop – she is my little firecracker – she was here.

Wow, she was good at it. I never saw her reach up to gently pull the fabric of time apart and, like Sam, she must have done it with her mind. I was in awe of my four week old daughter. Not many moms could say their kid could do that.

It was the same with Erin. she hugged Ariel one last time, said, "See you in a sec, Dad." And with the sound of fluttering wings – later I would come to think of those wings as fairy wings – she was here. Ariel clapped her hands; she never doubted. I was relieved and anxiously awaiting Sam. I took the girls into the kitchen, so Sam and Ariel could have some time alone.

Like Sam, the twins are always hungry and they love cheese fries, pizza, and cheeseburgers – and I had it all waiting for them.

I heard the sound of air rushing through a tube and turned to see my husband smiling at me from the living room. I rushed into his arms and we kissed – a quick kiss that left me wanting more. We were still newlyweds. I heard my daughters say, "Get a room!" and "Way to go, Mom!"

He took a step back and looked at me with a grin.

"What?" I asked.

"You're pregnant again," he said with a combination of mystification and exhilaration.

But that's another story.

# EPILOGUE

Sam had the best of both worlds – two loving wives and two beautiful daughters, who by the way, are both brilliant and psychic. He is deliriously happy and so am I. I was used to being alone most of the time and I liked my alone time – I still do. And truth be told, Ariel is wonderful, so if I have to share him and the girls with someone, it might as well be her. Her health has improved immensely. Between the foods I was sending to her, and lunch every day at Alice's restaurant, she not only feels better, she is looking more like herself. That is to say, she reminds me a lot of Jill.

We are the best of friends now. She never makes me feel stupid, and to her credit, she never makes Sam feel stupid. Because the truth is, Sam isn't stupid – he's probably a genius and here is why I am telling you this. Sam is psychic, that's true. Sam also has common sense and the ability to think things through and figure the outcome. He never took the test to categorize him as a genius – he refused to take it.

Ariel may have done the study to find out why some animals gestate for a shorter amount of time than humans, but Sam was the one who actually figured out how to make that happen. It was Sam who figured out that the artificial environment would only work properly in a healthy body. Each woman's body reacted differently to the artificial environment right up until the eggs were implanted. If the environment wasn't absorbed by the body by that time, all would go as planned and a healthy baby would be born.

One afternoon, near the time Sam finished his time traveling training, he and Ariel sat down together and she explained animal gestation versus human gestation to him – per her year of study and contemplation. They talked about what each body had to do.

The whole project was literally dumped on Sam's shoulders. If he couldn't make it work, they would have to go with plan B. However, to quote Sam, they were almost out of time, so normal gestation just wasn't the answer.

In a nutshell, this is how it works. After Sam restores health to the body – although, not everyone needed as much attention as I did – and the artificial environment begins to develop, at the moment Sam implants the eggs, he convinces the environment that a gerbil will be gestating in there – and gerbils gestate for twenty-four to thirty days. The artificial environment believes it and, four weeks later, a fully gestated human baby is born.

So, in reality, when all is said and done, Sam was the one who designed the artificial environment. Boo couldn't do it after Ariel explained the process to her – not even after Sam tried to explain it in the way he understood it. Neither could the other psychics on the project. They figured four psychics working on it at the same time would help the plan move ahead faster. But, when they realized that only Sam could do it, he became the architect of 'the schedule'.

And because of Sam's schedule, there were nine hundred and eighty-four artificial environments created, with only seven of them being absorbed by the body before conceiving. It's not magic – it's love – *pure love.*

So, nine hundred and eighty-one first generation babies and the twenty-third century is repopulating –

with no catastrophic changes and Sam is now retired. He has yet to take full credit for his accomplishments and he never will.

So, now, if by chance you were wondering if being a psychic healer is normal or if maybe they were engineered, the answer would be no. Psychics, psychic healers, mediums, and profilers have been around since the dawn of time. Unfortunately, they've been given many different labels throughout the centuries and not always treated with the respect they deserve.

For instance, in the seventeenth century, Massachusetts became famous for accusing and executing witches. In 1692, the courts tried twenty-nine men and women, and convicted them of being witches. You have to remember that witchcraft was considered a capital offense and the good people of that great state put people to death for capital offenses. There were several different methods of putting a witch to death. Some were burned at the stake, some had their hands and feet bound and thrown in the river, others were hanged, and some were thrown off a cliff. If they saved themselves, they were witches. If they died, they were normal. You guessed it – psychic healers.

As time passed, psychics had other labels attached to them. People with mental retardation, autism, ADHD and others with similar developmental disorders. These people drew into themselves. Some were diagnosed with bipolar disorder and others who had hallucinations were just deemed crazy. These people were born with such an incredible gift and abilities. Some just didn't know how to deal with it. Others kept quiet about their abilities, so they would be thought of as normal.

In the twenty-third century, psychic abilities are embraced. These people came out of hiding and are able to be exactly who they are. They are sent to a special school, so their abilities can be explored and developed. These people are as normal as you and I, and should be respected for exactly who they are. They are different, not less.

Sam's abilities, as it turns out, are just as strong and as potentially dangerous as Boo's – if not more so. But like all us, with our talents and abilities, it's all in how we choose to use them.

It is our choices that make us who we are.

# ABOUT THE AUTHOR

Bernice Erehart was born and raised on the Jersey Shore. She is the middle child of Howard and Vincenza, with two older sisters and an older brother, as well as three younger sisters.

Because of them, she is now called "aunt" by six nephews and five nieces, and great aunt by five great nephews and five great nieces. She lives a quiet life with her kitties Boo, Chipee, and Lucy.

*Out of Time* is Bernice Erehart's first novel.

Made in the USA
Lexington, KY
18 September 2014